THE
GREAT ORME
TERROR

THE GREAT ORME TERROR

Garnett Radcliffe

Introduced by
John Pelan

RAMBLE HOUSE

The Great Orme Terror — Thornton Butterworth 1935

ISBN 978-1-60543-654-8

Cover Art: Gavin L. O'Keefe
Preparation: Fender Tucker

Dancing Tuatara Press #30

THE GREAT RADCLIFFE TERROR

Years ago I was taught a great book collecting trick by the late Karl Edward Wagner . . . The occasion was a chat about his famous "Wagner List" of the top thirty-nine horror novels that appeared in the pages of The Twilight Zone Magazine and led to a resurgence of interest in the works of such authors as Walter S. Masterman, Mark Hansom, R.R. Ryan and others. I asked Karl, "how do you find this stuff?" or words to that effect and his reply was that where there's one book of the sort you're looking for there's likely others, so if you discover an interesting supernatural thriller, don't just look for more books by that author, but look at the publisher's catalogue from that time period and check for promising titles . . .

This approach led me to continually look at titles published by Henry Drane between 1900 and 1930. After all, the brilliant collection *The Weird O' It* by Clive Pemberton appeared from this publisher and was joined by Richard B. Gamon's *The Strange Thirteen* in 1925. I've been able to release the former through my imprint of Midnight House and the latter title has been issued by Dancing Tuatara Press. Among the other Drane titles that I took note of was a volume entitled *The Return of the Ceteosaurus* by Garnett Radcliffe. My friend and mentor, George Locke actually possessed a copy and was kind enough to give me a run-down on the contents . . . Only the titular tale contained any fantastic elements and as such there didn't seem to be any reason to spend several hundred dollars simply to obtain the one story . . . However, something about the book stuck in my mind and I finally realized that there was a Garnett Radcliffe active in the dying days of the pulp magazines and that the stories I'd read by this author were pretty good.

A further examination of my collection and notes turned up the information that Garnett Radcliffe was a regular contributor to *Weird Tales* as well as a couple of the science fiction digest magazines of the early 1950s. With this information in hand I started the slow process of assembling a collection of Radcliffe's fantastic fiction . . . Somewhere along the line I discovered the small clutch of novels he authored in the 1930s which include the present volume and such thrillers as *In the Grip of the Brute*, *The Thirteenth Mummy* and the humorous fantasy *The Lady from Venus*. Like most of the British thrillers of the 1930s the target audience was the lending libraries and as a result of this marketing strategy Radcliffe's books were literally read to pieces and copies are extremely scarce today. As an example, the present volume commands prices in excess of three hundred dollars on the rare occasions that a copy is offered for sale.

The present volume is an excellent example of Radcliffe's ability to blend the humorous with the spine chilling. Our protagonist, Lord Basil Curlew seems to be a foppish fool, but underneath the ridiculous exterior is a steely reserve well suited to combat a master criminal such as the Lizard. The Lizard is a master criminal in the best pulp tradition, fond of macabre pranks and an early master of robots . . . Robots that are put to dire purposes in the course of events.

It's a shame that Garnett Radcliffe's work has been ignored for so many years; he certainly deserves a place on the shelf alongside authors such as Walter S. Masterman, Mark Hansom, and Gunnar Johnston. We intend to follow up this volume with new editions of his other fantastic crime novels and a collection of all of his weird fiction.

John Pelan
Midnight House
Gallup, New Mexico
Summer Solstice — 2012

THE
GREAT ORME
TERROR

CHAPTER I

THE MAN WITH THE MOCKING EYES

IT SEEMED THAT MISS MONA VACHELL was a well-known person in Minrhyn Bay. Dr. Constandos, who had come all the way from Port Said in order to interview the young lady anent a matter that will presently be made clear, got an agreeable surprise at the station. Instead of having to go to the police as he had anticipated, he was given all the information he required by the porter to whom he had entrusted his suit-cases.

"Miss Vachell, sir? You mean the tennis player, don't you? 'Er father's rector of Brig-y-don. Is that the young lady you want, sir?"

Dr. Constandos wasn't sure. He knew very little indeed about the Miss Vachell he had come from Port Said to find. But what he did know he proceeded to put into slow, but not precise English.

"Ze lady I wan'—'er family zey lived in Minrhyn Castle long time ago."

"That's Miss Mona," said the porter. "I know where you'll find 'er, too. She'll be in the covered tennis 'all at Brig-y-don, most likely practisin' for the tournament. Playin' yourself, sir?"

The question was a natural one. Dr. Constandos, who was slight and sallow and wearing a straw hat, was obviously a foreigner. And foreigners seldom came to Minrhyn Bay, North Wales, save for the purpose of playing tennis.

But this foreigner had come for a more serious purpose. And now that he was so near the end of his quest he had almost begun to regret the impetuousness that had sent him dashing from Port Said. Would the English, or rather Welsh, girl laugh at him? Would the sum of nine hundred thousand pounds, which appeared so immense to him, a not very successful little Port Said doctor, mean nothing to Miss Mona Vachell? Like many foreigners he had a naive idea that all upper-class English and Americans were multimillionaires.

"You've come all the way from Egypt about a paltry little sum like that! How perfectly ridiculous! As if it could matter to me!"

It would be terrible if Miss Vachell received his great news in that spirit.

His delusion about the wealth of the English received an impetus from the opulent appearance of the great white building the taxi-driver told him was the Brig-y-don Hydro. By the same person's advice he booked a room and left his suit-cases. Then he crossed the road to a smaller building, also white, which was the covered tennis hall attached to the hydro.

A Rolls-Royce stood near the entrance to the hall. It came into Dr. Constandos's head that it was Miss Vachell's property, and his spirits sank even lower. Glancing into the car as he slunk past, he encountered the gaze of a pair of dark, deep-set eyes, cold and hard as jewels and mocking in expression. Whether the owner of those remarkable eyes was a man or a woman he could hardly have said in his confusion, but he did get the impression that he or she, whichever it was, knew all about his errand and was laughing at him for a fool. He grabbed at his straw hat and positively trotted into the covered tennis hall with a numb feeling that the only thing to do was to get the worst over as soon as possible.

He had never been in a covered tennis hall before. An attendant gave him a ticket in exchange for two shillings. While he fumbled for the right change he heard mysterious sounds, reverberating thuds, rubber shoes pounding on a wooden floor and the voice of an umpire calling the score, coming from the other side of a curtain.

"Mees Vachell? She ees 'ere?" he asked.

"No. 2 court, sir. Up those steps into the gallery, please."

Dr. Constandos blundered somehow through a glass door. He was in the gallery overlooking the courts. There was only one other spectator. An elegant young man with a monocle who listlessly sucked the silver knob of a malacca cane while he regarded the play.

Once Dr. Constandos had seen that young man—or rather his double—before. It had been in a theatre in Cairo. There had been an actor who had played the part of a feeble-witted young English aristocrat complete with top-hat, monocle and idiotic, chinless smile. And though the young man he now beheld was wearing an ordinary lounge suit and a fedora, he was otherwise the exact ditto of that actor who had left Dr. Constandos with the impression that the average young English nobleman is not fit to be entrusted out without a nurse.

Although he would have preferred not to have had to seek information from an obvious half-wit, there was no one else to ask, so he sidled along the wooden bench until he could sit down beside the vacuous-faced youth.

"Mees Vachell. Could you please to tell me which lady ees Miss Vachell?"

"A pleasure, my dear chappie," the young man said affably. "She's the one on the left on No. 2 court. Playing positively foully for her."

Miss Vachell was much younger than Dr. Constandos had expected. A little sturdy figure in a short skirt that swung like a ballerina's, she looked a mere child. A pretty, mutinous child, who appeared to be bursting with laughter at some secret joke. Suddenly she picked up a ball and drove it hard at the young man beside Dr. Constandos.

"Go away, Basil. I can't play while you're watching. Take your face outside and bury it,"

The ball would certainly have hit Dr. Constandos on the nose had not the young man shot out his hand and caught it in the nick of time.

"Now, now, now," he drawled as he tossed it back. "Keep cool in the hour of defeat. You can't expect always to win."

"Will you bet a shilling I don't win this set?" the child below fired.

"What's the score? Mrs. Flant is leading you five games to nothing and it's her service? Yes, I think in the circumstances I'll wager a shilling. Deuced rash of me—what?"

Miss Vachell became a white flame that flickered and danced about the court. Dr. Constandos drew closer to the young man who was evidently a fairly intimate friend.

"So zat ees Miss Vachell! I 'ave come from Port Said to see 'er."

"People do. She's hot stuff when she's on her game," was the languid reply.

"It ees not 'er tennis I 'ave come to see. It ees something quite different. You know 'er? You can make ze introduction?"

The young man looked at him. And again his open mouth and the way he screwed the monocle into his eye reminded Dr. Constandos of that actor.

"With the greatest pleasure, dear old soul. You see Mona and I are sort of engaged—that's why we're so beastly polite to one another. What's this? Your card? Oh, thanks awfully . . . Here's my—er—dog licence."

With satisfaction Dr. Constandos saw that his guess as to the young man's social status had been correct. He *was* a nobleman. Lord Basil Curlew. Underneath his name appeared *Royal Household Lancers,* and in the corner of his card was the address of a club known to even Constandos as the most exclusive in London.

But this was even worse than he had feared. Miss Vachell was "all but" engaged to an English peer, to a gilded youth who, for all Dr. Constandos knew to the contrary, received a million pounds a day for doing nothing.

Peer or not, Lord Basil seemed a friendly soul. Dr. Constandos was much less afraid of him than of Miss Vachell, now performing miracles of activity on the court.

"I am thinkin' it may not be worth my while to trouble Mees Vachell after all. It ees only about a vaire small sum of money. Nine honderd tousand pound only. In England 'e ees not moch—no?"

"Light of my life, is this a confidence trick?"

"I do not understan'. I zay nine honderd tousand pound ees not moch."

"I won't argue," said Lord Basil languidly. "Have it your own way. I expect you're right. Everyone always is except P.B.C."

"P.B.C. Who ees 'e?"

"It's short for poor bloomin' Curlew. They christened me that at Malchester and it stuck. Poor bloomin' Curlew. The chappie who's always wrong. It's no use asking me riddles. Try Mona. Here she comes."

The set on No. 2 court was finished. Miss Vachell was climbing up the wooden seats towards them, hampered by two rackets, a box of balls and a fur coat.

"You owe me a bob, Basil."

Lord Basil rose. He was very tall and very slim. Dr. Constandos remembered that that actor had confessed to wearing corsets.

"I've a riddle for you," said his lordship holding out Miss Vachell's coat. "This fellah has come all the way from Port Said to ask if nine hundred thousand pounds isn't a very small sum. It is, isn't it?"

"It is to me," said Miss Vachell, after a suspicious stare at the doctor. "I never consider anything under a million."

"Nor do I," drawled Lord Basil. "Nine honderd tousand pounds! Pouf! The mere thought of it makes me feel ill. Doesn't it you, Mo?"

"Very ill," said Miss Vachell. "Quite green."

Dr. Constandos stood up. Their gravely scornful faces had confirmed his worst fears. They were laughing at him.

"It ees no matter," he muttered. "You would not be interested. I 'ave made a mistake. I am zorry."

He groped short-sightedly out of the tennis hall. The April sunlight made him blink after the subdued light. Brig-y-don Head, on which the hydro had been built, was one of a series of similar high rocky promontories which jutted out into the sea along that portion of the North Wales coast. Across the curve of Minrhyn Bay, looking above the roofs of the little seaside resort that lay in the valley, he could see the towering whale-shaped mass of Minrhyn Head. And beyond that, looming dark between sea and sky more ultramarine than the posters, were the Little Orme, the Great Orme and Penrhyn Point.

It was at Minrhyn Head that Dr. Constandos gazed. Even at that distance he fancied he could make out the battlemented silhouette of a castle. It could be no other than Minrhyn Castle itself.

He stared at it, fascinated. There was the guerdon of all his hopes. Like a grey finger it had beckoned him across those leagues of land and sea. In it—

"Dr. Constandos of Port Said, ain't it? Bless my soul, doc! Who'd have thought of seein' you 'ere?"

The speaker had emerged from the Rolls-Royce Constandos had imagined to be Miss Vachell's property. He was middle-aged, short and stout and wearing "plus-fours" of striking design.

Dr. Constandos looked at the red face, the little cunning eyes and waxed moustache.

"I am zorry. I cannot remember. My memory—"

"Seems a bit bad," said the stranger, shaking his head. "My name's Goldburg, Sir Jasper Goldburg. Got me now? I met you in Port Said. We'd drinks at some pub. Are you makin' a long stay in Minrhyn Bay?"

"I am not," Constandos said bitterly. "I find I 'ave come on ze chase of ze wild goose. I wish to go back to my work as queeck as I can."

An observant person would have noticed something like a gleam of satisfaction in Sir Jasper's cunning eyes.

" 'Ow would you like to go back on my yacht?"

"Your yacht?"

"Yes. She's sailing shortly for Egypt. Plenty of room for another passenger. Say the word, doc, and I'll tell Mr. Cusper to fix it. It will be all right, won't it, Cusper?"

Another man had appeared. So far as clothes, height and figure went he was not unlike Lord Basil Curlew. But there the resemblance ended. Whereas Lord Basil's face was good-nature itself, Mr. Cusper's expression was cold, supercilious and sneering. Also, he affected side-whiskers, ornaments of which Lord Basil was innocent.

And Constandos had become conscious of a third man who had remained in the Rolls and who was now watching them through the glass. He was the owner of the dark, deep-set mocking eyes that had made Constandos feel so uncomfortable. Now that the doctor could observe him more closely he got the impression of a long, clean-shaven, whimsical face that might have belonged to a musician or an artist.

"This is Mr. Cusper, my secretary," Sir Jasper was saying. "Cusper, the doc's goin' to join us on the yacht. 'E doesn't like Minrhyn Bay. 'E wants to go back to Port Said as soon as 'e can."

"One applauds," said Mr. Cusper, who had a high-pitched cultured voice. "One considers Minrhyn Bay a very unhealthy locality—in certain circumstances. You'd be better in the yacht, Dr. Constandos."

"It's settled," Sir Jasper said. "See 'ere, doc, you get your traps an' come to the yacht straightaway. She's lyin' off Llandudno. Come along."

Dr. Constandos was on the verge of acceptance. He had come to the conclusion that it wouldn't be the slightest use telling Miss Vachell what he had come to tell. She wouldn't be interested. She and Lord Basil evidently thought nothing of nine hundred thousand pounds.

But then a loud "coo-ee" made him turn round. The subject of his thoughts had come out of the tennis hall. She had seen him and was waving her racket.

Sir Jasper saw her too, and his face changed. There was something almost threatening in the way he grabbed the doctor's arm.

"Let's be off. Don't mind 'er, doc. Little pauper, that's what she is. Wants a lift, I dessay. She won't get one in my car. Come on."

Mr. Cusper had the doctor by the other arm. Between them they were urging him towards the car. And Constandos felt no inclination to resist. The dark eyes of the man who looked like a musician were drawing him like invisible wires.

And then Lord Basil drifted on the scene. He had possessed himself of one of Mona's rackets and was bouncing a ball up and down. But apparently he was too inane to perform even that simple operation with success. The ball dropped and rolled under the Rolls-Royce.

Lord Basil made a clumsy rush to retrieve it. Unfortunately he trod on Mr. Cusper's toe, collided heavily with Sir Jasper, and all but put the racket through the window of the car. And when the mix-up had straightened itself out Dr. Constandos found himself no longer between Sir Jasper and Mr. Cusper, but behind his lordship's elegant back, while his lordship bleated abject apologies for his clumsiness.

"So frightfully sorry, doncherknow. I say, old chappie, have I really hurt your toe? You'll want some jolly old embrocation, what! I'll send you a bottle and you rub it in with a jolly old what-d'you-call-it. What? What?"

His apologies were not received in the spirit in which they were manifestly meant. Both Sir Jasper and Mr. Cusper swore at him. The man inside the car put an end to the scene by pulling down the window and leaning forward.

"I think we had better be going, Sir Jasper," he said quietly.

They got in without a word, Cusper at the wheel, and the great car moved off. Sir Jasper turned to the man like a musician.

"That's torn it, Count," he said hoarsely. "Who'd 'ave thought that little runt would 'ave come all the way from Port Said to tell 'er? Well, I did me best. We'd 'ave 'ad 'im in the car if that young fool 'adn't barged in. Who is 'e?"

The man he had addressed as Count laughed.

"Nobody who need make the slightest difference to our plans. A more perfect specimen of a society idiot I have rarely seen. Really, I don't think it matters in the least if Dr. Constandos docs tell Miss Vachell. A puppy with an eyeglass and a schoolgirl who thinks of nothing except how hard she can bang a tennis ball—I don't think they'll be very formidable opponents!"

Sir Jasper felt reassured. Looking at the clever, sinister face beside him and comparing it with what he remembered of Lord Basil's inane physiognomy, he felt the odds were indeed upon the former.

The man he had called Count was laughing quietly.

"I think I shall send Dr. Constandos a warning to keep off the grass," he said. "A mild fright now might save him a lot of unpleasantness in the future. If he's wise he'll take the hint and leave Minrhyn Bay."

"And if he doesn't?" Sir Jasper ventured.

But the Count didn't answer that question. Perhaps he felt it would be a pity to mar the serenity of that sunny April afternoon by mentioning such a sordid topic as murder.

CHAPTER II

THE SEVERED FINGER

LORD BASIL CURLEW watched the retreating Rolls-Royce through his monocle. "The fellah seems peeved!" he burbled. "Poor bloomin' Curlew! Whatever will auntie think when she hears?"

Mona turned to Dr. Constandos. And annoyed as the doctor was, he had to admit that she was more than pretty.

"I don't think I understood you just now. That fathead Basil put me off. What were you saying about nine hundred thousand pounds? Is it a joke?"

"It ees no joke. But if you think ze sum is so small—"

"Small! I didn't know there was so much money in the world. But what has it to do with me?"

"You are Mees Vachell? Your ancestors—zey built ze castle on Minrhyn Head?"

"Yes, but—"

"Then 'ave you nevaire 'eard of ze *Cinco Llagas?* Ze Spanish treasure-ship?"

"What?" Mona turned white and spun round to face Lord Basil. "Basil, I believe he's come to tell us the legend is true. But it's been proved the gold isn't there. Dozens of people have tried to find it and failed."

"It *ees* there," Constandos shouted, his face dusky with excitement. "It ees to tell you that I am come from Port Said. You 'ad an uncle called Major Vachell—yes? 'E died one, two months ago in Port Said on 'is way back to England. I treated 'im, I was 'is doctaire. I 'eard 'im tell ze story when 'e was dyin'. But there were two ozzer men. Criminals, thieves—"

The pent-up torrent of words choked him and he could only gesticulate. Mona, hardly less excited, was shaking Lord Basil's arm.

"It's genuine. He means Uncle Jack. Uncle Jack was coming back to England, nobody could understand why. He died of malaria in a Port Said hotel."

"Poor old chappie," drawled Lord Basil. "But, Mo old thing, I wouldn't go off the deep end just yet. I hate to damp the exuberance and all that, but we haven't actually found the treasure yet. What exactly is the scheme, Dr. Constandos? To float a company with yourself as treasurer to recover the *Cinco Llagas* gold? If so, nothing doing."

"No, no," Constandos shook his head. "I know what you think. You ees wrong. This ees true story."

Lord Basil stared at him. And just for that flicker of time his lordship's face looked anything but inane.

"Righty ho," he said. "We'll risk it. Let us hence and to the hydro. Can't talk about hidden gold in this glare of publicity, what!"

The walk up to the hydro was short, but it sufficed to calm Dr. Constandos. He was feeling much happier. From Mona's exclamations he gathered that she regarded nine hundred thousand pounds with at least as much awe as he did himself.

They found a secluded table in the lounge. When drinks had been brought Lord Basil turned to the doctor.

"Now then, old fellah. Let's have the works. I gather you were present when Major Vachell died?"

"I will tell you all zat 'appened," Dr. Constandos said. "Major Vachell came to ze 'Otel Cairo from ze ship. 'E was vaire ill—too ill to continue ze journey, you onderstan'. But 'e would not go to ze 'ospital as I advise. 'E was vaire obstinate man.

"From ze first I see it was 'opeless. 'E was in ze 'otel three, five day an' zen 'e stopped ravin' an' began to talk sense. 'E knew 'imself 'e was dyin'. An' 'e cursed an' cursed because 'e said 'e 'ad to die like a poisoned rat in Port Said instead of goin' 'ome to be a millionaire.

"Presently on ze sixth evenin' 'e became vaire oneesy in 'is mind. 'E told me 'e 'ad a secret 'e wished to tell someone before 'e died. I said why not tell me, but 'e wouldn't. 'E did not trust me, you onderstan'. Because I was not English 'e thought I could not be honest man."

Dr. Constandos paused to sip an unfamiliar cocktail. Mona was leaning forward, her eyes starry with excitement. For her ears the story held the hallmark of truth. Uncle Jack, who had been a peppery gentleman with a taste for "burra pegs", would have behaved just as Dr. Constandos was describing.

"Then I said who will you trust if you will not trust me? Shall I fetch ze priest? But 'e wouldn't 'ave ze priest any more zan 'e would 'ave me. An Englishman, zat was what 'e wanted. So at list I went from ze room for I saw 'e was dyin' an' I asked ze manager if zer were any English in ze 'otel. 'E told me zer were two gentlemen just arrive. 'Zen fetch them queeck,' I said. 'If zey do not 'urry it will be too late.'

"Five, ten minutes we wait an' then zey come. Misters Gravenant and Crane were ze names. An' when I saw them I think to myself if you entrust your secret to these you are indeed a fool, Major Vachell.

"For zey were not honest mens. Gravenant, 'e was vaire beeg with a red face an' white moustache an' white eyebrows that stuck up. Oh, a fierce, 'ard man! 'Is eyes were like ze eyes of a tiger, bright an' cruel, you onderstan'. I 'ave seen men with eyes like zat in ze madhouse.

"Ze ozzer man, Crane, was not frightenin' like Gravenant, but I did not trust 'im either. 'E was short an' smilin' with red lips. A Jew, I think."

Again Dr. Constandos paused. He was recalling to his mind the picture of those two men standing on the threshold of the death-chamber. Crane, oily and plausible; Gravenant, brutal and domineering, with fierce eyes and snarling voice. He resumed:

"Major Vachell was too weak to see them clear as I did. All 'e knew was zat zey were English, an' zat was enough. 'E waved 'is 'and for me to leave ze room an' Gravenant 'imself pushed me through ze door. Ah, but I was vaire angry. To treat me, ze doctor, like zat!

"But I could not make a scene in ze room of death. I went into ze next room an' I listened wiz my 'ead against ze wall. For I did not trust those men. I knew Major Vachell could not give 'is secret into worse 'ands."

Mona gave a sort of groan.

"Don't say he told them how to find the *Cinco Llagas* gold!" Dr. Constandos nodded.

"I 'eard 'im tell ze whole story. 'Ow 'is family used to live in Minrhyn Castle an' 'ow zer was a legend zat at ze time of ze Armada a Spanish treasure-ship called ze *Cinco Llagas* 'ad been blown on to ze rocks at ze foot of Minrhyn 'Ead. An' ze legend as I remember 'im tellin' it was zat ze Vachell who was livin' in ze castle got ze gold."

"Sir Gwilliam Vachell," Mona cried. "He was my great-great-great-something or other. When he saw the galleon helpless on the rocks he collected his retainers and they rushed down the cliffs and sacked her from poop to stern. They killed the crew and fired the *Cinco Llagas.* According to the legend they literally waded through blood to get that gold. But since then nobody has been able to discover what Sir Gwilliam did with the gold. People have often looked, but they've been unable to find it."

" 'E 'id it in ze castle," Constandos said. "I 'eard Major Vachell tellin' those two men, Misters Gravenant and Crane, 'ow 'e 'ad an old walnut bureau that 'ad once been in ze castle. 'E 'ad taken it out to India with 'im. One day quaite by chance, 'e found a secret drawer an' in ze drawer were papers. Those were ze plans that show where ze treasure is 'id. 'E know zey were genuine an' 'e was comin' back to England to look for ze gold when 'e took ill. But when 'e knew 'e was dyin' 'e gave ze copies of ze papers 'e 'ad made to Misters Gravenant and Crane an' 'e begged them to 'and these to 'is niece, Miss Mona Vachell, livin' in Minrhyn Bay. I 'eard it all, you onderstan'. I was listenin' with my 'ead against ze wall."

"How long ago was that?" Lord Basil asked.

"Two muns to-day."

"Two months! Well, if these fellahs had been honest Mona would have had the papers from them before this. You've heard nothing, have you, Mo?"

"Nothing," Mona said. "Oh, Dr. Constandos, couldn't you have stopped them and made them hand you the papers?"

"I tried," Dr. Constandos said. "After 'e 'ad 'anded over ze papers I 'eard Major Vachell give a long gasp an' zen I heard Crane tellin' Gravenant 'e was dead. Gravenant 'e laughed like one beeg devil. 'This ees ze best bit of luck ever come my way'—zat was what I 'eard 'im say.

"Then I went into ze room vaire queek where ze dead man was an' I began to tell them zat if zey did not send ze papers to Mees Vachell I the police would inform. But Gravenant 'e drew back 'is fist an' zen pouf! It was as if ze ceiling 'ad tumbled on my 'ead. 'E 'ad knocked me unconscious, you onderstan'. An' when I 'ad recovered myself Misters Grave-nant and Crane 'ad gone with ze papers. I told ze police but they could do nossing. Egyptians are no good. All they said was they could not find Misters Gravenant an' Crane, so they must 'ave left Port Said on a sheep."

"But, my dear chappie, why didn't you write to Miss Va-chell yourself at once?" Lord Basil cried. "Don't you see that if these birds are really out to get the treasure for themselves, you've given them the deuce of a long start?"

"I did write," Constandos said. "But ze only address I 'ad was Mees Vachell, Minrhyn Bay, an' ze letter was returned. Then I thought I 'ad better come myself. It ees a vaire beeg sum of money zat ees at stake. Nine honderd tousand pounds. Zat was what I 'eard Major Vachell tell those two men."

"Did he say exactly what the treasure consisted of?"

"All in gold. Ingots and doubloons and pieces of eight. Ze *Cinco Llagas* was takin' ze gold for ze Spanish Army in ze Netherlands when she got wrecked."

There was a long pause. Mona looked at Lord Basil Cur-lew, who was polishing his monocle.

"What do you think, Basil?"

"I say thumbs up," said his lordship. "It all fits in. We know Major Vachell *did* return very unexpectedly from India. We also know—at least I do—that he had in his possession some very old furniture that used to be in the castle. I think we can take it for certain he did find some papers connected with the *Cinco Llagas* treasure, and that he was sufficiently impressed by them to try to get back to England, or rather North Wales. But whether the papers were genuine or not, and whether the gold really is still in the castle—those are other matters."

"Then all we've got to do is tell the police and ask permission to begin searching," Mona said. "You see," she added, for Dr. Constandos's benefit, "the castle doesn't belong to my family any longer. There was a mortgage and it fell through. At the moment the castle is the property of a bank. They've been trying to lease it for years."

"We can't appeal to the police," Lord Basil said.

"Why on earth not?"

"Because if we did it would be good-bye forever to the *Cinco Llagas* gold. I'm a bit hazy about the law, but I do know that all treasure-trove is Government property. Besides, in this case the gold was booty of war. Even old Sir Gwilliam had no right to keep it. I expect that's why he hid it so deuced carefully. Afraid of getting his head chopped off by good Queen Bess.

"To put the doings in a nutshell," his lordship continued, "the issue lies between Gravenant and Co. and ourselves. The odds, I'm sorry to say, are heavily on the former. They've got the plans and they've got a long start. If the plans are anyway clear it should be the simplest thing in the world for them to find the gold. Then all they've got to do is to cart it away and sell it abroad. If they'd a yacht—"

Dr. Constandos started.

"A yacht! Sir Jasper, ze man who spoke to me outside ze tennis 'all 'as a yacht. 'E wanted me to go on 'er at once. 'E was vaire pressin'."

"By Jove!" said Lord Basil. "That's a hot point, laddie. Sir Jasper has his yacht here and he nearly burst his braces to get you away from Minrhyn Bay. Looks fishy, what!"

"You know 'im?"

"Only by repute. What I do know isn't in his favour. He's a shady customer. That was why I—er—barged in just now. I thought you looked a bit green and innocent, you know, and I knew if Sir Jasper did get you to one of his parties it wouldn't be exactly for the good of your purse. They play high on that yacht. Follow?"

Dr. Constandos stared at him. He was beginning to change his opinion of Lord Basil.

"You mean you drop zat ball on purpose?"

"Even so, sweet pippin. The great idea was not to let you, a stranger, be fleeced by Sir Jasper and his pals, but it looks now as if there were more behind their maneuvers than hit the eye, what! In fact, I'm open to bet that if they had got you into that car Mona would never have heard a word about the *Cinco Llagas* treasure."

"But neither Gravenant nor Crane were there! 'Ow did they recognize me?"

"From a description supplied by one of them, of course. You see what's probably happened is that Gravenant and Crane decided this was too big a job for them to handle alone. They knew they'd want a yacht, money—possibly explosives. So they've roped in other people, one of whom is Sir Jasper Goldburg. And another, I presume, is Mr. Smiling Sam."

"Who?"

"I mean the amiable gentleman who was in the back of the Rolls. He seems to be the big noise in this affair. At least I gathered that from the way Sir Jasper jumped to obey his orders. Mr. Smiling Sam. A gentleman whose face I did not like."

He stopped suddenly. Sir Jasper Goldburg and two other men had entered the lounge. One of his companions was the secretary, Cusper, and the third was a heavily-built individual whose pink skin and shaven head proclaimed him a German.

"Another bird of prey," Lord Basil murmured. "Take a squint, doctor. I suppose yonder Teuton isn't Gravenant by any chance?"

Constandos shook his head.

"I 'ave nevaire seen 'im before. Zey are lookin' at us now. It ees of us zey speak." Lord Basil rose suddenly.

"The jolly old bean has had a flicker. Excuse me, sweet ones, I will return anon."

Tall and elegant, he drifted across the lounge. As he passed Sir Jasper's table he favoured that person with a bland smile. Sir Jasper scowled and Cusper sneered. The German gave an insolent chuckle and laid a fist like a ham ostentatiously on the table.

In under five minutes Lord Basil was back. "As I feared," he murmured, hitching up his trouser legs preparatory to seating himself. "I've been on the phone to Messrs. Bracknall and Dogsbody. They're the house-agents who've been trying to let the castle. One of their young men, Reilly by name, is a pal of mine. Reilly tells me the castle was let as recently as this morning."

"Let!" Mona cried. "Who to?"

"A Mr. Sylvester from Manchester. He's taken it for three months. From what Reilly said I gather he can't take immediate possession although he wanted to. There are some legal formalities in connection with the lease that will take about three days to complete. So much breathing-space for us!"

"Did he describe this man Sylvester?"

"Yes. Of course 'Sylvester' is only a composite name for the gang, but I'm pretty sure the bird who interviewed Reilly was no other than the chappie you knew as Crane. Short, stout and Jewish in appearance. He paid for the lease in advance in ready cash. Reilly says he spun some yarn about being keen on archaeology and wanting to make a careful study of the interior of the castle . . . Well, what about that, my chickens?"

His chickens were looking blank. Mona indeed was near to tears.

"It's heartbreaking," she wailed. "I almost wish I'd never heard about the gold at all. They've got the castle and they've got the plans. We haven't a hope."

"In fact," Lord Basil drawled, "they're leading us by five games to nothing and it's their service. Time we went up to the net, what! In plain English, if we're going to beat these blighters we'll have to get a move on. What about paying a visit to the castle to-night?"

"But we can't find the treasure without the plans."

"Quite. All the same it mightn't be a bad scheme to have a nose round before they actually take possession. Sort of re-connoitre the ground, what! Well, doctor?"

Constandos was squirming with excitement.

"Lord Basil, may I a favour ask? I should like vaire moch to 'elp. May I assist you and Mees Vachell to beat these mens?"

"I call that deuced sporting of you," said his lordship. "Are you a married man, by the way?"

"I 'ave a wife an' four children. An' I am not a vaire reech man. I—I 'oped—"

Dr. Constandos blushed and stammered miserably. Mona guessed what was in his mind and rushed to the rescue.

"Dr. Constandos, if we do get that gold you'll be a rich man for life. I promise you that. You'll find yourself sailing back to Port Said on your own yacht."

Constandos wiped his eyes.

"Zank you, Mees Vachell, zank you. An' zer ees anozzer reason why I should like to 'elp. To be avenged on zat man Gravenant. 'E threw me out of ze room where my patient lay an' 'e 'it me on ze jaw. I am Greek. I do not forgive zings like zat easily. It ees Gravenant I 'ate. I tell you you will find 'im ze most dangerous enemy of all."

Ten minutes later Dr. Constandos received a fresh cause of offence. He found it when he went up to the bedroom where his suit-cases had been placed.

Lord Basil, who had accompanied him to show the way, had lingered for a moment in the corridor outside. He heard a cry of horror. Running in, he saw the doctor leaning sick and faint against the wall.

"On ze pillow . . . Look . . ."

Lord Basil looked and he too experienced a spasm of horror. For on the pillow lay something that looked like a long black slug. But it was even more unpleasant than a slug. It was a severed finger once the property of a Negro.

Suddenly Lord Basil laughed. Closer inspection had revealed that the supposed finger was only a clever imitation made of wax.

"A joke, Constandos. Not a very pleasant one, I admit, though. But the meaning is pretty obvious. It's a hint to you not to interfere."

He examined the gruesome little object. The workmanship was superb. Whoever had fashioned that finger had been an artist with a strong taste for the *macabre.*

Lord Basil looked thoughtful. It had come to him that they were opposed to a criminal of a very unusual type.

"We're up against something hot, sweet pippin. A crook who's something of an artist and has a devilish sense of humour. I can't swear it was the gent I christened Mr. Smiling Sam, but he certainly looked the part."

CHAPTER III

THE HOWL IN THE DARK

MONA'S HOME, Brig-y-Don Rectory by name, stood in the woods at the back of Minrhyn Bay, about a mile from the hydro. It was fortunate for her intentions with regard to the *Cinco Llagas* treasure that her father was temporarily away delivering a series of Lenten addresses. For he was an orthodox person who certainly would not have countenanced her endeavouring to cheat the Government of its lawful rights.

And it is also certain that if Mr. Vachell had seen what his daughter found on her pillow—an object that was seemingly the severed finger of a Negro—he would have hied himself straight to the police. Not so Mona. After a moment's shuddering nausea she nerved herself to look at the thing more closely and found, as Lord Basil had done, that it was merely a clever imitation fashioned of wax.

Someone must have placed it there during her absence. She locked it in a private drawer and rang the bell.

"Who's been in here except yourself, Ellen?" she asked of the housemaid who answered.

"A man from the gas company, miss. He said he'd been sent to inspect the meters. I hope there's nothing missing."

"Nothing," Mona assured her. "You didn't happen to notice what he looked like, did you?"

But barring the fact that the visitor had had a peaked cap and had been what she called "nicely spoken" Ellen could remember nothing. Mona dismissed the girl. After she was gone she unlocked the drawer and had another look at the finger.

"It's been sent as a warning," she decided. "The gang who stole the plans from Uncle Jack have found out Dr. Constandos is in Minrhyn Bay. They've sent that horrible thing as a hint that it would be wiser for us not to try to interfere."

In the meantime Dr. Constandos, still somewhat shaken, was sampling his first dinner on Welsh soil. Opposite him sat Lord Basil, looking as monocled and vapid as ever did that Cairene actor.

His lordship had elected to dine in the hydro that night for two good reasons. The first was that he wished to give Constandos some information about Minrhyn Castle before they actually visited it; the second was that he had judged it might be advisable to keep a fatherly eye on the little Greek.

"Y'see it's like this," said Lord Basil. "Mo and I have been hearing about the *Cinco Llagas* treasure ever since we were so high. It's one of those good old family legends one respects but doesn't believe. In fact, I don't think anyone's ever bothered to have a serious look for the gold. There may have been a few spasmodic attempts, but nobody really got down to it properly.

"All the same," he went on, crumbling his bread with a white, manicured hand, "there's no earthly reason why the legend shouldn't be based on fact. Ships from the Spanish Armada were wrecked on the Isle of Man—that's how the tailless cats got there, incidentally—and there's no reason that I can see why the *Cinco Llagas* should not have drifted to Minrhyn Head. And if she did, Standy, you can bet that straw hat of yours those old Welsh laddies wouldn't have let the Dons push off again with the gold. They'd have done exactly what they're reputed to have done in the legend—have waded through blood to get it."

He swallowed a mouthful of fish, drank his sherry and went on:

"So we'll say, Standy, there's at least a good sporting chance that treasure is really in the castle. Very well then. We'll now proceed to glance at the geographical position of the castle. That's going to be important if these fellahs take possession and begin searching. We may find ourselves having to squat outside like a besieging army, if you get what I mean.

"Minrhyn Castle, Standy, is, or would be, a deuced tough nut to besiege. It was built in the dark ages by some jolly old pirate of a Vachell who didn't mean it to be sacked by his neighbours if he knew it. You've seen Minrhyn Head—that big rock striking out into the sea? Well, the top of the head is a sort of plateau of rough moorland covering about three square miles and triangular in shape. The apex of the triangle is to the sea, and it's on the apex that the castle's built. On each side there are three-hundred-foot cliffs, not exactly un-climbable, but pretty risky unless you know what you're about. Generally speaking, you can say the castle is unap-proachable from the sea.

"Inland there is one road by which you can get up to the summit of the Head. It branches off the Minrhyn Bay-Llandudno road, and winds up past a lot of abandoned slate quarries until it reaches the triangular plateau I was speaking of. But it's a rotten road and hardly ever used. In fact, you can say that between the cliffs and the slate quarries Minrhyn Castle is almost as much cut off as if it were on an island. You see, there's nothing to bring anybody up there. Only this rough stretch of moor and an empty castle which isn't even particularly picturesque. And in addition to the difficulties of getting up there, there's the fact that the castle has a local reputation for being haunted."

"Zen if these men go to look for ze gold zey will not be interfered with!" Dr. Constandos said.

"Precisely, Standy. That's what I wanted you to grasp. Once they're up there they can blow away the Head without anyone bothering. There are one or two cottages on the Head, but they're empty. Apart from one or two camping parties in the summer, sea-gulls and sheep have the whole Head to themselves."

"Your plans?" Dr. Constandos asked. "You 'ave made any—yes?"

"Heavens, no," Lord Basil said cheerfully. "Apart from a foggy idea it mightn't be a bad scheme to have a squint round this evening, I haven't the vaguest how to proceed. We'll just have to trust to luck and see what turns up."

About an hour later Dr. Constandos found himself shivering in front of the iron gate that barred the approach to Minrhyn Castle. He was not surprised that no one cared to live on the summit of Minrhyn Head. It was simply a bleak stretch of rough moorland, very high and commanding magnificent views, across which the wind blew perpetually. The castle itself, grey and storm-battered as the cliffs on which it stood, looked to the doctor a habitation fitter for birds than human beings.

Lord Basil was drawing a rug over the radiator of his car. Mona stood beside the doctor, her feet wide apart, her hands in the pocket of her blazer and her bobbed hair tossing in the wind.

"There you are," she cried. "The ancestral home of the Vachell family. If my great-grandfather hadn't invested in the South Sea Bubble I suppose I'd be living there now."

"Perhaps you will live there when we 'ave found ze treasure!" Constandos suggested.

"Perhaps not," said Mona. "I'd much rather be down in the Bay, thanks. Now, Basil, be intelligent. Having brought us up here, what do you propose?"

"A look 'round," said his lordship vaguely.

"Where? Outside or inside?"

"Outside first. You see, I'd like to make certain there aren't any of those fellahs knocking round before we go poking into cellars and things. It looks deserted enough, but you can't be sure."

The night was fast closing as they walked across lawns that had once been well-kept and were now almost as wild as the moor beyond the twelve-foot wall encircling the castle grounds. Behind the castle were the yards and beyond those an orchard with half the trees uprooted by the wind. They crossed the orchard and were confronted by the encircling wall.

A little to the right Lord Basil found a gap where someone had levered out half a dozen of the uncemented stones, leaving a tunnel through which sheep might pass into the orchard. With a sigh for his Saville Row suiting his lordship crawled through on hands and knees. He found himself on a strip of turf about twelve yards wide that ran between the wall and the edge of the cliff.

The others found him stretched full length on the turf with his monocled visage protruding over the abyss.

"A fellah could spit into the sea from here if he wanted to," he announced over his shoulder. "It's a sheer drop—about three hundred feet. Standy, my friend, if you go too near the edge you'll assuredly topple over. Pull him back, Mo . . ."

Mona pulled the doctor, who had incautiously wandered too near the edge, back into safety by his coat-tail. On hands and knees she wriggled forward until she could lie alongside Lord Basil.

"It's not the precise locality one would select for fun and games with a gang of cut-throats if one had one's choice," Lord Basil murmured. "I've visions of P.B.C. being cast on to yonder rocks in the near future. In fact, I feel decidedly goosey at the moment. What about you, Mo?"

"I'm all right," said Mona, whose teeth were chattering partly with cold and partly with terror of the depth into which she looked. "Can you see anything useful?"

"Yes. If you'll open your eyes for a second you'll see a black rock at the base of the cliff a little to the left. From there there's a gully that might be climbed in case of necessity. I'll remember that. It'll be an alternative route by which to reach the castle if those fellahs are watching the front."

He wriggled back, rose and brushed himself with care.

"That's that. Shall we go home now?"

"Home!" cried Mona. "But we haven't been inside the castle yet!"

"My sweet pippin, are you really serious? Inside a reputedly haunted castle on this extraordinarily uninviting evening! Tell you what. You go alone while Standy and I sit in the car and hold hands. How's that? What?"

Dr. Constandos looked at the Englishman with amazement not untinged by contempt. Apart from one or two flashes when he had displayed something approaching intelligence—noticeably when he had spoilt Sir Jasper's scheme for enticing him to the yacht—his lordship seemed quite as fatuous as that actor.

"I will escort Miss Vachell through ze castle if you are nervous," he declared.

"And leave me alone!" Lord Basil twittered. "Why that would be worse still. Auntie said I was never to be left alone even at night. I'll walk in the centre and you two hold my arms. And if you hear my teeth chattering remember it's with fright not cold. Er—the other way round, I meant to say."

There was a flash-lamp in the car. Armed with this they entered the castle by the main door which, rather surprisingly, proved to be unlocked.

The interior was in better repair than might have been expected from the appearance of the exterior. Mona, who had memories of the place from having visited it as a child, conducted them through the chain of vast, empty rooms. Rats scampered away like the ghosts of dead feet and bats and owls circled where once all had been light and laughter.

After inspecting the rooms on the ground-floor, they made their way to the kitchens. Here the dirt and disorder was indescribable. His lordship's face was a study in disgust as he stared round him.

"Well, all I can say is this," he said. "If those fellahs actually contemplate sojourning in this rat-haunted ruin they must be deuced anxious to get the gold. I'm hanged if I think it would be worth it for fifty *Cinco Llagas* treasures. Look at the bats on those beams. Thousands of them. All black and crinkled."

Mona looked and shuddered.

"But perhaps they won't have to sojourn," she said. "For all we know they may be able to get the gold quite quickly. We haven't seen the plans. It may be just a case of pulling away a few stones and walking off with the treasure."

"It may," Lord Basil agreed. "On the other hand, the fact that the treasure has remained undiscovered for about four hundred years points to its having been pretty carefully concealed. And Reilly said that Sylvester, otherwise Crane, had taken a lease of the castle for three months, giving the rather thin reason that he wanted to make an archaeological survey of the inside. If it had been simply a question of nipping in and taking the gold he wouldn't have troubled to do that. It looks to me as if the gang anticipated a longish job."

He dusted a space on a window-sill and sat down. He had switched off the flash-lamp to avoid wasting the battery, but they could see his pale face and slim shoulders silhouetted against the fading light.

"Gang," he repeated. "A noun of assembly implying more than a few. We're not a gang because we're only three. May I offer the suggestion that we enrol at least two more accomplices?"

"Men," Mona insisted.

"Yes, men. Stout-hearted chappies for preference. As a first nomination I propose my friend Stan Hastings. You've heard me speak of him, Mo."

"The American detective?"

"If Stan heard you call him that he'd be annoyed. He's not a detective in the official sense. His job is keeping an eye on wealthy tourists from the States in the interests of the big insurance companies on the other side. I've heard it said that he knows more about the big Continental jewel-gangs than any other man living. I don't know if that's true, but I do know that Stan's a stout fellah. If we could get him he would be no end of a help."

"Write to him."

"I will if I can find his address. I'm afraid though he may have gone back to the States. Well, if I can rope him in we'll have four. Now what about a fifth?"

They discussed various names, but could arrive at no decision. Suddenly Mona lifted her hand in a warning gesture.

"I thought I heard someone. Listen!"

"A false alarm," Lord Basil said after a minute. "Well, I personally am feeling cramped and cold. Shall we call it a day and clear off?"

"The cellars!"

"What about 'em?"

"We can't leave here without having a look at them. If the treasure's anywhere it would be down there. Perhaps the gang have been searching already. Shall we go down and see if we can spot their handiwork?"

"I'm positive we won't see anything. And it will be infernally damp and unpleasant down there."

"Oh, do let's, Basil. You never know your luck. They may have unearthed the treasure already and have left it there ready to carry off to-morrow."

Highly improbable as Lord Basil considered this suggestion, he gave in against his better judgment—as he usually did give in where Mona was concerned.

A heavy door opening off a stone-flagged passage barred the entrance to the cellars. The wood had been warped and swollen with damp so that it required their united strength to jerk it open. A flight of stone steps leading into abysmal darkness confronted them.

They descended the steps and advanced some hundred yards along a damp, evil-smelling passage with cellars opening off either side. Lord Basil stopped.

"Not another inch. It's too like being buried alive for my taste. Think what would happen if the lamp gave out."

"I too think we 'ave come far enough," Constandos said. "If Mees Vachell ees satisfied I advise we return."

The two men looked hopefully at Mona. She was swinging the beam of the flash-lamp into the darkness ahead as if she expected it to show her the *Cinco Llagas* treasure.

It did show her something, but it was not the ruddy gleam of gold. It was a black, shapeless thing that dodged swiftly and noiselessly from the beam.

The glimpse of that movement in the darkness was too much for Mona's nerves. She dropped the lamp and screamed. And as if in answer came a howl that was more bestial than human.

Lord Basil had found the flash-lamp. It was uninjured by the fall. Again the comforting little beam shot forth.

"I wonder what the deuce that was?" Lord Basil murmured. "A dog that has got lost in these catacombs and gone mad, or one of the gang playing a trick? Shall we—er—beat it?"

He addressed empty darkness, for Mona and Dr. Constandos were already "beating it" with undignified haste. Lord Basil trotted after them wailing like a lost child.

"For the love of Mike, don't leave a fellah alone," he panted. "It's catching me up . . . I can feel its hot breath . . . 'Elp . . . Go on, Standy, you ass . . . I'm only ragging."

Mona threw herself down on the bottom step.

"Topping," she panted. "I got an honest-to-goodness thrill out of that. Did you, Basil?"

"Of course I did. Not as good a one as old Standy though. He only touched ground at ten-yard intervals."

He glanced at the doctor, who was still white and breathless, and became serious.

"Not that I blame anyone if they did get the wind up. That howl coming from the darkness like that was the most unpleasant sound I've ever heard. Could you see what it was, Mo?"

"I only got the merest glimpse. It might have been anything."

"Well, we'll say it was one of the gang who heard us coming and decided to give us a scare. They seem strong on giving scares—these people with their wax fingers and all the rest of it. They . . . Hullo?"

"What's up?"

"Look up the steps and you'll see. I left that door open. This is getting past a joke . . .."

The heavy door at the top of the stairs had been shut. Lord Basil sprinted up the steps and hurled himself against it. A bolt creaked, but it stood fast.

"Well, we have been had for mugs!" Lord Basil cried. "Not content with scaring us, they've locked us in. Hi, you on the other side! What the deuce does this mean?"

Someone laughed. It was a sinister sound, more like the snarl of a vicious animal than a human laugh.

Dr. Constandos started violently. He clutched Lord Basil's arm and his face turned the colour of snow.

"Gravenant," he whispered. "Ze beeg devil with ze mad eyes. I tell you Gravenant ees ze worst of all."

Gravenant was speaking now. He must have put his mouth to the keyhole, for they could hear him plainly.

"Good evening, my dear young friends. So you've wasted no time in coming for the treasure! Is Dr. Constandos there?"

Dr. Constandos made no reply. They could hear his teeth chattering in the darkness.

"I'm anxious to have a word with you, doctor," Gravenant went on. "You filthy little spy! God, I wish I'd cut your throat that evening. I had Vachell's razor in my hand—I'd have done it if that cowardly Jew hadn't stopped me. The Tiger told me to. If I'd listened to him and not Crane you'd never have got here."

Lord Basil touched Mora's arm.

"He's as mad as a hatter. Go down to the bottom of the steps. If he opens the door run for your life."

But Mona preferred to remain where she was. She drew close to Lord Basil and his arm slipped about her waist.

Again Gravenant was speaking. And there was a note in his snarling, furious voice that made Mona's blood run cold.

"I tell you that gold belongs to me. I captured it from the Spaniards four hundred years ago. Why are you trying to rob me now? We waded through blood and flames and there were men screaming and great black waves thundering over the rocks. And I was the first on the *Cinco Llagas*. I pulled away the bodies and there was the beautiful raw red gold glistening in the flames. But it caught fire and has been burning ever since. Only blood can quench the fire. The Tiger told me. He knows—he knows the gold is mine. But I must kill, kill, kill, before I get it . . . I'll drench it in blood and then the Tiger will lick it clean . . . He told me . . . He told me the secret of the burning gold . . ."

Constandos had taken something from his pocket. He was levelling it at the keyhole when Lord Basil seized his wrist.

"Heavens, man, you can't do that! It would be murder. The poor devil's as mad as a hatter."

" 'E is 'omicidal lunatic of most dangerous type. I tell you 'e would be better dead . . ."

But Lord Basil removed the automatic from his fingers and dropped it into his own pocket.

"I'll use it as a last resort—not otherwise."

Gravenant was still speaking, but they could no longer distinguish the words. It was a senseless, snarling mumble of sound they heard—exactly like the sound that might be made by a furious tiger in a cage.

Suddenly he began to attack the door. Howling and screaming like a wild beast, he hurled himself against the unyielding wood. But it seemed he was too demented to draw the bolts. He was tearing and scratching at it just as the tiger he evidently believed himself to be might have attacked the confining bars.

Lord Basil had now drawn the revolver. He had resolved that if Gravenant got the door open he would shoot.

And then—as suddenly as it had commenced—the attack upon the door ceased. There was a sound of heavy feet plodding away along the passage.

"Exit human tiger dancing and singing," murmured Lord Basil. "Pleasant little pet, isn't he? Fairly powerful, too— judging by the way he shook that door."

"The whole castle trembled," Mona declared. "He's a monster. But what are we going to do now? We're still locked in."

"Try to find another way out, I suppose . . . Listen!" A sound like a shout, seemingly uttered in some distant part of the castle, had come to their ears. There was a shot and then another shout. And a second later three shots rang out in sharp succession.

"That's why Gravenant went away," Lord Basil said. "Someone else has come and he heard him. Let's hope the new arrival shot him dead . . . Shout for help . . . Altogether . . ."

Their cries were heard. Quick feet came along the passage. A man's voice, sharp and authoritative, spoke on the other side of the door.

"Who the devil are you? If you're friends of that other lunatic you can stay where you are while I fetch the police."

"He shut us in," Mona cried. "Do pull the bolts."

"Good heavens! Do I hear a lady's voice?"

"It's Mona Vachell speaking. Lord Basil Curlew and Dr. Constandos are here too. The lunatic took us prisoner."

"Miss Vachell the tennis champion? Well, I'm blowed—"

Already the unknown was tugging back the heavy bolts. He opened the door and the flash-lamp showed him standing before them, a vast figure of a man with a leonine head and a curling, golden beard.

"Commander Eggington, late of the Royal Navy, very much at your service," he said. "Miss Vachell, you won't know me, but I've been one of your most devoted fans ever since you first appeared at Wimbledon. Allow me to congratulate the most promising player Wales has produced for many a long year."

He took Mona's dirty little paw and bowed over it with the gallantry that is the hallmark of the old type of British naval officer.

As he did so Lord Basil remarked a little trickle of blood running down the back of his left hand.

CHAPTER IV

LORD BASIL GETS SOME GOOD ADVICE

"YOU'VE CUT YOUR HAND," Lord Basil bleated. "Hadn't you better tie it up in a hanky or something, what?"

The commander laughed with a shade of contempt.

"It's only where that lunatic's bullet grazed me. Nothing for an old shellback to bother about. Let's get out into the air."

"But where 'as Gravenant gone?" Dr. Constandos asked nervously.

"If you're alluding to the lunatic you needn't worry," Eggington laughed. "He's run away and I don't think he'll come back in a hurry. He knows by now that I'm a pretty good shot."

They followed him into the yard, and so out on to the moor. A full moon had risen, its beams revealing a mighty panorama of sea and mountain with the crescent lights of Minrhyn Bay twinkling far below.

"Magnificent country," said Commander Eggington. "Give me North Wales every time. And now, come along to my cottage. I prescribe a good tot of rum for all hands."

"Your cottage? Are you living on the Head?" asked Mona, trotting at his elbow.

"For a week or two. I like it up here better than the Bay. Air like wine and sunlight and sea-gulls. I've taken a cottage and furnished it. Very rough and ready, but good enough for an old pensioned sailor."

The cottage was the one nearest to the castle wall. It stood in a dip some distance from the road. To reach it they had to wade knee-deep in heather.

"Private and sheltered from the wind," the commander said. "I can sun-bathe here without offending anyone's susceptibilities. Walk in."

His description of the cottage as being rough and ready seemed well justified. The furniture in the sitting-room they had entered would have been dear at ten shillings. But a bright wood fire gave the room a pleasant, homely aspect.

Dr. Constandos, observing their host by the light of the fire, thought to himself that here was the finest specimen of an Englishman he had ever seen. Tall as Lord Basil Curlew was, he was dwarfed by the naval officer. With his immense stature and golden beard the commander might have been a reincarnation of some old Viking chieftain.

When he had mixed the rum, Eggington produced a pipe of size to match his figure.

"May I, little lady?" He looked at Mona. "It's Navy Shag. I can't smoke that scented hay young fellows use nowadays."

He looked contemptuously at the Turkish cigarette Lord Basil was taking from a monogrammed case.

"Do light up," said Mona. "Basil, I wish you'd smoke a pipe."

Clouds of smoke enveloped the commander's leonine head. He gave a grunt of satisfaction.

"That's better. I can't talk unless I've a pipe going full blast. Now I'll tell you what happened my side of that door. I was lying out on the heather when I saw your car going along the track of the castle, then I saw you get out and go round towards the cliffs. About half an hour later a man came running across the moor from the direction of the old slate quarries. He passed so close that I could see his face. He was a big chap with a red complexion and a white moustache. I thought he looked a bit queer. There was something furtive in the way he ran."

"Zat was Gravenant," cried Dr. Constandos.

"Is that his name? Well, he went into the castle and as I didn't see any sign of your reappearing I began to wonder what was up. In fact, my curiosity was so strong that I followed myself. I couldn't see anyone in the upper part, so I went down to the kitchens and began to rummage round there. Gravenant evidently heard me. He came charging down a passage with a gun in his hand, snarling like a wild beast. First I knew was when he fired and the bullet cut my arm. I thought that wasn't quite good enough. Luckily I always carry a gun myself—it's a habit I picked up when I was in China and have never dropped—so I whipped it out and let fly. I saw he was off his head so I didn't shoot to kill. I just put them near enough to scare him off."

Dr. Constandos shook his head sorrowfully.

"Zat was a mistake. I tell you Gravenant ees a dangerous man. 'E should be shot like a mad dog."

The commander had left the room to fetch lemons. Mona made a long leg and kicked Lord Basil's shin.

"Basil, he's just the sort of man we need. Do you remember what you said about getting Stan Hastings? The commander would be twice as good."

"M'yes," drawled Lord Basil. "He's a stout fellah without a doubt. Only thing is, would he approve of our trying to cheat the Government? We're on the wrong side of the law, remember."

"Ask him. He looks an old sport."

The old sport had returned with the lemons and had heard the last words.

"What am I to be asked, little lady?"

"Mona was wondering if you'd care to join us in an—er—enterprise," Lord Basil Curlew explained. "I suppose a very strait-laced sort of bird might say it wasn't legal, but you see—"

The commander glared at him.

"Not legal! Speak plainly, young man. You don't imagine an officer of the Royal Navy would connive at anything that wasn't absolutely above-board?"

"It's perfectly above-board," Mona cried. "Basil has muddled things as he always does. What we're trying to do is to recover a treasure that is really mine. My ancestor captured it in fair fight. But we think—in fact, we know—that a gang of criminals are after it, too. They've stolen the plans and—"

Miss Vachell's story-telling capacities were hardly on a par with her tennis. Aided, however, by Lord Basil and the doctor, she succeeded in giving a fairly coherent account of the events leading up to the evening's adventures.

Commander Eggington gave a roar of laughter and slapped his thigh.

"Well, I'm blessed! Who said the days of adventure were over and done with? Miss Vachell, you're perfectly right. It would be criminal to let the politicians touch that gold. They'd only appoint a lot more inspectors to stop people earning money. That's what the politicians do when they get a windfall, isn't it, Lord Basil?"

"That's what I say," Lord Basil laughed. "If the gold is there it ought to go to Mona. But you see, dear old Commander, not being able to appeal to the police is going to make things a bit awkward. I mean to say, we've got to fight these crooks with their own weapons. And they're a dangerous crowd. I don't suppose they'd even stick at a murder or two to get that gold."

"Are you trying to scare me off?"

"Not a bit of it, my dear old fruit. If you do come in you'll be as welcome as what-d'you-call-it's in June. But remember the odds are on the other chappies. They've got the numbers, plans, organization, everything."

"I wouldn't miss it for a farm," Commander Eggington declared. "It's the best thing that has come my way since Zeebrugge. Gad! Just think that there's nearly a million pounds' worth of gold, red gold, lying five hundred yards from where we sit. Makes one long to run for a spade and start digging the castle up. But of course that would be ridiculous. It must have been very cleverly concealed or it would have been found long ago. Well, well, well! To think that the *Cinco Llagas* legend may be true after all, and that you're the heiress!"

He beamed on Mona, who was looking like an excited untidy child. She laughed back.

"You're the right person for a treasure-hunt, Commander Eggington. You've got the authentic 'yo-ho-ho-and-a-bottle-of-rum' flavour. I could imagine you making a splendid pirate."

"In another age and environment I believe I might have been one," the commander confessed. "Adventure has always appealed to me strongly. Well, Lord Basil? What are your plans? Or haven't you made any yet?"

"I—er—really don't know," Lord Basil said feebly. "I suppose the rough idea is one should—er—hang about, doncherknow, and—er—watch the other chappies, and—er—butt in when a suitable moment offers, and—er—generally make oneself a bally nuisance, what!"

Commander Eggington looked at him sternly. "Are you serious about this, young man? Do you really mean to try to get the gold for the little lady?"

"Dear old soul, I'm positively oozing," said his lordship. "All clammy and strung-up, doncherknow."

"You don't look it. Instead of lounging there in that blasé way and talking about making a bally nuisance of yourself, you ought to make a definite plan. Bless my soul, if I was your age I'd be up and doing. Now, look here, I've got a suggestion to make."

"Pip, pip," said Lord Basil, with a wink at Mona.

"Yes, pip, pip, exactly. Everything, it seems to me, hinges on the plans that were stolen from Major Vachell. Without them you can do nothing. Now, why don't you, instead of waiting for the other side to make the first move, try to get the plans yourself? Find out where this gang is and go for them properly. That's the only way. If you wait until they're actually in the castle, you'll never see that gold. You've got to take the initiative."

"Oh, quite," said Lord Basil feebly.

"Another suggestion I'd like to make is that you use my cottage as your headquarters. This will be the bridge of the ship, so to speak. Bring your reports here. You'll always find me on the bridge ready to help with advice or in any other way. What do you say to that idea, little lady?"

"I think it's a splendid idea," Mona cried. "But what's the matter with Dr. Constandos? He seems quite overcome."

She was looking at Dr. Constandos on whom the toddy seemed to have worked with unusual effect. The little man in his neat blue suit was lying back in his chair, snores issuing from his open mouth. His straw hat and cane had fallen off his lap to the floor.

Commander Eggington bent over him.

"Fast asleep, poor little beggar. I suppose he's had a tiring day. You'd better leave him here for the night. I'll give him a shake-down with pleasure."

Lord Basil sat up.

"Thanks awfully and all that, but we couldn't put you to so much trouble. I'll take him back to the hydro."

"No trouble at all," the commander insisted.

"Dear old flick, it's frightfully kind of you to make the offer, but you see, I feel responsible for the doctor. In the hydro he'll be as safe as houses. I don't think even the gang could touch him there."

Despite the commander's protests, he woke Constandos, who struggled yawning and stretching to his feet.

"And now," Lord Basil said, "I think it's time the party broke up. Auntie doesn't like her little Basil to be out too late."

Outside the moonlight coated rocks and heather like freshly-fallen snow. The bleat of a sheep, the distant whistle of a train and the mumble of the sea far below were the only sounds that broke the stillness.

"*Look!*" Mona cried. "Gravenant."

She was pointing to the castle. The front was in shadow, and in one of the upper windows they could see a light.

A black form moved between them and the light. For a moment of time they saw Gravenant's silhouette, shapeless and crouching. Then the light vanished and the castle was in darkness.

"If I were you, Commander," Lord Basil twittered, "I'd vacate the cottage to-night and move down to the Bay. You've got a deuced dangerous neighbour."

The commander gave him a contemptuous glance.

"Thanks for the warning. I've settled tougher customers than that fellow before now. No, I don't think he'll trouble me. He knows I've got a gun and can use it."

They walked through the heather to the car. The commander slipped his arm round Mona's waist. She gave a squeak when his beard touched her cheek.

"The privilege of an old seadog," Commander Eggington laughed. "Don't scowl, Lord Basil. Remember that I'm old enough to be Miss Vachell's father."

CHAPTER V

THE LIZARD SPRINGS

IT MIGHT HAVE BEEN EXPECTED that Lord Basil Curlew would have chosen one of the big, expensive hotels for his stay in Minrhyn Bay. As a matter of fact he had done nothing of the sort. His choice had fallen upon a quiet, unpretentious little place called Rose Bower which stood conveniently close to the front.

As he had dined with Constandos at the hydro and had gone straight from there to Minrhyn Castle, he had not entered his own bedroom since the doctor's arrival in the Bay. And when, after safely depositing Dr. Constandos at the hydro, he finally did enter it, it was with a certain amount of not altogether pleasurable anticipation.

Mona and the doctor had found those sinister wax fingers on their pillows. Had he been similarly honoured?

He had. The finger was on his dressing-table, acting as a paper-weight for an envelope that lay underneath.

Lord Basil did not trouble to inquire of the staff who had entered the room during his absence. He knew that if he did he would be told nothing helpful.

He slit the envelope and sat down to read the letter it contained. It was written in a beautiful, thin copper-plate hand, the calligraphy, he felt certain, of the strange, artistic-looking person he had nicknamed "Mr. Smiling Sam".

"DEAR LORD BASIL (the letter read):
"Don't be foolish. As the future Duke of Matchingham, you doubtless find life well worth living. Why not stick to your polo, your fox-hunting and your golf and refrain

from interfering in a matter that may very well cost you your life?

"I refer, of course, to the *Cinco Llagas* treasure. The plans are in my possession and I am convinced that the gold is really there. Furthermore, its removal should be a matter of no great difficulty. If Dr. Constandos had not come from Port Said to tell Miss Vachell what he had overheard, I should have procured it with ease and nobody in the world need have been any the wiser.

"Constandos's coming has rather altered the complexion of affairs. Now that you and Miss Vachell are aware that the *Cinco Llagas* gold is no myth, you may feel tempted to try to secure it for yourselves.

"Take my advice and do nothing of the sort. I bear no ill-feeling towards either you or Miss Vachell, but I warn you that if you try to hinder my plans in any way you will die. I am not boasting; I am simply stating an irrefutable fact.

"And I make you an offer. In return for you and Miss Vachell undertaking not to try to hinder my plans for the removal of the gold I will—subject, of course, to my finding the treasure—pay the sum of ten thousand pounds to Miss Vachell as a slight solace for her disappointment.

"If you decide to accept, please address your reply to 'G. Smith' and leave it at the sub-office in Greenfields Road to be called for.

"I am,

"Yours most sincerely,

"THE LIZARD."

"P.S. Please forgive the wax fingers. My purpose in sending them was two-fold. First to administer a mild scare, and secondly to show you that my organization is fairly efficient. Remember that those wax fingers might equally easily have been deadly bombs."

Lord Basil Curlew folded the letter with care and slipped it into his morocco note-case.

"Getting a bit windy, old darling," he murmured aloud. "Think it's not going to be all plain sailing, hence the handsome offer!"

He crossed to the writing-table, unscrewed a gold fountain-pen and wrote a reply in a round, schoolboyish hand.

"DEAR OLD LIZZIE,

"How nice of you to write! And what a kind suggestion to make! Ten thousand pounds in return for letting you walk away with a million! I think not, Lizzie. On Miss Vachell's behalf I most regretfully refuse.

"Yours sincerely,

"CURLEW."

"P.S. Many thanks for the fingers. I hope they taste nice for one day I'm going to push them down your gullet."

He addressed and sealed the envelope and a few minutes later was sound asleep.

Commander Eggington was the first person of any consequence Lord Basil met the following day. The encounter took place in Station Road, the principal shopping thoroughfare in Minrhyn Bay. The commander, a striking figure in a knickerbocker suit of shaggy homespun, was wheeling a push-bicycle with a reinforced frame. A basket containing groceries hung from the handle-bars.

Lord Basil waved his gloves and quickened his steps. He was wearing a new suit of pale lavender that reflected high credit on its designer, Mr. Snip, of Saville Row.

"Pip, pip, Commander. How's things? All merry and bright, what?"

"Gravenant came to the cottage," Eggington said gravely.

"No! How bally awful!"

"He did. Luckily I'd barred the doors and windows so that he couldn't get in. But I heard him prowling round. Nasty-looking devil when you see him close. He'd got a knife in his hand."

"I'm glad I wasn't in the cottage," Lord Basil said feelingly. "What did you do?"

"Fired a shot out of the window to scare him away. He went off then—making in the direction of the slate quarries. The fellow's a homicidal lunatic without a doubt."

"Oughtn't we to tell the police or something?"

"If you do it will be good-bye to the treasure," Commander Eggington said. "And Gravenant can't do any harm so long as he stays on Minrhyn Head. Nobody ever goes up there except myself." He consulted an old-fashioned watch. "It's five to eleven, the correct time for splicing the mainbrace. Where do you suggest?"

"The Station Hotel at the corner. I was just heading there to have a spot myself before tricklin' round to see Mona. By the way, I got this last night."

He handed Eggington the letter he had found in his room the previous night. The commander glanced over it and laughed.

"I don't suppose Miss Vachell would want to close with that offer. But it's a good omen that they've made it. It shows they're very anxious to keep you out of the game. You take my tip, my boy, and have a try at getting hold of the plans. Carry the war into the enemy country. Don't wait for them to start digging in the castle. Well, here's the Station Hotel. Shall we turn in and have one?"

Lord Basil led the way into the lounge, a large, lofty room with one corner partitioned off to form a bar. Leaning against the bar, engaged in dalliance with the dark-haired girl behind the counter, was a thick-set man with a deeply tanned face. When he saw Lord Basil he straightened up and stared.

"Lord Basil Curlew! Well, the world is certainly a small place. What's brought you to North Wales, you old son of a gun? Still busy kidding folk that you're wet?"

The monocle fell from Lord Basil's eye.

"Stan Hastings! I call this providential—dashed if it isn't. Only last night I was saying I wished I knew where you were."

They shook hands heartily, the tall, languid Englishman and the wiry, alert American. Stan was beaming.

"This is certainly the best surprise I've had since I hit this burg," he declared. "As I was saying to Miss Floss here just now, Minrhyn Bay is a nice little town, but a sight too quiet for my taste. I like a spot where there's something doing. Meet Lord Basil Curlew, Miss Floss. He's the wettest thing ever walked down Piccadilly in spats—till you get to know him."

"Miss Floss found me out long ago; we're old friends," Lord Basil said. "This is Commander Eggington . . . Commander, Mr. Stan Hastings."

"Drinks are on me," boomed the commander. "Darling— if you'll forgive an old seadog the liberty of addressing you thus—will you take the order? What's it to be, lads? A tot of rum for all hands?"

The younger men voted for beer. Tankards in hand, they adjourned to a near-by table.

Lord Basil beamed on Stan.

"This is the sort of thing makes a chappie believe in Providence, Stan. You're the one fellah I really wanted to find. I've a show on will suit you down to the jolly old what-d'you-call-it. The genuine goods and no mistake about it."

To his amazement the American shook his head.

"Sorry, old horse, but I'm booked up to the back teeth with a show of my own. It promises—well, I guess it promises too well. You fellows won't misjudge me when I say I'm scared stiff."

"We won't believe you—at least I won't," Lord Basil said.

"It's a fact. If the Minrhyn Bay police weren't so busy tracking down the criminals who sell cigarettes after nine, I'd ask them for protection. But I guess it wouldn't be much good if I did. As far as the Lizard is concerned the police just don't exist."

"The Lizard!" Lord Basil cried. "My dear old flick, he's the very bird we're up against. Look at this!"

He thrust the letter into Stan's hand. The American read it with expressionless eyes.

"I don't know what he's talking about, but if I were you I'd clinch with this. It's a mighty handsome offer—for the Lizard."

Lord Basil looked at him reprovingly.

"This isn't like mother's brave boy! Surrender to a crook? You surprise me, Stanley." The American laughed.

"I knew you wouldn't take my advice, but I had to give it to save my conscience. Well, it seems that you're somehow hitched up with the business that brought the Lizard to Minrhyn Bay. Suppose you give me your end first, then I'll hand you mine. How's that?"

"Righty oh. It doesn't matter the commander hearing for he's in it just as much as I am. In fact, we've made him captain of the ship on account of his age and wisdom. Well, yesterday afternoon a funny little toad called Dr. Constandos rolled up from Port Said—"

Stan listened attentively. When Lord Basil had finished speaking, he threw himself back in his chair and emitted a long whistle.

"If that doesn't beat the band! The *Cinco Llagas* gold! It's a big enough thing to attract even the Lizard. Close on a million pounds in raw gold. If he brings it off it will be the biggest kill he's ever made. Oh, you're up against something hot, old horse. When the Lizard starts sending those wax fingers it's a sign he means business."

"Is the—er—sending of wax fingers a habit of his?" Lord Basil drawled.

"It is. He's a freakish devil, quite apart from the ordinary run of crooks. But I'll tell you about him presently. First I want to identify the man called Crane. I have an idea I've got him down here."

He produced a thick red notebook from his pocket. They watched him flip over the closely-written pages.

"This is my private 'Who's Who' of the Underworld," he grinned. "I don't know if his lordship mentioned it, Commander, but big-crook hunting is my hobby. I don't reckon myself a professional detective, but I work for some of the big insurance companies in the States. They pay me a fee to keep an eye on their clients—especially the ones who've got a lot of jewels—when they're travelling on this side. In that way I may say without boasting that I've accumulated quite a useful lot of knowledge about big European jewel-gangs. In fact, I'm open to bet that Scotland Yard or the Sûreté would give me five thousand dollars any day of the week for a read of what I've got written here . . ."

He ran his finger down a page.

"Here we are . . . Rathenden, alias Smith, alias Lewis, alias Crane . . . Short with bald head and Jewish appearance. Educated man, speaks well. Clever actor. Specializes in confidence trick . . . Dangerous . . .' That's your man all right. He works for the Lizard's gang in the Mediterranean ports as a rule. It's a cert that it was he who put the Lizard on to the *Cinco Llagas* treasure . . . Now, for the other fellow. What was his name? Gravenant?"

"Alias the human tiger," Lord Basil murmured.

They waited while Stan searched the notebook. At last he shook his head.

"He's not here. If he's working with the Lizard's gang he must be a new recruit I haven't heard of. Frankly, I don't quite see how he comes in. He's a bit of the puzzle that doesn't fit."

"He was with Crane when Major Vachell died," Eggington pointed out.

"Quite—I've grasped that, Commander. But what I can't tumble to is what is he doing now on Minrhyn Head? Look here. The getting of the *Cinco Llagas* gold is going to be a job that demands secrecy above all else. Well, when you're on a job demanding secrecy you don't usually send a homicidal lunatic on ahead to get things ready. Take my point? If the police hear there's a lunatic running wild on Minrhyn Head they'll go after him and that will spoil the Lizard's chance of getting the gold. The Lizard must know that himself."

"What's your explanation?" Lord Basil asked.

"There are several possible ones. Perhaps Gravenant has quarrelled with the gang and is working on his own; or perhaps the gang don't realize how mad he really is. He may have gone off his chump quite suddenly, you know. Or again he may not be mad at all. All that raving may have been pretence to scare you out of the castle—the same principle as sending the wax fingers. And you said something about a ghost howling at you down in the cellars. How do you know the ghost wasn't Gravenant playing another trick? He may have got round to the other side of the door by some way you don't know about."

Lord Basil stared at him, cigarette poised in air.

"That's a deuced ingenious theory, Stan. It never struck me Gravenant might have been pretending to be mad. But against that there's the fact that when Constandos saw him in Port Said he thought he'd got very queer eyes."

"Plenty of folk have queer eyes who aren't homicidal lunatics," the American argued.

"Well, I've seen him twice," Commander Eggington said, "and if he wasn't raving mad you can call me a Dutchman. Dash it all, the fellow's eyes were like blue flames when he came at me down that passage. And that shot he fired! You're not going to tell me that was all pretence!"

Stan shrugged his shoulders.

"You may be right. Well, leaving Gravenant as an unsolved riddle for the moment, I'll tell you fellows what I know about the Lizard. Count Saratini is his real name. He owes the nickname to the fact that the skin of his hands is discoloured. They're mottled green—most repulsive to look at. I believe it's the result of an accident in his laboratory. Some acid was spilt over them."

The American paused to take a pull at his tankard. He set it down and went on:

"I don't know how I'm to make you fellows grasp exactly what Count Saratini is. To start with he's not an ordinary criminal. The ordinary criminal has about as much sense of humour as a crab. Saratini on the other hand, delights in playing jokes—usually jokes of a very perverse and sinister nature. The sending of the wax fingers was typical of the man. Incidentally, I'll bet he made those fingers himself. He's an artist and also a brilliantly clever engineer."

"I," Stan went on, "would rate Saratini as one of the most dangerous criminals in Europe although I don't believe Scotland Yard or the Sûreté even knows he exists. He's the big brain behind one of the cleverest jewel gangs on the Continent. The French Riviera is his usual hunting-ground. It's unheard of for him to come so far afield as North Wales. But I suppose what attracted him was the value of the *Cinco Llagas* treasure and the comparative ease with which it could be secured.

"It was a certain little lady living in Calais who gave me the tip that he was going to Minrhyn Bay. She's got a boy friend in the gang called Heinman, who's a brute if ever there was one. God help that girl if Heinman finds she's been ratting, incidentally—he won't, though, for she's too clever. Well, when she put me wise about Saratini and some other leading lights of the gang going to Minrhyn Bay I could hardly believe her. Minrhyn Bay! What the blazes there could be in a little Welsh seaside town to make it worth Saratini's visiting I just couldn't imagine. But I knew there must be something pretty big. A guy like Saratini wouldn't go to North Wales just to look at scenery!

"So that's how I come to be here. Curiosity to see what the Count was up to—that's what brought me. And I don't mind telling you fellows that if Saratini finds I'm here he'll get me—if he can. He knows I've been on his trail for years. I told you at the beginning I was scared, didn't I? Well, that may have been an exaggeration, but it's the gospel truth I'd rather take risks with a man-eating tiger any day than with Saratini. He's a cunning devil who thinks as much of murder as you or I'd think of lighting our pipes."

He paused to glance at his listeners' faces. Lord Basil Curlew looked mildly interested; Commander Eggington was smiling sceptically. Stan took a photograph from his wallet and pushed it across the table.

"There you are, gentlemen. Count Saratini, the most dangerous man in Europe."

Lord Basil adjusted his monocle. The face in the photograph was that of the man he had seen in the Rolls. The deep-set eyes, the high forehead and the cruel, whimsical mouth were unmistakable.

Commander Eggington pushed back the photograph with a grunt.

"Are you pulling our legs, Mr. Hastings? D'you mean that dyspeptic, schoolmaster-looking fellow is really dangerous?"

"So much so that I advise you fellows to get Miss Vachell to accept his offer."

"And what about yourself?" The American grinned.

"I guess Saratini isn't going to make me any offers. Anyway, I'm an old hand and can look after myself, but you and Lord Basil are different. Take my advice and clinch the offer. At the moment Saratini is only laughing at you. If he'd thought you were really dangerous he'd have had you murdered long before this."

Lord Basil stared at him in mild reproof.

"Murdered! Sweet thing, this is North Wales, not Chicago. People don't get murdered here. It simply isn't done."

"It's done wherever Saratini happens to be—that's my experience," the American said grimly. "And sometimes it's worse than murder. That sense of humour of his has landed more than one fellow in an asylum before now."

They were astonishing words to hear in that orthodox setting. Behind the bar Miss Floss was polishing glasses; through the open window Lord Basil could see the sunlit square fronting the station, where a policeman was directing trippers to the front. Murder seemed as remote as the end of the world.

A pageboy had entered the lounge. He approached their table, the only one occupied.

"Lord Basil Curlew wanted on the phone, please." Lord Basil rose.

"An invitation to play tennis, I expect. Pip, pip, chappies . . . I'll be back in two two's."

When he did come back five minutes later he was looking unwontedly grave. Stan gazed at him.

"Anything wrong, old son?"

Lord Basil's slender fingers were drumming the devil's tattoo on the glass-topped table. But when he spoke his voice was light, drawling as ever.

"The Lizard has kidnapped Mona. She never got back to the Rectory last night. I left her at the hydro, you see; she'd left her car there and she meant to drive herself home."

There was a moment's silence. Commander Eggington broke it harshly.

"If Saratini has injured that little lady, I'll wring his neck like a chicken's," he said.

CHAPTER VI

THE COWLED HORROR

AS LORD BASIL HAD TOLD STAN, he had left Mona at the Brig-y-don Hydro on their return from Minrhyn Head. Her car was there and she proposed to drive herself back to the Rectory which was only a mile or so from the hydro.

From the hydro steps she watched the tail-light of Lord Basil's car vanish down the drive. She turned to where Dr. Constandos stood swaying at her side. He had not as yet recovered from the effects of Commander Eggington's toddy.

"I'll be coming up here to play tennis to-morrow morning and I'll drop in to see if you're still alive," Mona said. "Will that be all right?"

Dr. Constandos declared with a hiccup that it would be very much all right. He was in a mood to agree to anything. His straw hat had been battered beyond repair, his suit looked as if he had been dragged backwards through an ash-pit, but his eyes shone behind his thick pince-nez with a love of adventure entirely due to the toddy. If Dr. Constandos's first day in North Wales had begun badly, there could be no question but that it was having a happy ending.

"If you do not find me 'ere, Miss Vachell, you will understan' I am somewheres else. You need not make ze search. Remember I can take care of myself bettaire zan most mens. Please do not you or Lord Basil be anxious on my account."

"We won't," Mona assured him. "But why shouldn't you be here? I thought you were so keen to help us to get the treasure."

"Keen! *Bacchos,* you ask if I am keen! I tell you I am keener zan a razor, Mees Vachell, you do not know what sort of mans I am. If Gravenant was 'ere now I would take heem by ze throat an' keel 'im with my bare 'ands. I will get ze treasure for you, I, ze brave Dr. Constandos. Long live Greece! 'Ooray!"

Mona giggled.

"I'll have to tell the commander not to give you any more toddy; it evidently doesn't suit you. Well, good night, Dr. Constandos. Don't dream about ghosts and tigers."

She waved her hand, ran down the hydro steps and vanished in the direction of the garage. Dr. Constandos walked uncertainly into the lounge. Love of adventure was pulsing strongly through his veins. He had not the least desire to go to bed.

He hailed a waiter on night-duty.

"A beeg 'ot toddy, please. Vaire strong an' in a tankard," he ordered.

In the meantime Mona had started up her little car and departed for the Rectory. As she flew along the wide, chestnut-tree bordered roads at the back of Minrhyn Bay, she thought of the *Cinco Llagas* treasure and all its possession would mean.

It was a wonderful dream. Nine hundred thousand pounds! Wealth beyond her wildest imaginings. She could enrich all her relations and have ample over for herself.

Mona was the most generous little soul alive. Having endowed herself with what she really wanted, a Chrysler sports model and a fur coat like Mrs. Flant's, she began mentally to give away the *Cinco Llagas* gold by bucketfuls. And it may be taken as an indication of where her heart lay that in the dream it was Lord Basil Curlew who got the lion's share. Dear old Basil! Superior-minded people scoffed at his monocle and his elegant clothes, but he was a man for all that. A loyal, kindly man who never let his friends down . . .

Yes, she'd marry him if she got the treasure. She'd be an heiress then; no one could accuse her of having "caught" him. Her poverty and the fear of doing him a wrong had made her hold back. But if she had the *Cinco Llagas* gold as a dowry she could become Lady Curlew with an easy conscience.

And then the dream-castle came down with a crash. Close to the Rectory gate a car had been pulled into the side of the road. A policeman stepped into the road and raised his gloved hand as a signal for her to stop.

A guilty conscience lent added sweetness to Mona's smile.

"Only thirty-five according to the clock and the road was empty. And I've written for a new licence. I have really. I posted the letter only this morning."

"Are you Miss Mona Vachell?"

"Yes."

"Only daughter of the Rev. Thomas Vachell, Rector of Brig-y-don?"

"Yes."

The policeman gazed at her like a sorrowful sheep. He was a tall man with a drooping moustache.

"I'm afraid I've bad news to give you, miss. Mr. Vachell is 'urt."

The sparkle died out of Mona's face.

"Hurt! What do you mean?"

"He was involved in an accident. Near the Deganway Pass. He was in a charabanc; it skidded going down the Pass and turned over. Your father was flung out and hit his head against a rock. They've taken him to Dr. Jones's house between Deganway and Pwllchywchi. The Deganway super sent me over in his car to fetch you."

Mona listened like one in a dream. Her father dying! Dear old dads! She felt stunned, incapable of thought.

"Better come quick as you can, miss. Not a minute to lose if you want to see him alive. I've been up to your house and told them there . . . He's asking for you . . . Dr. Jones doesn't think he'll last an hour."

After that Mona wasted no more time. The Deganway superintendent's car was a sports Bentley, much faster than her own. At the policeman's suggestion she backed her own car up a side lane. Then she got into the Bentley and in a moment they were off with the policeman at the wheel.

The car was fast, and he was evidently a driver of more than average skill. Even on the winding Mochdre road leading inland from Minrhyn Bay he contrived to keep the speedometer needle hovering in the neighbourhood of sixty.

And then the incident occurred—one that made but little impression on Mona's mind at the moment, but that later she was destined to recall. At the four cross-roads close to the old Conway Bridge a long black car, recklessly driven, shot out of a side-turning. For perhaps half a minute it roared alongside the swaying Bentley. And then the windscreen in front of the policeman's face suddenly starred.

He stepped on the accelerator pedal. The Bentley leapt ahead. As the black car dropped behind he turned to the white-faced girl at his side.

"Some fool trying to race us. Wish I'd got his number. D'you see the glass in front is broken? Must have been a stone flung up off the road did that."

Mona made no comment. She was so preoccupied wondering if they would find her father alive that she had hardly noticed the incident.

They were now traversing hilly, lonely country, typical of the inland districts of North Wales. The head-lamps showed heather-covered hills criss-crossed with stone walls and bare stretches of moor. At last they saw a white iron gate. The Bentley slowed to a crawl. They turned and bumped up a rough drive to a small farmhouse built of grey stone.

Mona flew up the steps. Evidently she was expected. An elderly, hard-faced woman opened the door before she could knock.

"I'm Miss Vachell. Is my father—?"

"Come in."

The door slammed behind her and a key grated. She was standing in a dark passage. The woman had vanished and she heard a murmur of voices.

Then a door on the left opened and she saw a man she imagined must be the doctor. He was thick-set with a markedly Jewish appearance. When he spoke his voice was suave and cultured.

"I see you've arrived safely, Miss Vachell."

She sprang towards him.

"My father? Is he—?"

The full red lips parted showing excellent teeth.

"As far as I know Mr. Vachell is enjoying his usual health. To be quite candid, I've never seen the reverend gentleman in my life. If he's half as charming as his daughter I wish I had."

Mona stared, anger and surprise gathering in her eyes.

"Then there hasn't been an accident? The policeman told me—"

"Forget what the policeman told you," the Jew laughed. "He's no more a policeman than I am. I'm sorry you got such an alarm, Miss Vachell, but it was imperative you should be brought here to discuss a certain matter. Don't blame us. If you blame anyone blame that infernal little eavesdropping doctor from Port Said, the real cause of all this trouble. Will you come in here?"

Her feelings were a mixture as she followed him into a stuffy little sitting-room. Relief that her father was all right, anger with herself for having walked so easily into the trap. It had been the policeman's uniform had thrown her off her ground. That and the plausible manner in which the man had told his story.

There was a lamp in the sitting-room. By its light she studied the Jew's face. A clever, unscrupulous rogue was how she summed him up.

"Are you Crane?" she asked.

"Ah, you've recognized me from Dr. Constandos's description! Yes, I am the man he knew as Crane. I had the melancholy distinction of being one of those present when your late uncle made his last behest."

He laughed softly and Mona felt she hated him.

"Miss Vachell," Crane went on, "you have been brought here to listen to an offer that is also being made in writing to your friend, Lord Basil Curlew. It relates, of course, to the *Cinco Llagas* treasure. Now we—that is to say myself and my friends—want if possible to settle this matter without any sort of unpleasantness. We believe the gold to be in the castle; we want to take it and go away. That is what we would have done if Constandos hadn't interfered. We'd have leased the castle, quietly removed the gold and neither you nor anybody else in the world would have been any the wiser. And if you're sensible and accept our offer that is what we shall still do."

"What is the offer?"

"Give me your word as a lady not to interfere in any way with our operations at the castle and I'll send you home tonight with a cheque for ten thousand pounds in your pocket."

Mona's eyes flashed.

"In other words, make you a present of nearly a million pounds. No thanks, Mr. Crane. I give you my word as a little lady that if the gold is really there we'll get it and not you."

The Jew gazed at her for a moment without speaking.

"I was afraid you'd take that attitude, Miss Vachell. You're Welsh and fiery and—if I may say so—childishly wilful. Indeed, I said so much to the Count. But he wished you and Lord Basil to be given every chance. He's not usually so forbearing. I was surprised."

"I'm not," said Mona. "Perhaps the Count, as you call him, is afraid we'll stop him getting the treasure and that's why he's made the offer!"

Crane laughed—with genuine amusement it seemed to Mona.

"That remark only shows how little you appreciate what you're up against. The notion that either you or Lord Basil Curlew could oppose Count Saratini in any way is simply ludicrous. Do you know Sir Jasper Goldburg?"

"I know of him."

"Then you're probably aware that in England Sir Jasper is regarded as a fairly wealthy and powerful man. Yet to Count Saratini he is the merest puppet. In the past he has undertaken and accomplished far, far more difficult matters than the securing of the *Cinco Llagas* gold. And I warn you plainly, Miss Vachell, that the people who oppose Saratini— well, they don't usually enjoy their old-age pensions."

"Surely you're not suggesting he'd—he'd murder us?"

The Jew showed his perfect teeth.

"I can see you've led a very sheltered life, Miss Vachell. Does the idea of murder strike you as being so very out of the ordinary?"

"Of course it does. The police—"

Crane raised his hand.

"Please don't talk about the police. When Count Saratini has to—er—get rid of people he doesn't like, it's not done in such a way that the police have the least suspicion of foul play. They die as the result of an accident—always. Believe me, you'll be very foolish if you try to drag the police into this matter. For one thing, you'll ruin your own chances of getting the treasure."

"But if the Count is going to murder us—"

"He's not. All he asks is that you remain neutral while he secures the treasure. What I said just now was simply to try to make you understand what the consequences might be if you refuse his offer. But you won't be so foolish."

For a fraction of a minute Mona hesitated. Despite herself, she had been impressed by the Jew's manner.

But, as her opponents on the tennis court often learned, she was a game fighter. The thought of surrender was repugnant. Especially the thought of a surrender impelled by veiled threats.

She threw back her head and faced Crane.

"Foolish or not, I do refuse. I think I owe it to my uncle. You robbed him when he was dying! That was a brave thing to do, Mr. Crane!"

For any effect her angry words had upon the Jew she might have been speaking to the wall. The only response was an oily smile.

"Then I'm afraid, Miss Vachell, you will have to remain in this house. How long depends on how quickly we can locate the treasure. The fact that you're in our power will doubtless restrain Lord Basil from doing anything foolish. Not that we're in the least alarmed of that young man. I've never met him, but I'm told his friends allude to him as 'Poor blooming Curlew'. A charming person, doubtless, but—er— not precisely what you would call intelligent, is he?"

Mona flamed.

"That's all you know. Basil isn't one of your brainy people, but he's got a knack of getting there."

Crane was lighting a cigar. His smile at the mention of Lord Basil's name infuriated Mona.

"I'm rather a believer in brains as opposed to mere brawn, Miss Vachell," he said in a conversational tone. "I'll give you a concrete instance. Originally, as I daresay Dr. Constandos told you, I shared the secret of the *Cinco Llagas* treasure with a man called Gravenant. Now Gravenant had brawn in abundance, but he was lacking in grey matter. Also, he was very greedy. If it hadn't been for his greed leading him to want to secure the whole of the *Cinco Llagas* treasure for himself, he would not now be languishing in a French criminal lunatic asylum. Poor Gravenant! It's a pity he was so unreasonable."

"Why did they let him out?" Mona asked. "He was certainly very unreasonable to-night. First he got us shut up in the cellars, then he nearly shot—"

In the nick of time she stopped herself saying Commander Eggington's name. It had flashed into her mind that the gang didn't as yet know that he was one of their opponents. To have mentioned him would have been a tactical error.

But she needn't have troubled. If she'd shouted the name twenty times it would have been lost on Mr. Crane. He was staring at her in almost ludicrous surprise. The cigar had fallen on the carpet and every vestige of colour had fled from his florid face.

"Gravenant?" His voice was a croak. "Did I understand you to say you'd seen Gravenant?"

"We didn't actually see him," Mona explained patiently, "but we heard his voice, which was nearly as bad."

A faint look of relief crept over the Jew's face.

"It can't have been him. The Count got him put away. Someone was playing a joke."

"A poor joke," Mona sniffed. "He nearly killed us all. But it was certainly Gravenant. Dr. Constandos recognized his voice. I say, are you feeling ill?"

"Hell!" Crane muttered. "I knew they wouldn't hold that devil long. And now he'll be mad for his revenge . . . Oh, Hell!"

The change in his manner was balm to Mona. His suave nonchalant bearing had completely vanished; he looked like a man who has heard his death-sentence announced. Jumping from his chair he began to pace about the room, muttering to himself.

He seemed to have forgotten Mona's existence. Suddenly he stopped and rang a bell furiously. The man in policeman's uniform appeared.

"What's up now, Mister?"

"The devil's up. Gravenant has escaped."

"Escaped! I thought the Chief had had him given up to the French police and he was booked for the guillotine!"

"That's what the Chief intended, but he tricked them he was mad. He's clever enough for anything. I believe even the Chief himself is afraid of him, Morgan."

Mona was almost enjoying the situation.

"I thought you said Count Saratini was so powerful, Mr. Crane! Surely he's not afraid of a wretched madman! Tell him to send Gravenant a little wax finger."

Neither man paid the least attention. They were staring at one another with white faces. The man called Morgan took an automatic from his pocket.

"Wish I was safe back at headquarters. There's only you and I and Mrs. Jones in this house. I wonder if it could have been 'im followed us from Minrhyn Bay to-night. It was queer the way the windscreen splintered. Almost like a bullet had gone through."

"What are you talking about, you fool? Who chased you?"

"I'm not saying anyone chased us," Morgan said sulkily. "All I know is that someone in a black car sat on our tail for a mile or two. I'd to push her up to eighty to shake him off.

At the time I thought it was some young fool trying to race us."

"What makes you think differently now?"

"Hearing that Gravenant's knocking 'round—that's all. The windscreen starred when he was close behind. It might have been a stone—or it might have been a bullet."

"Did you hear a shot?"

"You wouldn't—not with the din the engines were making. How about phoning headquarters?"

"No good. The Chief's on the yacht with Sir Jasper. But we'll have to let him know somehow."

The two men went to a writing-table at the further side of the room. Mona threw a hurried glance round. Now if ever would be her time to escape.

Despite the boldness with which she had faced Crane, she had inwardly been shaking with terror. The prospect of having to remain a prisoner in the hands of these brutes was horrible. If she could get away from them she would.

She felt almost grateful to Gravenant for having switched their minds so completely away from herself. The Jew had now seated himself at the writing-table and was composing what was evidently intended to be a message of warning for the Count. Morgan was leaning over his chair, his back towards her.

It would be impossible to reach the door without being heard. She stole a glance at the window on her right. The heavy plush curtains had been drawn, but through a slit she could see that the window itself had been left open to its fullest extent. And as the room was on the ground-floor she knew the drop to the ground outside would be inconsiderable.

Again she glanced at the gangsters. They were now arguing hotly. Crane had dropped his pen and was drumming on the table with his fist.

". . . we can do nothing till we get rid of Gravenant. He's as cunning as a fox and as dangerous as a tiger. And now he'll be out for revenge as well as for the treasure. He must have guessed who gave him up to the French authorities . . ."

Mona rose from the chair. Holding her breath and moving as silently as a shadow she slipped behind the plush curtains. They were still arguing. She swung her shapely legs over the sill. Her rubber-soled shoes touched the mould of a flower-border. From the room behind came Morgan's angry voice:

"I'd back the Count to settle fifty Gravenants. Go and shut yourself up in a monastery if you're scared."

Mona waited to hear no more. The sports Bentley was standing at the foot of the steps. Morgan had turned it 'round so that it was facing the gate. And the head-lamps, which he had omitted to switch off, showed her the gate itself was open.

Could she get away before they heard her? She braced herself to make a dash.

But the head-lamps showed her something else, a monstrous apparition standing beside the drive that made her shrink half-fainting against the wall. It was the vast figure of a man clothed in black from head to foot. His face and head were covered by a cowl similar to those worn by the Spanish inquisitors, and the remainder of his body was hidden by a loose robe of black material.

Suddenly the monk began to creep across the grass towards the window under which she crouched. And she noticed now that the top of his cowl had been gathered up to form two black ears, which gave him a weird resemblance to a great cat walking on its hind-legs.

Gravenant! The thought rushed into her mind. She turned and ran for dear life while behind her she heard the padding of swift feet upon the turf.

CHAPTER VII

MR. CUSPER TAKES MEDICINE

"MY LITTLE LADY," Commander Eggington repeated. "If Saratini has hurt her I'll wring his neck like a chicken's."

He glared at Lord Basil and Stan as if daring them to challenge his statement. But neither of the younger men spoke. His lordship was staring out of the window with narrowed eyes; Stan was whistling soundlessly between his teeth, a habit of his when seriously disturbed.

Miss Floss broke the silence. The sweet girl behind the bar was quite ignorant of what had taken place. All she knew was that there were three well-dressed presentable males in the lounge, and she not unnaturally desired a little of their attention.

"Here, Mr. Hastings, could you tell me what this is, please?"

She had selected Stan for her inquiry as the handsomest of the trio.

The American moved mechanically towards the bar. Commander Eggington followed. Lord Basil remained where he was, tankard reversed above his face.

"What what is?" Stan asked.

"This. Looks like it might be an old coin to me. Eddie thinks it's gold. D'you think it's worth anything?"

Stan took the coin indifferently. It was about the size of an English half-crown and deeply crusted with red rust.

Suddenly the American's casual air vanished. He whipped out a penknife and began to scrape. A dull yellow gleam showed through the rust and he gave a cry.

"Well, I'm sugared! See what it is, Commander? An old Spanish gold piece; those are the arms of Castile and there's

King Philip's profile on the other side with the date 1557. Jumping snakes!" He lowered his voice. "What's the betting this didn't come out of the *Cinco Llagas?*"

Commander Eggington snatched it from his hand. "I do believe you are right. Who gave you this, darling?"

Miss Floss tittered and looked coy.

"Ah, that would be telling. No names, no pack drill. Perhaps I picked it up on the beach."

The Commander bent his enormous frame across the bar so that he could whisper in her ear.

"Won't you tell an old sailor? I won't be jealous. Which of the boy-friends was it, darling?"

The delighted girl tried to push him back.

"Who are you calling darling? And stay your own side of the bar, please. I'm not saying who it was, so there!"

Stan had returned to where Lord Basil was staring into the empty depths of the tankard. He slapped his shoulder.

"Buck up, old son. We may be all wrong about what we think."

"1 hope to blazes we are," his lordship said. "If those fellahs have got Mona . . . I mean to say, it would be the beastly limit, what?"

"We don't know they have for certain," Stan said.

"No, but it seems devilish probable. And if they have I'm dead sure of one thing—that it would be no use appealing to the police. I'm not bothering about the treasure; I'm thinking of Mona herself. The police would never be able to find her, and if those fellahs knew we'd called them in they might turn nasty and take it out of poor little Mo."

"I'm with you," Stan nodded.

"Of course," Lord Basil went on, "if we knew they'd—they'd murdered Mona it would be another matter. But I'm pretty certain they haven't. Ten to one their game is to hold her hostage until they've got the treasure."

"That's likely enough. But what about the folk at the house? They may have gone to the police already."

Lord Basil shook his head.

"The old man's away. It was Mrs. Galbraith the house-keeper phoned me just now. She's not seriously bothered as yet because Mona's got a school friend living in Rhos who sometimes gives her a shake-down. Old Bannock-Face—that's Mona's pet name for the Galbraith woman—asked if I thought she'd gone to this girl, and I, doing some devilish quick thinking, said I knew she had. All the same, I'd better see old Bannock-Face, worse luck. She scares me stiff."

"Scares you? How's that?"

"She's a verra sensible woman with a gey strong mind of her ain," mimicked Lord Basil, putting on his hat. "But we Curlews know no fear. Coming with us, Romeo?"

Romeo, otherwise Commander Eggington, shook his head.

"I think not. You young fellows will do better without an old hulk like myself in tow. I'll stand by ready to assist. Eddie "—he addressed the page—" I propose to lunch here. Avast, lad, and tell them I want an underdone steak sharp at one. Good luck, boys, good luck . . ."

As the page hurried away the commander winked at Stan.

"I guess it's not for the sake of the steak only he's dropped anchor there," the American chuckled as they strode up Station Road. "Nothing dumb about the commander. He's out to find who gave the girl that Spanish coin. If it isn't one of the *Cinco Llagas* lot it's a mighty queer coincidence. Looks almost as if some guy had been riflin' the treasure already."

"Not necessarily," Lord Basil told him. "It's not unusual for Spanish coins to be picked up on the beach round here."

Opposite Smith's bookshop Stan grasped his companion's arm.

"On your left, Saratini himself and Sir Jasper."

A great yellow Rolls was purring down the street in the direction of the station. Lord Basil caught a glimpse of the long whimsical face of Count Saratini. Had he imagined it or had a thin gloved hand waved in mocking salutation?

"If we'd had a car handy we could have followed," Stan grunted. "No use now. Cool devil, isn't he? Riding round Minrhyn Bay as if he owned the place!"

They hurried on, his lordship's long legs covering the ground at a pace with which Stan found it difficult to keep up. It was the fashionable hour at which to be seen in Station Road. Many people hailed Lord Basil as he strode past.

Ordinarily his lordship would have liked nothing better than to prop himself on his cane and talk tennis or golf by the hour. But now it was different. There was a sharp fear in his heart that drove him relentlessly on.

Mona? Was she alive or dead? If they *had* harmed her . . . Lord Basil swung his cane so that it whistled viciously through the air.

"One thing, old flick."

"What?"

"I'd rather it was Saratini had her than Gravenant. You don't think . . ."

"Hell, no!" Stan exploded. "If anyone has kidnapped her it's the Count."

Brig-y-don Rectory stood in what were locally called the Min-y-don woods overlooking the Bay. At the gate Stan halted.

"No sense two of us going up. You carry on."

At the end of ten minutes he saw Lord Basil returning. "That's all right. I braved old Bannock-Face and pledged her my Curlew word that Mona was at Miss Robinson's house in Rhos. The Bannock swallowed it like a hungry trout. No fear of her going to the police. I should have been a giddy old diplomatist, what?"

Lord Basil polished his monocle with a violet-scented handkerchief. Despite the pace at which they had ascended the hill he was quite unruffled so far as his outward appearance went.

"I elicited one other thing from the Bannock. I'm not sure though if it's got any bearing on the present situation. What do you think?"

He handed the American a filthy scrap of paper. With difficulty Stan deciphered the pencilled words:

"dere lady,
"you meet me at end of Maiden's Nose to-night you
will here sumthing to your avantage. Don't fail
"your respectful frend."

"Where did it come from?"

"It was pushed under the Rectory door some time last night, addressed to Mona. Nobody saw who brought it Mrs. Galbraith found it on the floor this morning. I'd told her I was lunching Mona at Sumner's, so she gave it me to deliver. In case you don't know what the Maiden's Nose is . . . Come here and see."

He led the American to a spot whence they could see the whale-shaped mass of Minrhyn Head through the trees. On that clear sunny day the castle and cliffs were plainly visible even at that distance.

Lord Basil pointed.

"Five o'clock from the castle and two fingers down. D'you see a sort of grey blur against the green? Imaginative people say that it looks like the profile of a girl's head looking towards the Bay. I can't see the resemblance myself except when I've had a couple . . . Well, that patch of rock is called the Maiden's Head. The Maiden's Nose, therefore, is a little to the right of the castle and about a hundred yards down the cliffs."

"You'd have to do a spot of climbing to get there?"

"You would. It was a deuced queer spot to choose for an appointment Looks to me as if the writer was a shy bird. Didn't want any publicity, what? D'you think Saratini sent this as a second trap in case the first didn't work?"

Stan shook his head.

"The Count wouldn't do anything so obvious as sending a faked message. And his traps don't fail. I should say this came from Gravenant."

"I shouldn't. Gravenant is streets too balmy to concoct even such a clumsy plan as this . . . Hullo!"

Glancing up a side lane a few hundred yards from the Rectory gate Lord Basil had seen a shabby little red two-seater pulled close to the hedge.

"Mona's car! Then she came this far at any rate. Now perhaps we'll learn something."

His heart was thudding uncomfortably as he approached the car. But there were no signs of a struggle. The car had been neatly parked on the grassy verge of the lane, the engine and lights properly switched off.

Stan nosed round like a terrier. After a minute he showed Lord Basil a little pool of oil on the side of the main road a few yards from the corner of the lane.

"I guess I can reconstruct what happened. There was a car drawn up here when Miss Vachell came along from the hydro. See these skid marks? That's where she pulled up in a hurry. Presumably someone had jumped into the road and made her stop. Then he must have talked to her, spun her some yarn that induced her to reverse up that lane and leave her car where it is now. You can see the tracks where she reversed quite plain. It looks to me as if she knew the person who stopped her by sight. If she'd suspected anything wrong she could have jumped on the gas and driven on to the Rectory. By the way, was she in the habit of parking up that lane?"

"When she was in a hurry. It saves her going up the Rectory drive and round to the garage."

"Then we'll take it she was in a hurry last night. I picture her running from her own car and jumping into Mr. Unknown's. Now let's see if we can follow his tracks? Yes, here they are. He swung right-handed down the King's Road. He was travelling fast for the near wheels went up the bank when he took the corner. Well, I guess that's all I can tell you. There are a dozen turns after that he may have taken."

"Good work," said Lord Basil. "We know now she was decoyed into a car close to the Rectory and taken off. The chappie who tricked her must have known his job all right. Mona's as sharp as a needle."

"Not sharp enough for the Count, though," Stan said. "I told you his plans don't fail."

There was no more to be learned in the vicinity of the Rectory. They began to walk down the King's Road to the Bay. Lord Basil broke the silence.

"Next thing is to find Saratini's headquarters, what?"

"How about Sir Jasper's yacht?"

"Probable, but not certain. It's quite likely he's taken a house on shore prior to moving into the castle. Or he may be in an hotel in Llandudno. The knotty point is how to make sure."

"And when you do make sure?"

"Go there, my dear old flick. What else do you suppose?" Lord Basil said cheerfully. "Jove, I know how I can find out where he is too! Who says we Curlews can't think?"

Stan reeled from a slap between the shoulder-blades. At the prospect of action Lord Basil's spirits seemed to have gone up with a bound.

"Keep your love pats to yourself, confound you? What's the big idea?"

"The big idea," said Lord Basil, "is Cusper. He's an objectionable person with side-whiskers who writes disloyal poetry that doesn't scan. But that's beside the point. What does matter is that he's Sir Jasper Goldburg's secretary and, as I happen to know, is staying at the Brig-y-don Hydro. He'll know where Saratini's headquarters are if anyone does."

"What then? Are you going to trail him?"

"No, dear soul. Our time is too limited to admit of such a tedious performance as trailing. We've got to take the jolly old bull by the what-do-you-call-its. But the snag is that Cusper has seen me and knows I'm a pal of Mona's. He doesn't know you from Adam, but I—"

Lord Basil stopped, rubbed his chin and stared at the roadway. Again he smote Stan painfully in the chest.

"Got it, my sweet pippin. A disguise is what's indicated. And I know the very bird who'll do it. Little Jabez in the Greenfields Road. He made me up for some amateur theatricals once so that auntie herself didn't know me. Yes, Jabez is our bird. If he can't fix me up well enough to deceive Cusper I'll eat my cane . . ."

Mr. Jabez was a quick worker. Less than an hour later Mr. Cusper got an unexpected compliment. To him, languidly sipping creme-de-menthe in the smoke-room of the Brig-y-don Hydro, appeared two men. The taller of the two—a weird object with a beard who looked like a Communistic poet after a bad night—held a highbrow weekly in his hands. Lord Basil had purchased it round the corner two minutes before.

"Have I the honour of addressing Mr. Ignatius Cusper?"

His appearance and his manner alike pleased Mr. Cusper. He felt he could recognize another great soul.

"One," he said, "believes so."

"Ignatius Cusper the poet? The second Shakespeare?"

That was a blunder. Mr. Cusper winced.

"One hopes not. Shakespeare? You mean the person they teach in schools?"

"I guess not," said the shorter man. "Old Bill Shakers couldn't have written the poem you've got there once in a blue moon. *'I spit on the Union Jack'*, by Ignatius Cusper! Mr. Cusper, I'll tell the world you're some poet. Have another drink."

"One," said Mr. Cusper, "might."

After that the friendship ripened amazingly. It wasn't long before Mr. Cusper was taking his new friends up to his bedroom that they might listen to him reading "*I spit on the Union Jack*", aloud.

But hardly had he closed the door when he got a nasty surprise. The tall thin man with the beard took him by the shoulders and shook him until his teeth rattled.

"My dear fellah," said Lord Basil in his natural voice, "I wouldn't listen to your poisonous tripe without a gas mask.

Now sit in that chair and look as pleasant as nature will allow. Stan, old fruit, there was a bottle."

The American produced it. They had stopped at a chemist's on the way to the hydro as well as at a newsagent's. A funnel such as is used for dosing horses had been another purchase.

"The quality of mercy is not strained," Lord Basil drawled. "That, Ignatius, is a quotation from a fellah called Shakespeare. Neat and full strength, Stan."

Mr. Cusper had glimpsed the label on the bottle. He swore and tried to bite Lord Basil's hand.

"No, you don't, laddie!" Those slim, manicured hands were holding him with amazing strength. "Nor will you attempt to treat my face like you treat the Union Jack if you're wise. Now, Cusper, old heart, what you're going to do is tell us the address of your pal Count Saratini. Don't try to bluff for it's no use. We know that you and that scrubby little employer of yours are helping Saratini to steal the *Cinco Llagas* treasure. What we want is the address of the headquarters of the gang, and Mr. Abraham Lincoln here is going to continue to pour until you tell us. Pour away, Abraham. It's doing him good although you wouldn't think so from his expression."

Fear of Count Saratini rendered Mr. Cusper unexpectedly obstinate. The dark blue bottle was almost empty before he raised a hand in token of surrender.

Lord Basil stood back.

"Well?"

Mr. Cusper spluttered.

"A house called Sperm at the foot of the Great Orme— damn you. I hope they wring your blasted throat, you grinning puppy. I'll have the police after you for this—see if I don't."

"Ingratitude," sighed Lord Basil. "Give a fellah a free dose and he tries to bite your hand. Well, well, well! Stan, will you reduce him to what they call the semblance of a mummy in the detective novels while I erase the good Jabez's handiwork in yonder mirror."

By the time he had removed the disguise Stan had expertly bound and gagged Mr. Cusper. They rolled him under his bed and left him there to seek inspiration from a bottle that had once held castor oil.

CHAPTER VIII

THE HOUSE OF DEATH

IN THE CORRIDOR outside Mr. Cusper's room Lord Basil paused to select a Turkish cigarette from his gold and platinum case. Slowly he expelled a cloud of fragrant smoke.

"That's that. If yonder great Thinker wasn't telling a lie—and people don't usually lie when they're half-suffocated—our objective is a house called Sperm at the foot of the Great Orme. I wonder if that's where they've got Mona. Better call there this afternoon and inquire, what?"

Stan put his hand on his arm.

"You're crazy. That would be just plumb suicide. If you knew what I know about Saratini . . . Wait till night."

"I can't wait," said Lord Basil. "This uncertainty about Mona is like a damn toothache. I'm going to find her if I have to shoot up Sperm like a fellah in a Wild West show. I'm—er—deuced fond of that kid."

He polished his monocle and replaced it in his eye. Stan, glimpsing the expression on his face, thought to himself that anyone who ran across his lordship in his present mood would find trouble.

"Constandos," Lord Basil said suddenly. "He was the last person to see Mona. Let's find him and get his report."

But Dr. Constandos was not forthcoming. It appeared that he had not slept in his room in the hydro the previous night.

Lord Basil ordered that the waiter who had been on night-duty should be produced.

After an interval that person appeared. Yawning, unshaven and obviously cross at being roused from his well-earned repose, he denied having ever seen such a person as Dr. Constandos at all.

Lord Basil stared at the man. Suddenly his hand shot out and seized his shoulder.

"You open up, Cocky, or you'll get your head knocked off."

It was the waiter's turn to stare. His mouth fell open.

"Strike me pink if it isn't Percy! They told me it was a blinking gentleman wanted to see me. How's yourself, Percy? Remember the night you socked the corporal of military police in the estaminet? Coo, I didn't 'alf larf! It took five of 'em to put you in the clink!"

"Six if you count the gendarme," Lord Basil said modestly. "Stan, meet Mr. Cocky Huggins. It was once hotly debated in military circles whether Cocky or I was the worst soldier in the Tenth Toughshires. I think I won, but it was a very close thing. In the near future, Cocky, you and I must re-fight our battles with the red-caps over many glasses of the best. But not now, Cocky. The burning need of the moment is information regarding last night's movements of one Dr. Constandos by name."

"The little dago bloke with the straw 'at?"

"The very one, Cocky."

"I can tell you about 'im," the waiter said. "About 'alf-past ten 'e came into the lounge, a bit squiffed by the look of 'im. 'E ordered a 'ot toddy in a tankard. Three 'ot toddies 'e 'ad one after the other and then 'e began to talk, which wasn't surprisin'. Told me 'e was goin' up to Minrhyn 'Ead to shoot a tiger. 'You go an' shoot tigers in your bed, sir,' said I, but 'e wouldn't listen. 'E 'd another 'ot toddy, then 'e clapped 'is little straw 'at on 'is 'ead, took 'is little cane, and went dancin' off. That was the last I seen of 'im. Runnin' down the drive shoutin' about gettin' a tiger—"

"And he never came back to the hydro?"

"Not that I know of. Only 'ope 'e didn't go up to the 'Ead. It's dangerous up there at night with them cliffs."

After the waiter had gone Lord Basil turned to Stan.

"Our numbers are fast diminishing, what? Jove, I hope the doctor didn't get as far as Minrhyn Head with Gravenant lurking about there. Well, I can't help him. Getting Mona back from Saratini is going to keep me busy."

After a hurried snack they left Minrhyn Bay in Stan's car with Sperm as their objective. As they tore along the Llandudno Road, Lord Basil began to speak.

"Look here, old chappie, I think this afternoon's performance had better be a one-man show. I mean to say if—er—anything happens to me, you'll still be there to assist Mona. As a matter of fact, I don't suppose that even Saratini would care to run the risk of murdering me in broad daylight, so to speak, but one never knows. All things considered, I think I'd better pay the call alone."

Stan protested, but Lord Basil was adamant. And the American had to admit there was sound horse-sense in what he said. For Mona's sake it was better that one should go under than both.

But the idea of this lone-handed daylight raid on the headquarters of a man he knew to be one of the cleverest and most unscrupulous criminals in Europe seemed to Stan almost tantamount to suicide. He knew Count Saratini and his methods better than did Lord Basil.

They were on the road skirting the western slopes of the Great Orme. On the stretch of reclaimed land between the road and the beach stood a number of hotels and palatial houses built for lovers of the sea. The name Sperm showed in bold black lettering on a white gate.

Round a corner out of sight of the house Stan applied his brakes. Lord Basil stepped languidly from the car.

"Pip pip, old squeak. See you sixish, what?"

"If you're lucky," the American said grimly. He made no further protest. While his lordship was in his present mood he knew it would be useless.

The car drove on, leaving Lord Basil propping himself on his cane in the centre of the road.

From where he stood he could obtain an excellent view of the house called Sperm. It faced seawards so that what he beheld was really the back.

Sperm was long and white and modern. Approach save by the drive was impossible. The few acres of garden and lawn surrounding the house were encircled by a twelve-foot high wall topped by criss-crossed iron spikes.

The white ornamental gate opening on the road was open. From his coign of vantage, however, Lord Basil could see a large individual pushing a lawn-mower over the grass in its immediate vicinity. Both from the inexpert manner in which he handled the machine and the fact that he always contrived to remain facing the gate from which he never moved more than five yards, it was patent that his real mission in life was to keep unwelcome visitors at a distance.

Lord Basil glanced at his platinum wrist-watch. To give yonder chappie twenty minutes in which to finish the piece of grass and remove his obnoxious person—that would be the scheme. If he was still there at the end of that time other methods would have to be employed. And thinking of what those other methods would probably be Lord Basil glanced dubiously at his white, manicured hands.

"They've got deuced soft," he thought. "I haven't had a proper rough-house since I ceased to be a private in the Tenth Toughshires. Still, we'll hope for the best."

He dusted a rock and sat down carefully. And no passer-by who beheld him sitting there as elegantly as a tailor's dummy in a Bond Street window would have dreamt that he was contemplating an assault on a man who could have given him two stone.

Before the allotted time was up, however, the toot of a horn made him turn round. He recognized the approaching car. It was the property of young Reilly, junior clerk of Messrs. Bracknall and Dogsbody, house-agents of Minrhyn Bay.

Reilly was the youth who had informed Lord Basil of the leasing of Minrhyn Castle to the so-called Mr. Sylvester. And as he was managing the negotiations of the lease, it seemed highly probable his present destination should be Sperm.

Lord Basil stepped on to the road with his cane raised. The car stopped and Reilly's spectacled face appeared round the windscreen.

"Want a lift? I've just to call at Sperm to get some papers signed, but then——"

Lord Basil sauntered alongside.

"I do want a lift—up to Sperm itself. They're an inhospitable crowd there and I rather think if they saw me walking up the drive they'd shoot at sight. That gorilla-like person with the lawn-mower has obviously been posted there to keep visitors away. He's in love with the same scullery-maid as I am, which makes things awkward."

Reilly grinned.

"Scullery-maid my elbow. Are they wrong 'uns?"

"If you insist upon the plain and brutal truth, they are."

"I thought there was something fishy about them," Reilly said. "As a matter of fact, I mentioned it to old Dogsbody, but he said as long as they'd the dough to pay for the lease it was none of our business who or what they were. But if you're certain they're crooks, why don't you tell the police?"

"Circumstances, laddie, circumstances. But it's imperative I should get into the house. With your permission I'll conceal myself under those rugs at the back and if anyone asks questions you can easily explain that I'm the latest thing in hot-water bottles. While you're getting your what-nots signed I'll nip out and into the house. After that you can quietly fade away and forget it ever happened." Reilly restarted his engine.

"I'll do it, but I'm hanged if I would for anyone else. If I was caught smuggling people into clients' houses I'd be sacked as sure as eggs. But those birds in Sperm are a rum lot, I'll grant you. Do you know what I saw just here the other night?"

"What?"

"I was returning from a dance at Llandudno; I'd a bird with me, and she chose this road as being more romantic. About two, or it may have been a bit earlier, we passed Sperm. Just about here there was a black car drawn up close under the wall. And there was—well, you'll think I'm quite mad when I tell you—"

"During the last twenty-four hours I have ceased to be surprised at anything," Lord Basil said. "What did you see?"

"A man dressed up like a monk of the Spanish Inquisition standing on the back seat so that he could look over the wall. He had his hands to the slits in his cowl as if he were using a pair of night-glasses. I'm not rotting. The girl with me saw him too. I remember she said, 'Oh, look at Felix the Cat!' You see the top of the cowl was bunched up so that it looked as if he'd a pair of black ears. I can tell you he was a pretty sinister apparition."

"He's a new one to me. You didn't stop and ask him to explain himself, I suppose!"

"Heavens, no. I accelerated. I was scared stiff and so was the girl."

Lord Basil was frowning at the ground. Here was a new complication. Had the man in black been Gravenant? But somehow he could not picture the man he had heard raving through the door as being rational enough to drive a car.

Anyway, Reilly's story seemed to have no bearing on the present situation. He stepped into the back portion of the car, lay down on the floor and pulled a rug over his form. Thanks to the fact that the side-screens were so dirty and yellow as to be almost opaque, it would have required more than a casual glance from outside to detect his presence.

The car moved forward. As Lord Basil had anticipated, the man with the mower stopped Reilly at the gate. But Reilly's explanation that he had come to see Mr. Sylvester in connection with the signing of the lease proved satisfactory and they were allowed to proceed.

In less than a minute they stopped again. Lord Basil knew they must have arrived at Sperm. He heard Reilly alight and run up some steps, then the sound of voices. Next there was silence. Apparently the servant who had admitted Reilly had conducted him into the house.

Lord Basil rose to his knees. Peeping through a corner of the side-screen he could see through an open door into a large, luxuriously furnished hall. There was nobody within sight.

Now or never was his chance. He opened the door of the car and stepped on to the gravel. Then—moving for a person of his apparent languor with incredible swiftness—he darted into the hall. A stairway presented itself on the right. Without hesitation he ran up it, his feet making no sound upon the thick carpet.

He was on the landing. A curtained doorway offered a convenient hiding-place. He slipped behind the curtain and stood motionless, listening.

Feet were crossing the hall below. He heard Reilly's voice wishing someone "good afternoon", then a door shut. The feet returned across the hall and died away. And then a silence almost uncanny in its intensity seemed to fall upon Sperm.

Patience was not one of his lordship's virtues. He waited for three minutes and then thrust his pale, monocled visage through the folds of the curtain. All clear. He stepped out on to the landing and stood looking about him, temporarily monarch of all he surveyed.

It was difficult to believe the house in which he stood was the headquarters of a criminal gang. From all outward appearances it was simply a luxurious English house of the modern type. The sort of house where there are well-trained maids and the vicar comes to lunch on Sundays. Indeed the only thing that hinted there might be anything queer about Sperm was the fact that the silence was almost too intense to be natural.

It was a hushed, waiting silence—the silence death brings to a house. It affected even the unimaginative Lord Basil. He was aware of an inclination to keep glancing over his shoulder.

A long corridor with doors obviously those of bedrooms branched to right and left of the landing. If Mona were really a prisoner in the house, the chances were that they had placed her in one of those upstairs rooms. Lord Basil, feeling as nervous as a cat because of the extraordinary silence, decided he could not do better than visit each room in turn.

Six rooms were empty. They were luxuriously furnished bedrooms of an appearance to match the remainder of the house. As he came out of the sixth Lord Basil heard a sound that seemed amazingly out of place in that silent, sinister house. The sound of a child's feet pattering across polished boards.

The child was in the hall. He glimpsed him from the landing—a boy with long fair curls, a deathly white face and what seemed to be a red bandage around his throat.

He trotted across the hall and disappeared through an open door.

Lord Basil wiped his forehead. The more he saw of Sperm the less he liked it. And yet he could hardly account for his growing terror. What was there alarming in these empty, sunny rooms and a little boy who ran with stiff, jerky movements?

After a long pause during which the child did not reappear he went to the seventh bedroom. It was occupied. On the bed lay a motionless form covered by a sheet.

Was it Mona? The palms of Lord Basil's hands were clammy as he walked across the room. He had to exert his will-power to make himself touch the sheet. Very slowly and with his heart pounding like a mad thing he pulled it down.

Relief and horror. It was a strange, glassy-eyed face—the face of a man he saw grinning up at him from the pillow. He was dead. And his staring eyes and swollen tongue, which seemed to be protruding in mockery of Lord Basil's horror, showed that slow strangulation had been the cause of death.

CHAPTER IX

THE LETHAL CHAMBER

ALTHOUGH THOSE MEN who knew him best would have scoffed at the idea of Lord Basil Curlew being in any way afflicted with nerves, the sight of the strangled man made him feel faint. His forehead was wet with cold perspiration as he walked backwards out of the room of death keeping his eyes fixed upon the thing on the bed.

In the passage outside he pulled himself together.

"Sperm doesn't appeal to me as the sort of house where one would send a nervous spinster for a happy week-end," he thought. "Strangled corpses in the first-floor bedrooms and Spanish monks peeping over the walls! I wonder who did that unfortunate chappie in? Was it a punishment of the Lizard's—or what?"

His nerve was more shaken than he would have cared to admit. It was an effort to turn his back on the door of the room where the corpse lay.

Despite the uncanny silence, he knew he was not alone in the house. In addition to the child he had seen in the hall, there was the servant who had admitted Reilly. And he could still faintly hear through an open window the sound of the indefatigable lawn-mower being trundled to and fro over the same patch of grass.

Lord Basil decided he had had enough of bedrooms. He began to creep downstairs. When he was half-way down he heard a sound that made the hairs on his head stiffen as if they were steel threads attracted by a magnet.

A bed had creaked; heavy feet were crossing a floor. He spun round and stood transfixed. The door of bedroom No. 7

was being slowly opened. A gruesome, white-robed form stood leering in the aperture.

Lord Basil waited for no more. With a yell that resounded through the house he sprang down the stairs. A rug skidded and he fell full length on the polished floor of the hall. And as he scrambled to his feet he heard a sound like a sob.

It came from the boy with the fair curls. He was standing in a doorway, his little face blanched like a sweetbread, and his head nodding while he clapped his tiny hands. But now Lord Basil could see what the supposed red bandage was. It was a gaping, crimson wound that stretched from ear to ear and almost severed the nodding head from the body.

"Your throat!" Lord Basil gasped. "Who—?"

The child had driven the other horror from his mind. But slow, heavy feet were descending the stairs. He spun round to see the strangled corpse following him with outstretched hands . . .

Waxworks! The explanation flashed into his mind, cutting short his yell of horror. They were life-like robots—great mechanical dolls designed to terrify.

Rage succeeded panic. He seized a chair and leapt towards the child, when a voice made him stop.

"Put that chair down, Lord Basil. I'm too proud of little Claude to allow him to be smashed by every puppy that strays into my house. Oh, dear me, you do look frightened! Your face is the exact colour of little Claude's."

There was an indescribably evil chuckle.

"Is it?" said Lord Basil. "Then what about that?"

He was too angry to bother about the consequences. The chair went across the hall like a stone from a catapult. It caught the robot-child squarely, reducing it to a shapeless ruin.

"Young fool!" The invisible voice was cold with contempt. "Little Claude can be repaired, but I'm afraid you can't. When you're carried out of this house it will require more than the united skill of Harley Street to make you as good as new. Now stand quite still. Remember one move will mean death."

This time Lord Basil obeyed. There was a quality in that sinister, mocking voice that made him realize the last statement was no empty bluff.

A door on the right opened and he saw the man he knew to be Count Saratini. His spare figure was enveloped in a dressing-gown reaching almost to his ankles. The deep-set eyes under the high, bulging forehead were alight with an amusement more devilish than human.

It was at his hands Lord Basil looked. For a second he imagined the Count to be wearing tightly-fitting gloves of a mottled green shade, then he remembered what Stan had told him about the origin of the Count's nickname.

It was a good nickname. Apart from the discolouration of his hands, there was something strangely saurian-like in those bright, darting eyes and in that large, whimsical mouth with the upward-twisted corners.

The Count spoke with half-humorous regret.

"I'm sorry I exposed little Claude to your violence. Well, Lord Basil, what do you think of my robots? An advance on anything to be seen in the London exhibitions, I flatter myself. I was afraid that after the episode of the wax fingers you might suspect a trick, but apparently you did not. Your terror was highly gratifying to my inventor's pride."

Lord Basil was cursing himself for having been tricked. Too late he had remembered what Stan had told him—that this extraordinary man delighted in the playing of sinister practical jokes.

"That was decidedly one up to you, old chappie," he drawled. "Enough to make a fellah take the pledge for the rest of his life, what? Well, I'll be pushin' along now. Pip pip, and all that."

To his secret surprise the Count made no effort to hinder his departure. Not until Lord Basil was almost at the door did he speak.

"One doesn't electrocute puppies. Come back, Fido."

Lord Basil turned and stared at him through his monocle.

"Addressing me by any chance?"

"I am. There's a high-voltage electric current passing through that door. I suppose even your vacuous mind can grasp what the consequences of trying to open it would be?"

"You're pullin' a fellah's leg, aren't you?"

"If you doubt my word you can test it by touching the handle. Do. I don't mind in the least."

For the life of him Lord Basil could not decide whether the Count was speaking the truth or not. Damn it, he'd call the bluff. He began to put out his hand . . .

Then came the remembrance that he did not yet know if Mona was in Sperm. Until he knew that, he was determined not to leave the house. He turned and came slowly back, watched by Saratini's contemptuous eyes.

The Count beckoned with a long, green finger.

"Come this way. And for your own sake don't try to do anything foolish."

The room into which they went was furnished as a library. Saratini seated himself and crossed his legs.

"Sit down, Lord Basil. Take a cigarette if you want one. No,"—he laughed softly—"they're not drugged."

Lord Basil took a cigarette from the silver box. Then he sat down facing the man Stan had described as being the most dangerous in Europe.

He could well believe the statement. Those sunken, malicious eyes were alive with intelligence. And the high bald forehead seemed to denote a brain of ability far above the average.

For a minute or two the Count smilingly regarded him without speaking. Then he tapped the ash from his cigarette.

"The first time I saw you, Lord Basil," he began, "I remember describing you as the most perfect specimen of a half-wit I had ever seen. And now that I'm beginning to know you a little better I see no reason to modify my statement. Anything more foolhardy than your action in coming to this house this afternoon it would be difficult to imagine. I should have thought it might have occurred even to your limited intelligence that I'd be expecting you."

Lord Basil might have retorted that he had considered that contingency, and that the thought had not in the least altered his determination to find out if Mona were in Sperm. But instead of saying so, he merely smiled inanely.

"Expectin' me, what?" he drawled.

"Of course I was. Cusper was found and released by Sir Jasper a few minutes after you'd left the hydro. Sir Jasper promptly telephoned to say that we would very likely have the pleasure of your society this afternoon. Acting on that hint, I took steps to arrange a—er—display of waxworks in your honour. It was very simple. The robots that caused you such alarm are controlled by wireless, invisible Phontgen rays making electrical connections through silenium bridges, that's the scientific principle on which they're worked. Doubtless you have seen similar toys on the music-halls. The designing of the robots is one of my hobbies. I never travel anywhere without my collection."

"Well, a chappie couldn't be expected to know that," bleated Lord Basil. "I mean to say if a fellah saw a bally corpse waltzing round in the sunlight—well, he's apt to be a bit scared, what? I call that a beastly, rotten trick. That sort of thing simply isn't done."

"You've only yourself to blame. You found your way in here uninvited."

"But, dash it all, I came to find Miss Vachell. Where is she?"

"She's not here," the Count said. "She's in an isolated farmhouse on the Capel Curig road about four miles from a village pronounced 'Pooku-Worky'. It's spelt P-w-1-1-c-h-y-w-c-h-i. No harm will come to her if she behaves herself. You see, I've no objection to your knowing where she is, Lord Basil. The time when you could have assisted her is past."

"What the deuce do you mean?"

"That you're not going to leave this house alive."

"I say!" Lord Basil drew himself up and stared. "I mean to say a joke's a joke, and all that, but I call this a bit too thick altogether. Do you mean you're going to murder me?"

"If getting rid of a useless puppy can be called murder, I suppose I am."

"Dash it all—you can't."

"And why not, pray?" Count Saratini smiled.

"Because that sort of thing isn't done," Lord Basil said feebly.

Count Saratini laughed shortly.

"My dear little Fido," he said, "you are very soon going to learn that more things are done on this earth than you've any conception of. Men have died by scores for the *Cinco Llagas* gold; you'll only be one more and, as far as I can judge, no great loss to the community. That robot you wantonly destroyed had more intelligence in its little finger than you've got in that brilliantined head of yours. Poor blooming Curlew—never was a man better named. When I look at you sitting there—chinless, vapid and inane, with your monocle and your rabbit's teeth, and your faultless clothes and your foolish mouth drooping open—I ask myself why such things as you are allowed to exist. If I had my way you and your like would be painlessly destroyed in a lethal chamber."

"You're—you're beastly rude," croaked Lord Basil.

"Beastly rude!" Saratini mimicked. "As if it was possible for a person of normal intelligence to be rude to an object like yourself! Anyway, I'm tired of your company. Playing with a puppy is amusing for a short time, but it soon grows wearisome."

He took a little silver whistle from his waistcoat pocket and blew two sharp blasts. Immediately two men appeared in the doorway. One was the big German Lord Basil had seen in the hydro with Sir Jasper; the other was an undersized individual with a swarthy skin and features like a rat's.

It was only then that the chilling knowledge came to Lord Basil that Saratini really intended to murder him. Until that moment he had fancied the Count was indulging his peculiar sense of humour by trying to frighten him.

Murder! It seemed an incredible thought to him sitting in that well-furnished, sunny library. Looking past Saratini's dome-like head, he could see the familiar outline of the Great

Orme. People were wandering about the green slopes. Golfers, men in flannels, women pushing perambulators . . .

Saratini seemed to possess an uncanny power of being able to read his thoughts.

"No use looking out of the window, Lord Basil. Those worthy trippers wouldn't help you even if you told them what was happening. Preposterous, they'd say. Such things don't happen in North Wales . . ."

He was crouched forward now, holding the dressing-gown to his chest with a thin, green hand. His restless, brilliant eyes rested on Lord Basil.

"Poor Fido! Such a harmless butterfly to have to meet death. But butterflies who flutter into places where they're not wanted have to be painlessly disposed of. That's what is going to happen to you, Lord Basil. The killing-bottle is ready.

"Carbon-monoxide gas, that is the approved modern method of getting rid of unwanted puppies. It's quick and, most authorities agree, quite painless. All that is required is an ordinary motor car and an unventilated room. If the engine is running slowly on a rich mixture the fumes from the exhaust contain a large percentage of carbon-monoxide, one of the most deadly lethal gases known to science. A puppy's death for a puppy . . . Don't you agree my plan is a very suitable one, Heinman?"

The big German laughed brutally. He was holding an automatic in uncomfortable proximity to the small of Lord Basil's back.

After a final mocking stare at Lord Basil's face, Count Saratini signed to the gangsters to take him away. Helpless as a sheep being driven to an abattoir, he was hustled out of the room, across the hall and down a flight of steps.

It was a bare room, measuring about eight feet by ten into which he was finally pushed. The window and fireplace had been blocked up and there was no other means of ventilation discernable. Even the edge of the door had been padded with felt to render the death-chamber completely airtight.

The door slammed and he was alone. Almost directly he heard a car being started up outside. By the sound he knew it must be standing close to the outer wall of the cell.

A small iron shutter in the door opened and he saw Saratini's sinister eyes.

"It won't be long, Fido. They've connected the exhaust pipe so that the fumes are flowing into the room. Already they are rising round you like water. When they reach the level of your head you'll drown like a kitten in a bucket of water. And so, Your Lordship, in your own elegant phraseology, I'll wish you pip pip and all that . . ."

He waved a long green hand in a humorous gesture of farewell and let the shutter click back into position.

While the Count was superintending the placing of Lord Basil in what was to all intents and purposes a home-made lethal chamber, a Rolls-Royce had arrived at Sperm. Its occupants were Sir Jasper Goldburg and Mr. Cusper, the latter looking like the whitewashed ghost of his usual supercilious self.

Nor did Sir Jasper look particularly joyful. He was scared of the Count down to the very depths of his vulgar little soul. Almost he had begun to regret having consented to assist in the taking of the *Cinco Llagas* treasure. He had been a rogue all his life, but the venture threatened to drag him far out of his depth in a stormy sea of crime.

As men of an irritable, bullying disposition are prone to do in moments of anxiety, he vented his displeasure upon his miserable secretary as the Rolls swung through the Sperm gates.

"Now, you blinkin' young idiot, you're goin' to catch it 'ot," he snarled. "Saratini'll 'ave somethin' to say to you. Givin' away the address of 'eadquarters an' all. I 'ope 'e shuts you up in a room with that Death-Robot of 'is."

They gave the password and were shown into the library, where the Count had interviewed Lord Basil. They had not been there a minute before the Count himself came in, smiling.

"Good afternoon, gentlemen!" He was all smiles and bows like an obsequious shopman while his eyes shone with diabolical amusement. "The pleasure of seeing you is in no way diminished by the fact that it is not quite unexpected. Won't you do me the honour of sitting down?"

" 'Ere 'e is," said Sir Jasper, pointing at the wretched Cusper. "Doesn't take much to make 'im rat. Little drop of castor oil they gave 'im an' 'e blabbed out the address like a baby. It wasn't my fault, Count. I tell you straight. I couldn't 'elp it."

"It doesn't matter in the least," Saratini purred. "I fact I'm inclined to think it was the best thing could have happened. Lord Basil lived up to his reputation for inanity by coming here alone. Thanks to your phone message, I had had time to make some preparations. His lordship got a very bad fright. It was excruciatingly funny."

"You scared him with them robots?"

"Yes. Unfortunately he smashed little Claude before I could stop him. He is now"—the Count paused to consult his watch—"yes, he is now dead."

"Dead!" Sir Jasper leapt to his feet with an exclamation. "But that's murder! . . . I didn't bargain for anything like that . . . D'you want to get us 'anged? . . . If the perlice . . ."

He pulled at his collar as if he already felt the noose encircling his thick neck. The Count only laughed.

"You need not be in the least uneasy. I promise you the police will never know how Lord Basil died."

"But 'is pal. That Yankee fellow! 'E'll guess."

"It doesn't matter. As long as Miss Vachell is in our hands there is nothing to be feared from Mr. Hastings. He's quite intelligent enough to know that if he gave information to the police Miss Vachell would pay the penalty. But in any case the hours of that American busybody's life are numbered."

"You're goin' to get 'im too?"

"I am. He knows too much and has become a nuisance."

Nothing could have surpassed the air of calm certainty with which Saratini spoke. Even Sir Jasper felt reassured. Some of its wonted colour returned to his face.

"Well, I s'pose you can manage it. But mind you, when I said I'd 'elp with my yacht an' all for a measly 'undred an' fifty thousand quid, I didn't bargain on any of this. A kidnapping first and now a murder! I thought we'd only to walk into the blinkin' castle, find the treasure an' take it away."

"So we would have done if Dr. Constandos hadn't arrived on the scene. His coming has completely altered the complexion of affairs. But if you want to draw out, Sir Jasper, don't let me prevent you. I can easily obtain a yacht elsewhere. Of course, you'll forfeit your share of the treasure when we find it."

Greed and terror struggled for mastery in Sir Jasper's face.

"I can't back out; I'm pretty well bust," he muttered. "If I don't get that 'undred an' fifty thousand quick I'll be in the soup. But what beats me is what are we 'angin' about for? Why don't we get the gold and clear off?"

"Because until the matter of the lease is settled we've no legal right to enter the castle," Saratini said patiently. "To do so and begin the search might attract publicity which would be fatal. But I'm doing my best to hurry matters up. It's now only a matter of hours before we can take possession."

"Orl right. I s'pose you know wot you're about. Me and Cusper'll stay in."

"Very well. You can stay in, but remember I won't tolerate any further criticisms of my methods. More transactions have failed through squeamishness and lack of nerve than from any other cause. The man who captured that treasure from the Spanish waded through blood to get it—literally. If necessary I'm prepared to do the same."

"I'll bet you are," Sir Jasper muttered. "Well, so long as you don't get me into trouble I don't mind 'ow many you kill."

"Perhaps you would like to view Lord Basil's body before it's disposed of?" Sir Jasper started.

"No thanks. Me stummick ain't wot it was."

"Then I won't press you. As an alternative proposal I suggest we drive to the farmhouse to see how little Miss Vachell is enjoying her incarceration. As a matter of fact, I'm a little surprised I have had no message from that quarter all day. But I know she arrived without mishap. Morgan phoned just before I left for your yacht last night."

"Who's with'er?"

"Crane, Morgan and a woman called by the not uncommon name in North Wales of Mrs. Jones. Shall we go over and see how they're getting on?"

"I'm agreeable."

"All right then, we'll go. But don't tell Miss Vachell what has happened to her half-witted admirer. For some unfathomable reason she's fond of that young man. Probably it's because she's sorry for him."

They went out into the hall. The robot that had been fashioned to resemble a man dead of strangulation still stood half-way down the stairs. Saratini went to where in an alcove off the hall there was an instrument not unlike a wireless loudspeaker. His green fingers began to manipulate switches and dials. The robot gave a shudder, turned, ascended the stairs with heavy, jerky movements and tramped back into his room.

Sir Jasper mopped his forehead.

"Don't wonder it gave that young chap a turn! You'd swear it was alive."

Count Saratini laughed complacently.

"And yet it's very simple. Clockwork controlled by electricity which is regulated by wireless rays. Aeroplanes can be guided, bombs dropped and ships steered on the same principle. I prophesy that the next war will be largely fought by robots. However, I won't bore you with a dissertation on my hobby . . . Steevens!"

"Sir?"

A coarse-looking man, attired like a butler, had appeared in the hall.

"Go and see what has become of the puppy I put in the lethal chamber."

Steevens grinned and disappeared. In under three minutes he was back.

"It's all right, sir. I didn't go in because of the gas, but I 'ad a look at 'im through the keyhole. He's dead."

"Splendid. Tell Heinman to open the shutter and let the gas disperse. In the meantime he can be lighting the large incinerator. Clothes and belongings can be left on a suitable spot on the shore to-night. You'll see to it?"

"Yes, sir."

The Count winked at Sir Jasper.

"To-morrow the public will be shocked to read of a bathing fatality in high society. Lord Basil Curlew, the popular and well-known son of the Duke of Matchingham drowned while bathing near Minrhyn Bay, North Wales. But as the body will certainly never be recovered, I don't think there'll be any occasion to open the family vault."

The drive to the farmhouse was a silent one. Mr. Cusper was naturally feeling indisposed for conversation, and Sir Jasper was too afraid of Saratini to break in upon the silence he evidently preferred.

They swept through a tiny grey village and took a rough road bordered by stone walls. At a white gate they alighted.

The Count preceded the other two up the drive. His eyes scanned the farmhouse which on that sunny afternoon had a singularly deserted appearance.

"No smoke! Surely Crane has not disregarded my orders and taken the girl elsewhere! I wonder—"

He quickened his steps to the front door. Seizing the antiquated knocker he rapped loudly. There was no sound of movement within the house. Saratini turned to Sir Jasper.

"There's something wrong. Remain here. I'll go and make investigation."

He disappeared round the side of the house. Sir Jasper fidgeted uneasily on the steps. For some reason he felt horribly afraid of what lay within.

Suddenly he saw something they had not noticed before. From beneath the door oozed a thin dark stream. He seized Mr. Cusper's arm.

"Look there! *Gawd!* It's . . . it's blood . . ."

They were staring in speechless horror when the Count reappeared. He was walking slowly, his head bowed. They saw him take a little phial from his waistcoat pocket, shake a few grains of white powder on to the back of his hand and sniff.

By token of that sight Sir Jasper knew something was terribly wrong. Saratini never used cocaine save in moments of crisis.

The Count spoke.

"Don't go into that house if you value your reason. The sitting-room is like a shambles. Crane and Morgan are there; Mrs. Jones is in the hall. Crane was torn to pieces; Morgan and the woman were shot."

He began to wipe his elegant shoes on the grass. After a long pause Sir Jasper found his voice.

"All three of them! Don't tell me little Miss Vachell—"

"She didn't do it," the Count said with a pale smile. "I haven't seen her body, but there's no question that it's somewhere about. If she was in the house she can't possibly have escaped."

"Then who did kill them?" Sir Jasper cried.

Count Saratini affected not to hear the question. He lit a cigarette with gloved hands as steady as a surgeon's.

"Wade through blood," he murmured. "History is repeating itself with a vengeance. And if what I fear is correct there'll be still more blood spilt before we touch the *Cinco Llagas* gold."

He spoke aloud for Sir Jasper's benefit.

"I've telephoned to Sperm for men to come over and remove what's inside the house. They'll be here shortly. All traces of what happened last night must be obliterated. While we're waiting for them to arrive I'm going to make a further search for Miss Vachell's body."

CHAPTER X

THE FAWNOG LAKE MURDER

ON FINDING HIMSELF a prisoner in a tiny cell into which invisible death was being pumped like water into a cistern, a more intelligent man than Lord Basil Curlew would have realized the position was hopeless and composed himself to await the inevitable with as much dignity as possible. Lord Basil did nothing of the sort. Indeed, for a young man afflicted by a drawl, a receding chin and a monocle, he showed a considerable amount of determination in his battle for life.

Hardly had Saratini closed the shutter when he was on his knees in the darkness and striking a match. There was one slim, desperate chance. He had been out-generalled, fooled, defeated, but while that one chance remained he would not lose hope.

Before being pushed into the cell he had had the presence of mind to draw a deep breath. He was holding it now—holding it with bursting lungs and pounding heart while he passed the tiny flame along the surface of the wall. Methodically. If he went too fast he might miss the flicker that would betray the flow of gas. Perhaps he had missed it. Perhaps . . .

The match dropped from his scorched fingers and went out. The agony in his lungs was almost unbearable. A red-hot cap was being screwed about his head. Already he must have inhaled some of the gas. He was drowsy and it was as if his limbs were weighted with lead. To take out another match and strike it was the supreme effort of his life.

Suddenly the flame billowed over and went out as if extinguished by a ghostly breath. He licked the back of his hand and felt hot puffs against the skin. Lying full length he groped for the inlet. He had it. The fumes were coming through a pipe about two inches in diameter whose mouth was level with the wall some six inches above the floor.

He couldn't keep his hand pressed there indefinitely. He rolled his silk handkerchief into a tight ball and screwed it into the pipe. Some letters and the lining of his note-case went to reinforce the dam. He tested his handiwork with a third match. The steadiness of the flame told him the flow of poison had ceased. If any gas were still leaking through it would be too infinitesimal an amount to be dangerous.

He was safe—for the time being, at least. The exhaust fumes would blow back into the engine, but it would be many hours before they choked it so that it stopped, thereby betraying what he had done to those outside.

What carbon-monoxide had already entered the chamber must be lying close to the floor. He stood upright and permitted himself the luxury of normal breathing.

After what seemed a long time and in reality was little over ten minutes feet came along the passage outside. He lay down and kept motionless. The shutter was raised and the beam of a flash-lamp passed over his recumbent body. There was a satisfied grunt and the shutter clicked again into position.

A little later he had another visitor. This time the door was opened to its widest extent and the iron plate blocking the window was removed. He guessed they were ventilating the cell prior to carrying out his body. But despite the temptation of the open door, he remained still; so still that when Mr. Niblett, whose duty it was to incinerate the body, entered the cell, he had not the faintest suspicion that it was not a corpse with which he had to deal.

The gangster, a burly individual who looked like a prize fighter, put his feet astride the body and spat on his hands preparatory to lifting.

"Come on, stiff 'un," he grunted. "Upsy-daisy, you blinkin' dude."

It was Mr. Niblett himself who "upsy-daisied". The corpse's hands fastened on his wrists and the corpse's feet doubled up and drove into the pit of his stomach. Mr. Niblett performed a complicated somersault. He landed on his face, his neck was bent back by the weight of his revolving body and there was a crack like a breaking stick.

Without troubling to ascertain whether he was dead, Lord Basil walked out of the cell. In the passage he encountered the German, Heinman. Heinman clawed for his hip-pocket. But his lordship's leap would have done credit to a mongoose. His long right whipped to the fleshy jaw and Heinman went down like a pole-axed bullock.

A door opened on to a yard. Lord Basil passed through unmolested and found himself on the terrace fronting Sperm. From an upper window came a hiss like a disturbed snake and something stung his cheek.

"Air-pistol," he diagnosed. "This is where a chappie removes. The sportsman at the window mightn't miss a second time."

He ran for the wall like a greyhound and pulled himself over regardless of the spikes. On the turf on the other side a family of trippers were picnicking. Lord Basil alighted in their midst as if he had fallen from the clouds.

"What d'you think you're playin' at, young man?"

"I'm frightfully sorry, but I'm escaping from a gang of murderers," Lord Basil explained. "I had to kill one of them just now. Topping afternoon, isn't it?"

He turned away leaving the trippers convinced that Sperm was a lunatic asylum and that they had just witnessed the escape of one of the inmates.

Having reached the road he paused to consider. On the whole he was inclined to the opinion that his afternoon call on Sperm had been a success. Certainly he had had a couple of bad scares, but on the other hand he had achieved his main object—finding out whither the gang had taken Mona.

A blue Rover car driven by a girl wearing a blue beret overtook him and stopped. A gloved hand beckoned.

"What's become of Mona, Lord Basil? We'd arranged a single at Brig-y-don this morning, but she never turned up. She's not ill, is she?"

Lord Basil recognized Mrs. Flant, one of Mona's tennis friends. He approached the car.

"Mo's got a chill. She won't be about for a day or two. Could you give me a lift as far as Minrhyn Bay?"

Before attempting Mona's rescue from the farmhouse he had decided to collect Stan Hastings and the commander.

"Jump in," said Mrs. Flant. Then as she let in the clutch: "What's all this I hear about a murder?"

"Murder!" The monocle dropped from Lord Basil's eye. "Er—which murder do you mean?"

"Which murder! You speak as if there'd been dozens. I mean *the* murder. The one the A.A. scout in Mostyn Road told me about. The girl."

The girl! To Lord Basil it seemed for a moment as if the Great Orme swung round as dizzily as one of its sea-gulls. The girl! Who could it be but Mona?

"Who was she?" he asked in a voice hardly to be recognized.

Mrs. Flant, busy with her gears, had failed to notice his perturbation.

"I don't know. All I know is what the scout said. They've found a girl's body in the Black Dingle close to the Fawnog lake. She'd been brutally murdered by someone."

"What was she like?"

"I don't know any more than I've told you."

Lord Basil sat very still. He felt numbed, sick. It was Mona's body they had found—he knew it. Little Mona . . . Brutally murdered by the human devils employed by Saratini.

The Count had talked of wading through blood to get that treasure. By Heaven he'd wade through blood to get his hands on the throat of that cold, smiling man. . . . As he'd done to Mona, so would it be done to him . . . He'd die slowly . . . slowly . . .

"You're very mouldy to-day," said Mrs. Flant's cheerful voice in his ear.

Lord Basil waked from his vision of vengeance. He contrived to speak in a natural voice.

"I wonder would you mind running me up to the Black Dingle?" he said. "I—I think I might know something about that girl."

"You really mean you want to gratify your morbid curiosity," Mrs. Flant laughed. "All right. But I'm not going near the spot. We dine at half-past six and I've got to be back."

Twenty minutes later they were at the Black Dingle, a small wood standing close to a lake on the Llanrwst-Llandudno road. Two empty cars had been parked by the stile leading into the wood. A little knot of farm hands and women from the neighbouring cottages were standing near the cars.

"I'll leave you here," Lord Basil said. "Thanks most frightfully for the lift . . . Good-bye . . ."

He joined the spectators. They were staring at a self-conscious young constable posted to guard the entrance to the wood. A farmer recognized Lord Basil.

"This is a bad job, sir. In there—about fifty yards beyond where the policeman's standing—they found her. Yess, poor thing. He done it in a car and carried her in there."

"Who was she?"

"Miss Floss. She worked at the Station Hotel in Minrhyn Bay, look you."

Lord Basil almost shouted in his relief. But the news, if not as bad as he had feared, was bad enough.

"Miss Floss! I saw her only this morning. I was in the lounge of the Station Hotel having a drink with some pals. She poured it out herself."

The farmer gave a dry chuckle.

"I'm afraid she's drawn her last beer, the poor creature. What time would it be you saw her?"

"About eleven."

"Ah, well, she'd be off duty at one. Reckon she had the afternoon off and came up here to meet the chap who killed her. They must have had a quarrel or something an' he did her in. She wouldn't have been found so quick only a young gipsy chap went in after a hare and his dog nosed out the body. They've taken her to Dutch Arms. The lil' inn just round the bend."

It was not morbid curiosity, but a desire to make certain the victim was not Mona sent Lord Basil to the Dutch Arms. But he was not allowed to enter. His path was barred by the sturdy, bowler-hatted form of Superintendent Fibkin of Minrhyn Bay.

Fibkin had a natural antipathy for Lord Basil, based partly on contempt, partly on envy. And as this was his first murder-case he was feeling worried and anxious. It was a relief therefore to vent his feelings on Lord Basil. Lord or no lord, he, Fibkin, was boss at the Dutch Arms, and he meant to show it.

"Sorry. Can't come in here. Sorry."

Lord Basil favoured him with his most inane smile.

"You're looking just as I've always hoped to see you look, Fibby. All strung-up and what-d'you-call-it. I'm backin' you, Fibby. I mean to say, if there's any fellah can catch the Johnny in the black car, it's you, Fibby. I can see it in your eyes."

The superintendent started.

"Who told you he was in a black car?"

Nobody had. It had been a sheer guess on his lordship's part, but it seemed to have hit the mark.

"Oh, I just heard it, doncherknow," he said vaguely. "Sort of picked it up, what?"

"It's damned extraordinary how things get round," Fibkin growled. "As a matter of fact, we have found a witness who claims to have seen a black car up here this afternoon. But I told him to keep his mouth shut. I suppose the fool's been talking already."

"They do, Fibby, they do. Tell a chappie to shut his beak and he goes bleatin' round like a bally sheep. I've noticed it myself . . . Deuced observant of me, what?"

The superintendent glared at him in grim contempt.

"You'd be an ornament to the force, Lord Basil."

"Really, I believe I would, Fibby. Jolly old Detective Curlew, what? Tell you what, Fibby, you put me on this case.

I've read the deuce of a lot of detective novels—I have, really ... Well, I mustn't keep you ... Pip pip, and all that ..."

Watching his lordship's elegant back, Fibkin thought to himself that there went the most vacuous young ass of his acquaintance. Had he known, however, that while making his inane remarks the vacuous young ass had contrived to look above his head into the room where the doctors were examining the body, he might have altered his opinion.

Lord Basil had only obtained the merest glimpse, but it had been sufficient. The girl murdered in the Black Dingle was not Mona. She was the barmaid who had shown the Spanish coin to Stan that morning.

The mystery was deepening. Had it been because of the coin the girl had lost her life? And had the man in the black car been the same individual that Reilly had seen spying on Sperm?

But he wasted no time pondering these questions. To get Mona out of Count Saratini's hands—that was his objective. Until that had been accomplished he cared nothing for the *Cinco Llagas* treasure.

A chance-met motorist took him down to the Bay. He made straight for the Station Hotel. As he had expected, he found Stan Hastings and Commander Eggington in the lounge.

They stared at him as if he were a ghost. Stan crashed his tankard down on the table.

"You old son of a louse! Why, the commander and I were dropping tears into our beer over your unfortunate fate. We were dead sure Saratini had nabbed you. As a matter of fact, we were trying to frame a rescue for to-night."

Lord Basil seated himself with his usual care.

"Quite unnecessary, sweet pippin. You can buy me a tankard of the usual instead; I see they've replaced poor Miss Floss already. That was a hellish business in the Black Dingle. You've heard, of course?"

"Sure. The whole town's humming with it. But it's not our pigeon."

"Don't be certain, old thing. I've a hazy idea it may have been Gravenant. Nothing definite; only the coincidence of a coin and a black car."

The commander shook his head.

"It can't have been Gravenant. I got a glimpse of him this afternoon on Minrhyn Head. He was prowling round the castle. That would have been—let me see—round about half-past two; just when I got back to my cottage from here."

"Then my theory's gone phut," said Lord Basil. "I was dead certain Gravenant had killed her for some motive connected with the treasure."

He set down an empty tankard and rose to his feet.

"Got your car?" he asked Stan.

"Sure."

"Then I'll tell you what happened at Sperm as we go along. We're going to a place called Pwllchywchi. They've got Mona in a farmhouse there. I don't think they've harmed her, but their idea is to hold her as a hostage until they've got the treasure. There may be a scrap. Does the prospect please you, Commander?"

"Nothing could please me better," the sailor declared. "My little lady! Stuck her away in a farmhouse, have they? Well, they'll get no quarter from me."

As the car tore along Lord Basil gave Stan a curt account of what had happened at Sperm. The American whistled.

"You'd a narrow shave. It isn't often anyone wriggles out of the Lizard's clutches. Anyway, you seem to have won the first round. If all goes well you'll have Miss Vachell back within an hour. What then?"

"That depends on Mona. If she wants to carry on with the hunt for the *Cinco Llagas* gold—and I bet she will—I'm game to have a shot at getting the plan from Saratini. I feel I owe that joker something. His confounded robots almost turned my hair white."

Stan chuckled.

"The Count must certainly bless Dr. Constandos. It was his coming from Port Said chucked the grit in the machinery."

Thanks to the fact that it was the only one of its species within miles of Pwllchywchi they located the farmhouse without difficulty. It was dusk when Stan pulled up at the gate. Lord Basil leant from the car to survey the house.

"No lights. Probably the garrison are round at the back. Come on, chaps. Don't shoot unless you have to, but if you do shoot don't miss."

The storming party went up the drive at the double. Before their combined weight the door went flat. With drawn guns they dashed into the dark and silent house.

But the Count's gangsters had done their work well. On receipt of his phone call six of them had driven over from Sperm in a fast car and had swiftly obliterated all signs of the struggle in which Morgan, Crane and the woman called Mrs. Jones had met their mysterious deaths. The bodies had been removed; the furniture washed. The carpet in the sitting-room being beyond cleansing had been taken away with the bodies.

In five minutes the would-be rescuers had satisfied themselves Mona was not in the house. They assembled in the passage that served as hall. Commander Eggington swore and Lord Basil's face betrayed his chagrin.

"My fault, chaps," he said gloomily. "I wasted time going up to the Black Dingle. When Saratini found I'd escaped from Sperm he simply telephoned the people here to take Mona somewhere else. Naturally he guessed I'd come here to try to get her. Well, we're no better off than we were before."

The commander's great paw fell on his shoulder.

"Don't lose heart, young man. Have another go at Saratini. Kill him next time."

As he spoke a telephone bell tinkled. Lord Basil answered the instrument which stood in a tiny room off the passage. At the sound of Saratini's mocking, high-pitched voice his eyes blazed in a manner that would have greatly surprised, say, Superintendent Fibkin.

"Is that little Fido? Yes, I expected you'd trot off to the farmhouse. I've been calling up at twenty-minute intervals. Well, Fido? Found what you hoped for?"

"No, damn you. The house is empty."

"How strange! I suppose it never occurred to your vacuous mind that I might remove her. By the way, you surely didn't imagine that I was in earnest about gassing you this afternoon? Hot air—that was all that was being pumped into that cell. And you wasted a perfectly good silk handkerchief! Really, Lord Basil, you're very easily frightened."

Again Lord Basil heard that devilish chuckle that set his teeth on edge.

His reason told him Saratini was lying. He had smelt carbon-monoxide in the chamber; had witnessed the cautious preparations made by the gangsters preparatory to removing his body. Yet, so convincing was the Count's manner of speaking, he felt almost inclined to believe that the "death-chamber" had been merely another sinister hoax.

"I had no intention of killing you," Saratini was saying. "My intention was to give a conceited young puppy a much-needed lesson. But you in your blind panic killed a harmless man with a wife and family. I'm surprised at you, Fido."

"You'll be more surprised before you're done," Lord Basil snapped. "Where's Miss Vachell? If you don't tell me I'll bring every policeman in North Wales to Sperm."

"Which would be the most foolish thing that even you ever did in your life," Saratini said coolly. "Miss Vachell is here now and alive and well, but I assure you she won't continue to be so if I hear the police are coming. By the way, she's anxious to speak to you. Will you hold on?"

Lord Basil heard a sound as if someone had snatched the receiver from Saratini's hand. There was a bubble of laughter, then a voice he could have sworn was Mona's.

"Hullo, P.B.C. Oh, Basil, you are a fatheaded, faithful old darling! They've told me what you did this afternoon. Have you been dreadfully worried? I'm quite enjoying the adventure, I am really, Popski."

Lord Basil's doubts vanished. It *was* Mona. "Popski" was
a private pet-name he believed to be known to nobody else.

"Thank goodness, Mo. I . . . I imagined all sorts of things.
Are those brutes treating you all right?"

"Oh, quite. But about this treasure—I think we had better
accept what Count Saratini offers. I know now we haven't a
hope of beating him. And if you do anything foolish again
they may take it out of me . . . Do you understand?"

His lordship's eyes narrowed. *That* wasn't like Mona.
That wasn't like the little Welsh fighter whose gameness was
proverbial in the tennis world.

"I understand," he said. "As a matter of fact, I thought it
would be wiser myself to scratch the match. You can tell the
Count that as far as I'm concerned he can get the treasure
without interference."

"Thank you, darling. Well, you'll see me safe and sound
in a day or so. Till then—"

"One second," Lord Basil said quickly. "I've got a message for you from Susie Coleman."

"Oh, yes. What did Susie say?"

"She'd like a single with you on Saturday if you're better.
You see I told her you were staying with Cecily Robinson
and had got a chill that kept you in bed. Will that be all
right?"

"Oh, rather. Good-bye, darling."

"Pip pip."

Lord Basil replaced the receiver. He was frowning
thoughtfully. Whoever the lady at the other end of the wire
had been, she had not been Mona. Mona knew as well as
Lord Basil that Susie Coleman was in the States, and that
Miss Robinson's maiden name was Gertrude.

It looked, therefore, as if Mona was not in Sperm at all,
but that the Count was anxious he should believe she was.
Why? Was it a trap to entice him back to the white house at
the foot of the Great Orme?

There was another and grimmer possibility. Suppose the
gang had murdered her and were anxious to make him imagine she was still alive! That was a common device of kid-

nappers. He remembered reading of an American gang who had driven a dead child past its father in a car so that he should believe it living—a trick that would have rejoiced the heart of Count Saratini.

He turned to see Commander Eggington behind him with a lighted candle in his hand.

"That was Saratini rang up. He got a girl to speak to me pretending she was Mona. She was a good actress and had evidently been coached what to say by someone who'd been shadowing Mona, but I caught her out."

"You're certain?" Eggington asked.

"Positive. And I'm also positive Mona is not in Sperm. If she had been Saratini needn't have bothered with a substitute. There'd have been no point in the deception."

"Then if she's not in Sperm, where is she?"

Lord Basil slumped down on a chair. He was feeling tired, dispirited and obsessed by an anxiety he strove to conceal.

"I'm beginning to think they've murdered her. The Count's idea is to keep me on a string until they've found the treasure and cleared off. Curse the treasure! I wish Constandos had never come. Do you know what I propose?"

"What?"

"That we chuck our hand in for Mona's sake. Yes, I know it's loathsome letting those swine beat us. If I'd only myself to consider I'd fight them to the last fence. But we can't expose Mona to danger like this just to save our own feelings. I'll tell the Count that if he'll only give Mona back we'll accept his offer."

He moved towards the phone. Eggington caught his arm.

"Wait till we hear what Hastings has to say. No sense in hauling down your colours before you have to. Besides, as you said just now, the child may be dead already. Anyway, have a talk to Hastings."

"All right," Lord Basil said wearily. "But I know he'll agree. Where is he?"

"He said he was going out to have a look round. Give him a shout."

Lord Basil went into the sitting-room and flung up the window. He could see the lights of Stan's car at the gate, but of the American himself there was no sign.

"Stan! Hullo there! Stan!"

No reply save the yapping of a dog. He was aware of Eggington towering behind him with the candle. Suddenly the blonde giant gave a roar.

"Look there! A figure all in black . . . That's one of them . . . Come on and we'll catch the swine."

With astounding agility for a man of his bulk he vaulted the window-sill. In a flash Lord Basil followed. Side by side, revolvers glinting in the moonlight, they raced down a turfy slope.

CHAPTER XI

THE BLACK KILLER

"WELL, I'M JIGGERED!" Commander Eggington said. "You can call me a Dutchman if the fellow hasn't given us the slip after all. The ground must have swallowed him up."

They had reached the spot where the turfy slope terminated at a stone wall. Beyond the wall was a field devoid of any cover. And the moonlight showed them cattle and sheep standing about apparently quite undisturbed.

Lord Basil leant his elbows on the wall. He was as puzzled as the commander. Then he advanced the only possible explanation.

"He ducked down and crawled along the further side of the wall. He must have gone at an amazing pace. There's a road of sorts crossing the valley down there. Probably he left his car there and is making for it now. Listen."

They listened for several minutes but could hear no sound of a car being started up. The commander mopped his forehead with a red bandana.

"I'm getting past the age for these games. It's all very well for you youngsters, but I'm stiff in the joints. D'you know what that fellow looked like to me? Like a picture I once saw of a Spanish inquisitor. Black cowl over his head and flowing black drapery, you know."

Lord Basil nodded.

"He's the same person Reilly saw at Sperm. Ten to one it was he did the murder in the Black Dingle. But what beats me if he's working for Saratini or not. He can't be Gravenant—at least not if he killed Miss Floss. That's pretty well proved by the fact that you saw Gravenant on Minrhyn Head this afternoon."

"What makes you so certain he did kill Miss Floss?"

"Simply the coincidence that the murderer was in a black car. Anyway, let's ask Stan what his views are. He's a clear-sighted sort of fellah."

"He is," the commander agreed. "I admire that American friend of yours. But I'm afraid he may have some bad news for you. From what he said to me just after you went to the telephone, I gathered that his theory is—"

He stopped, obviously unwilling to go on.

"What's his theory?" Lord Basil asked sharply.

"Don't take it too hard. I'm afraid Stan is inclined to think Miss Vachell was murdered in the farmhouse last night. He found clues that pointed to a crime of violence having been committed and steps taken to cover up the traces. Blood-stains hastily sponged out and that sort of thing. The carpet in the sitting-room is missing and there are damp patches on the furniture . . ."

"Then Stan thinks they killed her?"

"Well, it's pretty obvious *someone* was killed recently in that house. Suppose Miss Vachell had tried to escape? Saratini's men would have thought nothing of shooting her dead . . . That's why I was so anxious you should see Stan before you tried to make terms with the Count."

"If she's dead I'll break into Sperm and kill Saratini with my bare hands. But where the devil is Stan? I want to know exactly what he found in the house."

He led the way back to the farmhouse. On the drive he stopped and stared. The shifting moonlight had disclosed something previously concealed in shadow, the body of a man lying face downwards on the short grass close to the sitting-room window.

It was Stan Hastings. Lord Basil's first thought as he turned him over was that he was dead.

The commander ran for water from the yard. By the time he had returned with a bucket Lord Basil had investigated the American's injuries. It was plain he had been felled by a frightful blow from behind. Only the fact that he had been wearing a bowler hat with a specially strengthened crown and brim (a precaution against being blackjacked by Saratini's gangsters) had saved his skull from being crushed in like an eggshell.

Undoubtedly the Black Killer's work. Lord Basil could picture the sinister cowled form creeping out of the darkness with upraised arm. He must have come noiselessly over the grass and felled the American while his back was turned . . .

A crunch on the gravel heralded the commander's return with the bucket.

"Is he dead?"

"Fractured skull or bad concussion by the look of him. God knows if he'll live or not. Another life gone for that damned *Cinco Llagas* treasure . . ."

They were bathing the unconscious man's face and head. Eggington shook his head.

"He's in a bad way. This is Saratini's doing, of course. That fellow in black must be one of his gang. The Count posted him here to get Stan. I gather he was afraid of Stan because of what he knew."

Lord Basil's hand fell on his arm. He was staring in the direction of the gate. Was he imagining things or was there really a figure in black standing close to the wall? And then, while he was still hesitating, the figure emerged into the moonlight and began to approach . . .

Lord Basil's supposition that someone had been impersonating Mona over the telephone had been quite correct. The lady's name was Lydia Gratz. She was an actress of Russian extraction and striking appearance. Sir Jasper, whose property Lydia was, and on whose yacht she happened to be a guest, could pay highly for his fancies.

When Lydia had replaced the receiver she rose and swept a curtsy. For she had an audience. In addition to Count Saratini and Sir Jasper, there were half a dozen men and women belonging to the party on the yacht in the room. "Shady" is the most suitable word by which to describe these friends of Sir Jasper's. Not one of them was known to the police as a criminal, but they were all more or less connected with Count Saratini's gang, the most sinister crime organization in Europe.

It was to Count Saratini Lydia dropped her curtsy. That extraordinary individual, compound of scientist, practical joker and master-criminal, was sprawling in the depths of an easy-chair, his skull-like head bowed forward and his sunken eyes twinkling with amusement as he listened.

"Aren't I the clever girl?" Lydia chirruped. "Fido thought it was his love he spoke to. I'm glad she's dead, that rude little Welsh spitfire. She insulted me, Lydia Gratz, at a tennis tournament once. Just because I let my pom run across the court she called me a silly b——. She's no lady, that one."

Saratini gave his cackling laugh.

"You hadn't a difficult task, Lydia. Lord Basil has a vacuum where there ought to be grey matter."

"He believed me without a doubt. I called him P.B.C. and Popski—like I heard that little fool doing at Brig-y-don. Oh, yes, I played the part well enough to deceive a brighter person than Fido."

"When he realizes she's dead he'll say, 'How bally awful,'" mimicked Saratini. "'Beastly business, what? Enough to give a chappie the pip.'"

"We don't know for sure she is dead," Sir Jasper pointed out. "They couldn't find her body."

"She was very lucky if she escaped," the Count said grimly. "If she was in the house when the person who killed Crane, Morgan and Mrs. Jones arrived, I don't see how she can have escaped the slaughter. Or if she's not dead, she's in that person's power which, from her point of view, would be a hundred times worse. I can imagine nothing more unpleasant for a young girl than to be Gravenant's prisoner."

"Gravenant!" The name was echoed round the room in varying degrees of consternation and amazement. Count Saratini chuckled.

"I thought that would make you sit up. Yes, ladies and gentlemen, Gravenant has escaped. I suspected it at once when I saw what was inside the farmhouse. On returning here I put through a long-distance call to the criminal lunatic asylum in which he had been placed. He has been missing from that asylum for over a month. The French authorities are under the impression that he's dead. That accounts for the fact that so little notice has been taken of the escape."

"Why do they think he's dead?" someone asked.

"Owing to the great cunning with which he contrived to escape. On the day after that on which he left the prison a decapitated, unrecognizable body was found in the Vendome tunnel a few miles from the asylum. It had belonged to a man of about Gravenant's size and the clothes were identified as being those Gravenant had been wearing when he escaped. Naturally the French police concluded it was Gravenant had been killed by the train. They were wrong. Gravenant is in Minrhyn Bay now with a double objective. He wants the *Cinco Llagas* treasure and, even more I fancy, he wants his revenge on us."

He paused to glance at the anxious faces of his listeners. Then he went on—speaking for once quite gravely.

"All of you who know that Englishman can appreciate what this means. Gravenant is a supremely dangerous man, a compound of cunning and ferocity it would be hard to equal. He's well educated, of extraordinary physical strength and an actor of no mean ability. That he suffers from what I believe a mental specialist would call a tiger-obsession in no way impairs his formidableness. Saving when he gets one of those murderous fits in which he fancies himself a tiger he's as normal as anybody in this room."

There was an uneasy silence. People were recalling what they knew of the Englishman who had once been the terror of the underworld of the Mediterranean ports.

"Saved a lot of bother if you'd done him in, Count," a man said.

"For that mistake you must blame our late friend, Mr. Crane," Saratini said. "The Marseilles police wanted Gravenant for the atrocious murder of two girls in that city. He was to Marseilles, I may mention, almost what Jack the Ripper once was to London. Well, Crane held proofs, and when the quarrel arose about the disposal of the *Cinco Llagas* treasure he thought it would save trouble if he were guillotined by the French police. It was a bad blunder. Thanks to a clever counsel and also to his own powers of acting, Gravenant was found mad and, instead of being executed, was sent to the Vendome asylum."

"And he is in Minrhyn Bay—this dangerous man?" Lydia cried.

"Undoubtedly. He's made his first move by killing Crane and Morgan and, as far as I know, Miss Vachell. If I were you, Lydia, I should not go for any lonely walks in the vicinity of Minrhyn Head."

"But what do you propose doing about it?" someone asked.

The Count shrugged his shoulders.

"Deal with Gravenant as I should deal with any other mad dog. Formidable as he is, he can't do us much harm singlehanded. He's got no friends and very little money. And now, although I don't want to appear inhospitable, I must leave you to your own devices. Much as I should prefer to remain in your charming company, I am afraid there is work to be done."

"I thought you were going to make your robots give a display!" Lydia pouted.

"Not to-night, my dear. Another time with pleasure. *Au revoir,* ladies and gentlemen . . ."

And with the passing of his strange, sinister personality the atmosphere of the room seemed to become perceptibly warmer.

It was to his own private sanctum that Count Saratini went. This was a small room at the top of the house. Presumably it was a room after his own heart, but the average man would infinitely have preferred the Chamber of Horrors at Madame Tussaud's.

For it was a Chamber of Horrors, and of horrors a thousand times more blood-curdling than those exhibited to the public in the famous Baker Street exhibition. In the fashioning of those gruesome dolls the Count had satisfied both sides of his dual nature. His brilliant scientific brain had constructed the ingenious mechanism that gave them life-like movement, but it was his perverted, sadistic sense of humour that had led him to make them horrible.

For the robots were not of the square, geometric-looking design familiar to patrons of music-halls and scientific exhibitions. They were waxen effigies of people who had died violent deaths. Men and women who had been strangled, hanged and burned—distorted, leering caricatures guaranteed to sicken the mind and appal the imagination.

To Count Saratini they were only so many amusing toys. Nothing gave him greater delight than to use them for the purpose of scaring people. He had brought them to Minrhyn Bay on Sir Jasper's yacht and had enlivened the cruise by giving puppet-shows of a *grand guignol* character.

There was a rap at the door. The name of the man who entered was Hocking. A dark young man with a profile like a bird of prey, he had been promoted to fill the position in the gang rendered vacant by Crane's death.

Hocking caught his breath as he glanced round at the shrouded forms and distorted faces of the robots.

"I wonder you're not afraid to be in here alone, Chief. I wouldn't for a fortune even though I know they're only wax. Ugh! Their eyes follow you round the room."

"They are life-like," Saratini agreed. "Well, what have you found out?"

"About that killing in the Black Dingle?"

"Yes."

Keeping his eyes averted from the robots, Hocking made his report.

"It was Gravenant killed Miss Floss for a cert. I've been talking to Eddie, he's the page-boy at the Station Hotel, and I got out of him that she'd an old Spanish coin she'd been showing to customers in the lounge all morning. What I figure is that Gravenant must have been one of the people she showed it to. Well, if he thought it was part of the *Cinco Llagas* treasure, the natural thing for him to do would be to try and find out where she got it, wouldn't it? So I guess he decoyed her to meet him at the Black Dingle—you know what a way Gravenant has with the girls, don't you?—that afternoon, and then something happened that made him decide to kill her. Perhaps she twigged he was in disguise—or perhaps he got one of those attacks when he fancies himself a tiger. Anyway, I'm dead sure he killed her. And the police'll never catch him. He hasn't left the ghost of a clue."

Saratini was considering, his head sunk forward and the tips of his fingers pressed together.

"I agree," he said at last. "We can take it as proven that Gravenant killed Miss Floss. That shows he attached considerable importance to the Spanish coin. I suppose you haven't been able to learn how she obtained it?"

"I have, Chief. I got it out of Eddie she bought it."

"Bought it?"

"Yes. She bought it from an old beggar you can see on the front any morning. His name is Hare and the local people call him March Hare because he's supposed to be not quite right in the upper story. He's a mysterious old devil. No one seems to know where he lives or how he lives. Probably you've noticed him on the front yourself. Short with a ragged old trench-coat and a cap."

"I have noticed a man of that description," Saratini nodded. "So he sold Miss Floss the coin that led to her death! Had he any notion of its real value?"

"No—nor had she. Eddie says she gave him two shillings thinking she was doing a charity. But it doesn't follow that coin ever came out of the *Cinco Llagas.* He may have found it on the beach."

"It's queer that that solution did not suggest itself to Gravenant," Saratini said. "He would hardly have gone to the lengths of murdering the girl unless he had been desperately anxious to find out whence it came. It almost looks to me as if—"

"What, Chief?"

"As if Gravenant has already been to the hiding-place in the castle and has found out that the treasure has been removed or tampered with. It's not impossible. According to the plans Crane took from Major Vachell the gold was buried and sealed up, but then Gravenant was once a mining engineer and has an expert knowledge of the use of explosives. And he would have known where to look from having read the plan. Suppose he has been to the hiding-place and has found the treasure gone! Wouldn't that supply a motive for his murdering Miss Floss?"

He made an irritable movement. It was plain to Hocking that he was seriously upset.

"Waiting for that lease to be signed has wasted many precious hours," he muttered. "I suspect Gravenant has stolen a march. But it never entered my head that he and Dr. Constandos could both turn up in Minrhyn Bay. Confound them both!"

"I heard something else in the bay," Hocking said. "Constandos has been missing since last night."

"I'm delighted," the Count said savagely. "Let's hope Gravenant has mauled him to death."

CHAPTER XII

THE LIZARD HAS A NARROW ESCAPE

IT WAS EVIDENT Count Saratini was seriously disturbed. Hocking saw him take the little silver phial from his pocket and shake some white grains on to the back of his hand. He sniffed. His eyes brightened and he smiled. "That's better. It's always foolish to lose one's poise, but this case instead of proving as I expected the simplest of my career, bids fair to become one of the most complicated. As if it wasn't enough to have Gravenant and Dr. Constandos interfering, we are now faced by a doubt as to whether the gold is really in the castle at all. However, I think that doubt can soon be resolved. Lease or no lease, I'm going to the castle myself to-night to commence the search."

"You won't be able to see much if the gold's sealed up."

"I'll be able to see if Gravenant or anyone else has been tampering with the hiding-place. Before we go I'll show you the plans taken from Major Vachell. They have been read by Crane, Gravenant and myself and, hitherto, nobody else."

He crossed to a safe set level with the wall. When he returned he was holding a worn leather wallet in his sinister-looking hands.

The cocaine had done its beneficent work. He was smiling and humming a tune as he took the papers out of the wallet and spread them on the table.

"There you are, Hocking! Do you realize you're greatly honoured in being allowed to behold the documents? To a keen student of Elizabethan history such as I have no doubt you are they must be of enormous interest. And, incidentally, they are the key to a million pounds worth of solid gold. But of course the last sordid fact doesn't interest you, Hocking. It is your zeal for enlightenment about Elizabethan customs and not your lust for gold that impels you to lean so avidly across the table! Isn't that so, Hocking?"

Hocking sat back hurriedly. Somehow those mocking eyes and that purring voice had contrived to convey a threat. He knew that it would be most unwise to yield to the temptation to snatch the papers from the Count's hand and read the secret of the *Cinco Llagas* for himself.

"That's better, Hocking. All things come to him who waits. We shall proceed. First and foremost, let me inform you that the name of the original chronicler of the wreck and looting of the treasure-ship, *Cinco Llagas,* was Thomas Jones. He held the respectable position of clerk to the victualler-in-chief of the castle. A gifted young man, but I think we may conclude that his quill was mightier than his sword. Of his own part in the affair he simply says, 'I did helpe to binde and manacle such of the Spanish dogges as had the ill-fortune not to perish in the flames . . .' Note that he says 'ill-fortune', Hocking. It was a rude age in which he lived. Squeamishness had not yet become a virtue."

"That would have suited you, Chief," Hocking ventured with a grin.

"Probably you're right, Hocking. Let us proceed, however. I'll omit the excellent Master Thomas's vivid but long-winded description of the storm that drove the *Cinco Llagas* on to Minrhyn Head, and also his rather obsequious account of how 'That most excellente and puissante knight, Sir Gwylliam Vachell of Minrhyn, did rush down the cliffes at the head of his retainers and did hurle himself upon the amazed foe with shouts the like of which no mortal man ever heard before' and will hurry on to the plum in the pudding so far as we're concerned. The *Cinco Llagas* treasure. This is what Master Thomas tells us of the finding of that legendary gold:

". . . 'and in a secret place at the very bottome of the holde we did finde three stout chests which being opened were founde to be filled to the brinke with ruddy gold that shone in the lighte of the flames. And at sighte of that great abundance of precious metal a madness did falle upon certain ones of the company. Caring naught for the grievous wounds inflicted by the Spanish dogges nor yet for the fierce heat of the flames, certain men didde leap upon the gold and embrace it to their bodies as if it were cooling water and they perishinge of thirst. And scarce were they to be blamed for of a truth that golde around which the Spanish dogges had died by scores so that those who did reach the chestes had to wade in their bloode, was a sight to ravishe the senses . . .' "

Hocking smacked his lips.

"That old bird wrote sense, Chief. There's something about a lot of gold sends fellows off their chump."

"Beautifully and poetically expressed, Hocking. I implore you, however, to exert your self-control and not go off your chump when it comes to the actual handling of the *Cinco Llagas* treasure. And now we'll pass on in our chronicle to where Master Thomas describes the burying of the gold. And as his account is rather involved and difficult to follow, I'll read you the précis Major Vachell made for his own guidance."

He selected another sheet of paper and began to read:

" 'I think the chronicler means that the vassals buried the gold in a dungeon opening off an underground passage leading from the castle and emerging at some point on the eastern side of the cliffs. The rock he describes as marking the cliff end of the passage was probably the Maiden's Nose.

" 'As far as I can make out, the other end of the passage can be reached from the room called the old library. He describes Sir Gwylliam as "twisting the third Cupid from the right four times and striking, with the hilt of his sword upon the nose of the left-hand dragon". Beyond question he here refers to the fireplace in the old library. The mantelpiece is supported by two Welsh dragons carved out of marble, and there is a frieze of carved Cupids running between the dragon's heads. Doubtless the actions the chronicler describes set in motion some mechanical device which discloses the entrance to the passage.

" 'The dungeon in which the chests of gold were placed for safety from Queen Elizabeth's soldiers when they visited the castle was about two hundred yards along this passage on the right-hand side. There seems to have been a small well or pit (shades of Edgar Allan Poe!) in the centre of the floor of the dungeon into which the chests were lowered. When this had been done both the well and the door of the dungeon were blocked up with, to quote Master Thomas, "exceeding cunning". . .' "

Count Saratini put down the paper. Hocking, whose eyes were glittering, brought his fist down on the table with a bang.

"By God, it's easy, Chief! Locate that passage and we've got the gold. A pint of nitro'll soon open up the dungeon. Then we'll lower the chests down the cliff to a motor-boat to be taken to the yacht. It's easy."

By Saratini's orders a car was waiting at the door. In under half an hour they were standing on the slate-refuse road running across the plateau of Minrhyn Head. Before them loomed the dark mass of Minrhyn Castle, looking as impervious to time and change as the rock on which it stood.

They walked up the weed-choked drive and through the pillared entrance. Hocking's torch flashed round the vast, bat-haunted hall where their footsteps rang hollow on the marble floor.

The old library opened off the hall. Saratini knelt in the dust before the fireplace. His hand groped along the frieze of dancing Cupids and closed upon the third from the right. He pressed and found that the little marble figure turned on an axis like the handle of a door. From somewhere in the depths of the wall they heard a dull whining sound.

The Count raised his long, whimsical face to smile at Hocking, standing above him with a torch.

"We are certainly on the right trail. Now for the nose of the left-hand dragon. Sir Gwylliam struck it with his sword-hilt. I fancy that the butt of my automatic, although less romantic, should prove equally effective."

He had drawn the automatic and was holding it by the barrel ready to strike, when he paused. His sharp ears had caught a muffled sound of ticking. It might have been the noise of a death-watch beetle, or it might—!

Saratini leapt to his feet.

"Back for your life!"

They dashed for the door. Barely had they reached it when the fireplace vomited a sheet of red flame. The shock of the explosion flung them to the ground. As they scrambled to their feet they heard the thunder of falling masonry, like coal being poured down a chute.

"What the devil happened?" Hocking gasped, white-faced.

It was a moment before Saratini answered. The narrowness of the escape had for a second shattered his inhuman calmness.

Then he laughed aloud.

"It was Gravenant. He's been here already. I told you he was an expert in the use of explosives. He mined the fireplace, hoping to get me. A Ferris bomb wound up by the Cupid being revolved. Very ingenious! If I hadn't heard the ticking we should both have been blown to smithereens."

"That means he's got the gold," Hocking said.

The Count made no reply. He strode back into the library, now dense with acrid fumes, and inspected the gaping hole where the fireplace had stood.

"Vandalism! That fireplace was unique. Well, Hocking, my friend, shall we proceed? I don't fancy Gravenant will have laid any more booby-traps."

Bent double, they scrambled through the hole, stepping across a pile of smoking debris. A flight of narrow steps concealed in the thickness of the wall led downwards. They followed these and found themselves at the beginning of a tunnel hewed through the living rock.

For two hundred yards they advanced cautiously, their flash-lamps searching the fungus-covered walls of the tunnel. Suddenly the Count, who was leading, stopped. His torch had shown him a patch of mortar the size and shape of a door let into the rock.

It was evident the human tiger—to give Gravenant the name by which he was known to his fellow-gangsters—had passed that way. Two feet from the floor of the tunnel a hole had been blown through the thick wall, whose outer surface was a sheet of mortar large enough to admit a man.

Saratini pointed.

"Behold how modern ingenuity laughs at the erections of medieval labour. I dare say that when Sir Gwylliam's vassals erected that wall they congratulated themselves upon having placed an impassable obstacle before the mouth of the dungeon; yet I don't suppose it took Gravenant more than half an hour to blow that hole. Will you go first, Hocking?"

The gangster hesitated. The thought had come to him that the human tiger might be lurking at the other side of the wall.

The Count's bright, malicious eyes fastened on his face. "Will you go first, Hocking?" he purred. Hocking obeyed. Automatic in hand, he wriggled slowly into the hole.

Behind him Saratini stood waiting. He, too, suspected that Gravenant might be in the dungeon. He had drawn his automatic. Crouched and tense, he waited until Hocking's kicking feet had disappeared from view.

There was no shot; no yell of rage. Instead he heard Hocking s almost delirious cry of triumph.

"The chests are here, Chief!"

CHAPTER XIII

CONSTANDOS ESCAPES FROM THE FRYING-PAN INTO THE FIRE

HOCKING'S FACE APPEARED where his feet had been a minute before. He grinned up at Saratini.

"It's all jake, Chief. Not a sign of Gravenant. But he's blown open the pit in the centre and you can see the chests lying down there. Three of 'em. I suppose he was waiting his chance to get the gold away."

"How far down are the chests?"

"About eighteen feet. They look like three coffins down there. Come and have a look."

Saratini lit a cigarette. He was far less excited than his subordinate.

"I hate to damp your enthusiasm, Hocking, but, as little Lord Fido would say, I shall be deuced surprised if those chests contain anything more valuable than air. However, we'd better make certain."

He followed Hocking into the dungeon which proved to be a damp, foul-smelling cave measuring about twenty yards by ten. In the centre was the mouth of the well. It had been sealed by a layer of stones and cement, superimposed upon a sort of lid of massive oak beams, but Gravenant's explosive had blown the obstacle to fragments, which were now strewn about the floor of the dungeon.

Saratini flashed his torch into the well. He could see the brass-ornamented lids of three chests lying side by side like coffins. Considering they had been there for nearly four hundred years they were in a surprisingly good state of preservation.

Hocking swung himself into the well. For a second he hung by his fingers from the lip, then he let himself drop. He alighted unhurt beside the chests.

For a few minutes he wrestled with the cumbrous brass fastenings of the nearest. He raised the lid and then his shout of anger echoed up the shaft.

"It's empty! That devil Gravenant has got the gold!"

Looking up, he saw the thin, spectral figure of Saratini standing at the lip of the well. The Count was shaking with quiet amusement.

"Poor Hocking! Well, I warned you what to expect. But because the gold has vanished it does not follow that it's Gravenant who has taken it. By token of the murder in the Black Dingle I rather think that he is in the same predicament as we are. And I fancy that the owner of *these* is in a more unpleasant predicament than either of us. Open the next chest, Hocking, and let out Dr. Constandos—or what Gravenant has left of him."

The objects he was extending over the well were a straw hat and an ornamental cane which he had found in a corner of the dungeon. Next instant Hocking was dragging their unhappy owner out of the centre chest. He had been cruelly bound and gagged, but—as his rolling eyes testified—he was still alive.

Saratini had found a rope, evidently left there by the human tiger. By its aid they hauled the doctor to the surface.

The Count watched in silence while Hocking removed the bonds. Then he made a deep bow.

"This is a delightful surprise, Dr. Constandos. Next to the *Cinco Llagas* treasure itself the chests could have contained nothing that would have afforded me greater pleasure."

Constandos stared from one face to another. He was dazed, incapable of speech.

"Give him a drink," Saratini said impatiently. "I'm curious to learn what happened."

Hocking produced a flask. The undiluted spirit made Constandos cough and splutter. Slowly the fact penetrated his mind he was still alive.

Then he looked at Saratini's face and his joy at finding himself liberated from what he imagined his coffin vanished like a wraith of smoke. For the Count's face at that moment was a thing at which to shudder. He looked the very incarnation of cruel, devilish amusement.

A green, discoloured hand shot out and clawed the doctor's cheek. The fingers tightened until the pointed nails sank into the wincing flesh.

"Who put you in that chest?" he hissed.

"I—I do not know," Constandos stammered. He spoke the literal truth. Of what had happened on the previous evening he had no clear recollection. Dimly he remembered seeing a vision of his own face, very flushed and with excited eyes, reflected in the polished bottom of an inverted tankard. That must have been in the lounge of the Brig-y-don Hydro. Ugh! Nevaire—nevaire would he drink that vile drink of the English, 'ot toddy, again!

Another spasm. He saw himself dancing along a dark road under trees, brandishing his arms and shouting Greek patriotic songs as he ran. He, Dr. Constandos, to behave like that! Even at that moment he felt grateful that it had happened in Minrhyn Bay and not in Port Said.

He'd been going to shoot a tiger. And he'd found his tiger—or rather, his tiger had found him. A black, nightmarish figure with eyes like blue flames. Had it been some hideous dream, or had he really awakened in a strange bed to see a monstrous apparition with black garments like a bat's wings bending above him. The thing had raised him in huge arms. It had borne him, squealing, kicking and as impotent as a child, through darkness to this ghastly dungeon.

But how had it all happened? His recollections were distorted, fragmentary as a nightmare. Whose bed had he been lying on when the black-shrouded monster found him? Most certainly it had not been his own bed in the Brig-y-don Hydro. He had reached Minrhyn Head. He could vaguely remember stumbling over heather and hearing the mumble of the sea when he went perilously near the cliffs.

"You don't know?" Saratini's voice, aided by the pain of those cutting nails, brought him back to the present. "Then permit me to refresh your memory. It was Gravenant who buried you alive. How did he get hold of you?"

"I can remember nozzing. A big man all dressed in black—zat ees all I remember now. 'E may 'ave been Gravenant, or 'e may 'ave been someone else."

"I see," the Count nodded. "You're going to pretend you can't remember anything clearly. You're a remarkably foolish little man, Dr. Constandos. Indeed, with the distinguished exception of Lord Basil Curlew, I think you're the most foolish man I ever met."

There was a cruel, purring note in his voice that made the doctor shudder. He felt Saratini meant to play with him, to torture him as a cat tortures a mouse that cannot escape.

Indeed, there was something very feline in the Count's expression at that moment. Holding Constandos spellbound with his glittering, snake-like eyes, he went on speaking:

"Crane and Gravenant were both my servants. When Crane showed me the papers he had taken from Major Vachell, I came to Minrhyn Bay to secure the *Cinco Llagas* gold. And I would have got it without the smallest trouble if you hadn't interfered. It was a bad day for you, Dr. Constandos, when you came to North Wales. A wiser man would have remained in Port Said and have tried to forget what he had learned by eavesdropping."

His eyes had narrowed into slits of venomous light. He shook the doctor gently to and fro.

"Well, fool! What have you to say?"

Desperation lent Constandos a grain of courage.

"You dare not 'arm me. Miss Vachell an' Lord Basil— zey are my frien's. Lord Basil, 'e ees powerful man. If 'e think zat I am 'urt—"

Saratini's high-pitched laugh rang out.

"You fool! Arc you actually trying to frighten me with the name of Lord Basil Curlew! That manicured, drawling half-wit with a monocle! No, no, Dr. Constandos. Lord Basil won't help you for the very good reason that he's dead."

"Dead!" the doctor cried incredulously. "You murdered 'im?"

"If you can call the putting away of an unwanted puppy murder, I suppose I did. Miss Vachell is also dead, but that had nothing to do with me. She'd only her own foolishness to thank that she got killed by Gravenant."

Constandos staggered. With those mesmeric eyes fixed on his, he could not but believe every word the Count spoke.

Mona Vachell and Lord Basil both dead! Little as he had seen of them, he had found them vastly attractive. Their youth, their high spirits, their kindness to him, a stranger. They had gone after the *Cinco Llagas* treasure not for lust of gold but out of sheer love of adventure. And this inhuman, laughing man had murdered those two children as remorselessly as he would have drowned a couple of kittens!

He could not remove his eyes from the Count's. He saw him now as some obscene reptile grinning at him through a mist of blood. Although Constandos did not know it, Saratini was using his hypnotic powers to drive horrible visions into his mind.

In his weak, exhausted state, Constandos was an easy victim. He saw things such as men see in the tides of delirium. Birds with blood-bedraggled wings; snakes with human heads. He was wading in a lake of blood. Before him floated the maggot-eaten corpses of Mona and Lord Basil. They raised puffed, distorted faces and beckoned with decaying hands . . .

Probably it was his very weakness that saved his reason. Suddenly he collapsed in a faint from which even Saratini's will could not arouse him.

The Count laughed and lit a cigarette.

"A very amenable subject," he said. "I foresee a lot of amusement from Dr. Constandos. If he ever goes back to Port Said it will be in the charge of a couple of keepers."

"He deserves all he gets," Hocking said harshly. "What are you going to do to him? Send him bughouse?"

Saratini's thin lips emitted a cloud of blue smoke. He looked at that moment like some sadistic vivisector reaching for the knife.

"What crude expressions you use, Hocking! Send him bughouse indeed! As if I ever sent anybody bughouse! Once or twice I have diverted myself by exhibiting my robots to unsuspecting people, but if they were so foolish as to go mad, it wasn't my fault. The robots were entirely harmless. I'm not responsible for other people's weak minds."

Again he laughed. And even the callous Hocking felt at that moment a feeling of repulsion from the soft-voiced, smiling sadist with the discoloured hands.

Saratini flipped the ash from his cigarette and became grave.

"All this is a side-issue. Let us return to the main problem. What has become of the gold that was in those chests?"

"Gravenant has it. He's carted it away to some other hiding-place. It stands to reason."

"Then can you explain why he took the trouble and risk of decoying that girl to the Black Dingle and murdering her?"

"I can't. Not unless he's gone clean off his nut and wanted to sacrifice her to the Tiger or something."

"A feeble explanation, Hocking. My theory is that when he broke in here he suffered the same disappointment as we did; he found the gold already gone. When he saw Miss Floss with that coin he thought it might be a clue to the present whereabouts of the gold. Whether or not he succeeded in eliciting from her the fact that she had bought it from that mysterious person called the March Hare it's impossible to say, but I think it's fairly reasonable to suppose that he did."

"Then you think it was the March Hare, not Gravenant who took the gold from here?"

"I think that someone other than Gravenant took it. And since the March Hare was in possession of that coin, suspicion must rest upon him. In that case Gravenant is searching for him now."

"But how could he have got it, Chief? He hadn't seen the plans; it isn't likely an old beggar like that could use explosives. And if he'd found it—"

Saratini stopped him with a curt gesture of the hand.

"The only person who can answer those questions is the March Hare himself. It's imperative that we find him before Gravenant does. To-morrow, Hocking, you must devote yourself to that object. Go into the Bay and make all the inquiries you can about him. But beware of Gravenant. Remember that he's almost certainly running on the same trail."

"If the March Hare is above ground, I'll get him," Hocking vowed.

"All right. I'll take further steps to keep Fido quiet—not that I think that Lord Puppy will dare to do much so long as he imagines we've got Miss Vachell. And now I suggest we return to Sperm with the night's catch. Dr. Constandos, I hope you are sufficiently recovered to walk the short distance to the car?"

Constandos was. But, since all things go by comparison, he would almost rather have returned to the chest in which the human tiger had buried him alive.

A tall figure in black had appeared at the gate of the farmhouse while Lord Basil and the commander were attending to Stan. Had he really been the person they had nicknamed the Black Killer, then the Black Killer would have had cause to regret his intrepidity in appearing at that moment. For Lord Basil had passed the stage when a man sticks at trifles. Had the figure shown any disposition to turn and fly he would have fired—and he would have fired to kill.

But this visitor, who was nothing more alarming than an old farmer wearing a long black overcoat, calmly awaited their coming. Only when the moonlight showed him the menacing revolvers did he draw back a pace.

"What are you chaps playin' at? Comin' at me with guns like the Prussian Guard! I've as much right to be here as you—maybe more."

His tone of outraged innocence was too genuine to be assumed. Lord Basil put his automatic back where it belonged.

"Sorry, old chappie," he said genially. "We—er—mistook you for a friend."

"What do you want?" Commander Eggington demanded fiercely. "Who sent you spying round here at this time of night?"

The farmer looked at the herculean sailor. And what he saw in those fierce blue eyes made him decide that politeness would be the wisest policy.

"I was on my way to Pwllchywchi, sir, to hire a car for a young lady. She wants to get back to Minrhyn Bay in a hurry. And seeing your car here by the gate I thought as how you might be willing to oblige her with a lift."

"A young lady!" Lord Basil shouted. "Not Miss Vachell!"

"That's the lady, sir. My son and I found her lying in a lil' sandpit on the Curig Estate. Seems she'd lost her way and been wandering round the moors all night. She's not a ha'p'orth the worse for the tumble she had into the pit. But she's in a terrible fidget to get back to the Bay. You see, we haven't no phone and no car and it's a lonely—"

He stopped in amazement. The commander was pump-handling Lord Basil's hand as if he would never stop.

"Our little lady is safe, I knew she would be," he shouted.

Lord Basil began to polish his monocle. Outwardly, he was less excited than the commander, but his hand was shaking.

"That's a load off the old coco-nut," he said. "Where is she now?"

"In my cottage, sir. Only a couple of miles from here down in the valley yonder. Were you gentlemen looking for her?"

"Looking, my dear chappie! We were running round in small circles and chawing the ground—at least, I was. We'll go to your cottage at once, if you'll show us the way."

It wasn't until he was actually stepping into the car that he remembered Stan, so completely had the news that Mona was safe driven all else from his mind. The commander volunteered to remain with the wounded man while he went to fetch Mona, but not even his eagerness to see Mona again could make Lord Basil accede to that plan. He believed Stan to be dying. It was imperative he should be got to hospital without a second's delay.

Luckily, the cottage was on the way back to Minrhyn Bay. The commander drove; Lord Basil and the farmer sat behind supporting Stan between them. And despite his relief at hearing that Mona was safe, Lord Basil's anger against Saratini increased with every hoarse gasp he heard the American utter.

Mona was waiting impatiently at the cottage gate surrounded by the farmer's children. So far from being any the worse for her adventure, she looked in the very pink of health and spirits.

She flew to the side of the car.

"Basil! I knew you'd come sooner or later. You never let me down."

"Cheerio," said his lordship shakily. "Old thing, you've given P.B.C. the worst fright of his career. How are you? All the jolly old bones oke and all the rest? . . . Look at the commander grinning like a Cheshire Cat! . . . He was about as rattled as I was? Kiss him."

Mona saw Stan's white face and recoiled.

"Who's that?"

"Stan Hastings, the pal I told you about. He had an accident with his car." (This was loud for the benefit of the farmer and his interested family.) "We've got to get him to hospital as soon as possible. Well, shake off the babes and let's be going. By the way, old chappie, er—er—slight expression of gratitude, doncherknow."

The note he handed the farmer made that worthy person wonder if he were seeing things. He wished he could find a young lady in a sandpit every day of his life at fifty pounds a time—especially a young lady as pretty and friendly as Miss Vachell.

It was not until they had deposited Stan in the hospital and had returned to the Rectory that Lord Basil learned the details of what had befallen Mona.

Her story cast but little light upon the identity of the Black Killer. She told of her interview with Crane, how she had attempted to escape through the window and how she had seen the Black Killer standing on the drive.

"Basil, I simply flew," she said. "They say fear gives people wings, and it's quite true. I just ran and ran and ran. All the time I was certain he was just behind me. I heard his feet on the turf; I thought I'd feel his hands on my throat any second. Basil, it was frightful. I remember calling out your name . . . Oh, if I could have heard you shout 'All right, old thing,' and seen you go sailing into that great brute with that famous right of yours . . ."

"What a hope!" drawled his lordship. "I'd have run faster than you did, if I'd been there . . . Well?"

"Well, after a time I simply couldn't run any further. I stopped and found he wasn't chasing me after all. But I hadn't the vaguest notion where I was. It was terribly lonely and eerie on that moor. Wales is a haunted sort of country, you know . . . Oh, I did want you, Basil! You'd have made everything seem funny like you did that evening in the castle . . ."

"Alluding to my face?"

"No, you know what I mean perfectly. You're really rather a nice thing, Basil, although you hate people to think so. Well, then I thought I'd try to find a road back to civilization, so I started to walk. But in the darkness I didn't see the sandpit. I tumbled in and I suppose I fainted or something stupid . . . Anyway, that's where the farmer and his son found me early this morning. They took me to the cottage and Mrs. Farmer gave me something that made me sleep and sleep. What's that bit of poetry about sleep's gentle fingers erasing care, Basil? That's what happened to me."

"You look as cocky as a two-year-old," Lord Basil told her. "Game to continue the hunt for the *Cinco Llagas* gold?"

"Rather!"

"Splendid. We'll do Saratini in the eye yet. Well, I must sheer off or old Bannock-Face will be shooing me out with a broom."

Tired as he was, he visited the hospital before returning to Rose Bower. The night sister's report was highly reassuring. Stan's injuries were not nearly as bad as he had thought. An examination by the doctor had revealed the fact that the American was suffering from nothing worse than concussion. He was now conscious.

The night sister stretched the regulations and allowed Lord Basil to see his friend for a moment.

Stan grinned feebly from the pillows.

"Some little old welt," he said. "That baby certainly hits hard. Which of 'em was it?"

"The Black Killer. Don't you remember?"

The American moved restlessly.

"I can remember nothing that happened after we broke down the door. Sister says concussion often acts that way. A bit of the memory gets wiped out . . . Hell, I wish to blazes I could remember though."

"Why?"

"Because I've a sorta hunch there's something I ought to tell you. Something desperately important. . . . As if just before I was hit I'd made a discovery."

The night sister had entered the ward. She touched Lord Basil's arm.

"That's long enough. It's bad for him to try to remember too much. If he doesn't worry he'll find everything will come back in time. Now, Mr. Hastings, the best thing for you is to get some sleep."

Her instructions were difficult to follow. He was tormented by the feeling there was some warning he ought to give Lord Basil, but to save his life he could not remember what it was.

CHAPTER XIV

THE BAT

THE LITTLE HOUSEMAID at Rose Bower whose duty it was to bring Lord Basil his matutinal cup of tea, would have been vastly surprised—not to say shocked—could she but have seen into his lordship's mind the following morning. For Lord Basil had been making a mental précis of the events of the last twenty-four hours, and his mind was a medley of robots, lethal chambers and black-robed monsters guaranteed to keep the average housemaid in nightmares for a month.

But of what he had been pondering Lord Basil gave no sign as he wished Rose his usual cheery good morning. His smile, as he reached for his cigarette-case, was as inanely carefree as if he had spent the previous day playing croquet with a maiden aunt. Probably more so. He had the temperament that thrives on excitement, and with Count Saratini and the Black Killer still on the warpath there was a distinct possibility of more trouble to come.

Above all, Mona was safe. Now that his mind was relieved on that point he felt he could look forward to the campaign for the *Cinco Llagas* treasure with positive enjoyment.

What should the next step be? "Break into Sperm and steal the plans," was the advice Commander Eggington never tired of offering. Having been once into Sperm, Lord Basil had no bloodthirsty desire to go a second time. Still, he felt he owed Count Saratini something. Scaring him out of his senses with those filthy robots! His lordship was not vindictive, but he had vowed to make Saratini laugh on the other side of his mouth in the very near future.

His eye fell on a letter lying on the early-morning tea-tray. It was unstamped, showing it had been delivered by hand at

Rose Bower. When he opened it a cheque for ten thousand pounds, payable to Mona Vachell, fell out. The signature on the cheque was "N. Sylvester".

He was about to begin to read the letter when he was interrupted by a scuffle and a feminine squeak outside the door. The squeaker was Rose; the other person's identity was made clear by his trombone-like voice.

"Privilege of an old sailor, my lass. That's how we say good morning to pretty girls in the Royal Navy."

"Come in, Georgy Porgy," Lord Basil shouted. "I've a letter here that may interest you."

The commander burst into the room like a sea breeze. His checks were ruddy, his eyes bright and his blonde beard fairly bristling with vitality.

"Still in your bed, young fellow!" he roared. "Bless my soul, I've been having a plunge off the pier. Came down from the Head on my bicycle at half-past seven this morning. Yes, I've breakfasted, thanks. How are you and what's this letter you're telling about?"

Lord Basil had been glancing over the letter. There was flat disappointment in his voice as he answered:

"We're done. Saratini has found the treasure."

Eggington started violently.

"What's that! Found the treasure?"

"So he says."

"I don't believe him. It's a bluff or something. Read what he says."

Lord Basil began to read. The commander, who had seated his immense form on the side of the bed, listened attentively, his bearded chin resting on his hand.

"DEAR FIDO (Lord Basil read),

"So we have come to the end of a perfect day! The enclosed, which you will kindly hand to Miss Vachell with my compliments, may help to assuage her natural disappointment at not having obtained the *Cinco Llagas* treasure.

"For I am afraid she will never handle that gold now. It is safely stowed away on Sir Jasper's yacht. Last night we removed it from the castle without the smallest trouble.

"I'll not ask you to accept my bare statement. If you will go to the castle and enter the room called the old library opening off the main hall, you will see that the fireplace has been demolished by an explosion (I was regretfully compelled to take that means of entering the tunnel). Behind where the fireplace stood there is a flight of steps that leads down to a tunnel running beneath the castle in the direction of the sea. A couple of hundred yards along the tunnel on the left-hand side you will sec the hole we blew through the wall that sealed the entrance to a dungeon. Crawl through this and you will find the three chests that contained the *Cinco Llagas* treasure lying at the bottom of a pit. They are quite, quite empty. If you doubt my word go and see for yourself.

You will observe that I am aware that Miss Vachell has reappeared. My intelligence service is fairly efficient. It was reported to me that you and Miss Vachell and a large hirsute gentleman, whose name I have not the pleasure of knowing, returned to Minrhyn Bay late last night and that you had with you in the car your inquisitive American friend, who appeared to be either dead or dying—the former, I hope. Poor Mr. Hastings! Curiosity is not one of my failings, but I would gladly give a hundred pounds to know who laid him out. And I would give another hundred to be able to shake that person's hand.

"And now I really must end up. I trust I have made it quite, quite clear that so far as the *Cinco Llagas* gold is concerned your last hope has vanished. Take my advice and return to your tennis and your other infantile pursuits and be thankful you have escaped as lightly as you have done. Most people who try to interfere with my plans are not so fortunate.

"Little Claude, you will be glad to hear, is making good recovery. I am thinking of fashioning another robot, one with a monocle, rabbits' teeth and a fatuous expression. It will wear clothes of the latest fashion, have a vacuum inside its well-brushed head and will be called Fido.

"Pip pip, and all that,

"THE LIZARD."

"And that's jolly well that," said Lord Basil, refolding the letter.

The commander brought his clenched fist down on the dressing-table.

"Lies and bunkum, every word of it," he shouted. "He hasn't touched a grain of the gold. I know Saratini. His purpose in writing like that was to stop Miss Vachell and yourself interfering."

"But, my sweet pippin, he describes the hiding-place. If I go to the castle and look—"

"You won't find the gold. You'll find the dungeon and the three empty chests just as he describes, but that's no proof *he's* got the treasure. Man alive, do you think if he had really got the gold he'd have bothered to send Miss Vachell ten thousand pounds? Not him! He's sent that cheque because he wants you kept out of the way at all costs. He's up against a difficulty himself. Look here, suppose that when he went to that dungeon, which is obviously the hiding-place given in the plans, he found the treasure wasn't there after all. Do you see what that would mean? It would mean he'd lost the great advantage he had over you. Neither of you would know where the gold was. You'd be starting the hunt all over again from scratch, as it were."

"You seem very certain," Lord Basil remarked.

"I am certain," the commander declared. "I've a hunch, instinct—call it what you like—that Saratini has not found the treasure yet. Another proof is I noticed Sir Jasper's yacht this morning moored in the same place off Llandudno. Don't tell me that if they'd got the gold stowed away they'd be still hanging about there. They've got steam up and could sail in fifteen minutes if they wanted."

"Sweet pippin, you are highly convincing. I begin to feel hopeful again. But what you haven't told me is who has got the treasure if Saratini has not. I suppose Gravenant is the person you have in mind. From what Crane said to Mona it's pretty clear that he's at daggers drawn with the Count."

For a long moment Eggington made no reply. He was frowning at the carpet, apparently lost in deep thought. Suddenly he raised his bright blue eyes to Lord Basil's face.

"I've had a brainwave."

"How jolly," murmured Lord Basil.

"Yes, and my brainwave is this: Count Saratini, Gravenant and the man you call the Black Killer are the same person."

The monocle fell from Lord Basil's eye. The idea struck him as utterly preposterous. He stared at the commander to see if he were in earnest.

"My dear old banana, you've taken my breath away. Whatever makes you think that?"

"What I've learned about Saratini's nature. He's a brilliantly clever, unscrupulous man with a perverted sense of humour. To resurrect Gravenant would be a trick after his own heart. Why, it's history repeating itself. Have you ever read what those old pirate captains used to do when they'd stolen a treasure? Murdered their own crews. Massacred them by treachery so that there'd be no sharing-out to be done. I believe Saratini is at the same filthy game. He wants all the *Cinco Llagas* gold for himself. Conveniently for his purpose there was this fellow, Gravenant, apparently a ferocious, cunning customer of whom the other members of the gang were scared stiff. Saratini knows Gravenant has died in France; he brings him to life again in Minrhyn Bay for his own purposes. The Count is a tall man; to trick himself out so that he could be mistaken for Gravenant would not be impossible. I imagine him to be a good actor. He was in the castle wearing that disguise the evening you went down to the cellars. He barred the door and then raved at you just as Gravenant might have raved. Then he showed himself to me in the same disguise. Then—"

"But why should he want *us* to think he was Gravenant?"

"I suppose he wanted it to get round to the gang that Gravenant was in Minrhyn Bay. If they first heard it through one of us—as they did incidentally—they'd be more inclined to believe."

"One sec. though," Lord Basil said. "You saw Gravenant at your cottage on the night Mona saw the Black Killer at the farmhouse. That proves Gravenant and the Black Killer can't be the same person."

"Nothing of the sort. Pwllchywchi is no distance from the Head for a man in a fast car. I'm not certain what time he came to the cottage. The same applies to the following after-noon when I saw him in the slate quarries. With his car he would have had time to go from there to the Black Dingle to meet that girl."

"What about last night? At the same time Saratini was telephoning to me from Sperm you saw the Black Killer skulking round the farmhouse after he'd knocked out Stan!"

The commander made an impatient gesture.

"How do you know it was Saratini you heard speaking? Some girl imitated Miss Vachell's voice; the Count may have posted an accomplice to imitate his own. By the way, how is Stan?"

"Much better."

"Better! I didn't think he'd live through the night." Eggington sounded amazed.

"Nor did I to tell the truth. He must have a devilish thick skull. I'd a word with him last night after I left Mona. He couldn't remember the Black Killer knocking him out. The poor old bird was all hot and bothered about it. He said he'd a feeling there was something he ought to warn me about, but he couldn't remember what it was."

"Probably he never will remember, but I can guess what it is he wants to tell you."

"What?"

"The identity of the Black Killer. He may have seen Saratini's face before he was knocked out. That's what he wants to warn you about."

Lord Basil lay back among the pillows with a yawn.

"Commander, you make your theory devilish plausible, but I don't believe it for a second. Anyway, it's beside the point whether Saratini is the Black Killer or not. What concerns us is who's got the *Cinco Llagas* gold if Saratini hasn't. Tell me that, sweet pippin."

"I can't. It's up to you to find out for Miss Vachell's sake. You ought to get busy—not lie in bed all day. Do you know what I'd do if I were in your place?"

"Settle Saratini. You've told me before."

"Exactly," the commander said. "Get Saratini out of the way and you've won the game. The rest of the gang don't count."

"Oh, my hat!" Lord Basil moaned. "Not at this hour."

The commander stared at him.

"What d'you mean?"

"That pun. Didn't you mean it?"

The commander rose to his feet. His expression was contemptuous as he stared down at Lord Basil.

"You're disposed to be facetious. All I can say is that if you were half the man Miss Vachell apparently believes you to be, you wouldn't be lounging in bed while she's being robbed of about a million pounds' worth of gold. I tell you that to get Saratini is your only hope. And if you don't hurry up you'll find Saratini has vanished, taking the treasure with him."

"I hope not," said Lord Basil.

"Hoping isn't much use. You go ahead and see if you can't beat him; play hell with his plans generally. Shoot him if you get the chance. Remember he tried to murder your best friend. And let me know how you get on. I'm always in the cottage if you want me."

He stumped out of the room. The noise of the scuffle and the feminine squeak were repeated. And again the words "privilege of an old sailor" floated to Lord Basil's ears.

"Why didn't I join the navy?" Lord Basil thought wistfully.

For half an hour after the commander had gone he remained supine, smoking cigarettes and staring at the ceiling.

Although no one would have guessed it from seeing his face, he was thinking hard. A new and astounding possibility had presented itself. But as yet it was merely the vaguest shadow of a suspicion—nothing definite on which he could act.

Lord Basil spoke his thoughts aloud.

"If it *were!* God, what stupendous nerve! But it's impossible. Lord, I wish Stan were fit enough to talk things over . . . It would be a shame to worry the poor old horse just now . . . Question is, though, should I say anything to Mo? . . . If by any chance I *am* right . . ."

He gave his head an impatient shake. The possibilities of what might happen if his vague suspicions were correct were so unpleasant as not to bear thinking about.

Suddenly he sprang out of bed, stripped and began his accustomed morning exercises. Revealed thus, his body was a surprise. He was slim and small-boned for his height, but as he bent this way and that muscles like coiled snakes rippled under the white skin.

The cold shower that succeeded the exercises brought decision. He would say nothing to Mona as yet. It was a thousand to one he was wrong. Better to wait and watch. No harm could come to Mona if he kept his eyes skinned.

Ten to eleven found him sauntering down Station Road in the direction of the Station Hotel. Sunshine and the approach of Easter had brought a horde of happy, hatless trippers to the North Wales resort. And through them drifted Lord Basil Curlew, tall and willowy in a light grey suit, looking, as Superintendent Fibkin put it to himself, like a tailor's dummy that had escaped from its window.

All the same, the super was not averse to being seen in the Bay in company of a tailor's dummy who would one day be a duke. In response to a cheery wave of his lordship's cane, he left the constable he had been speaking to and came alongside.

"Pip pip," said Lord Basil. "How's things, Fibby? Boots full of feet and all that, what?"

"I'm damned busy," said Fibkin, wondering to himself if the honour of being seen in his lordship's society was, after all, worth the penalty of having to endure his lordship's inane conversation.

"Still huntin' for the fellah who killed Miss Floss?"

"I am."

"You know what, Fibby," drawled Lord Basil, "you made the biggest bloomer of your career when you turned down my offer to help. I'd have led you straight to the murderer like a jolly old what-d'you-call-it—doggie that bays, I mean. The infallible instinct, Fibby. That's what I've got. I'm a loss to the Yard, I am."

"I'm sure of it," said Fibkin gravely.

"Thank you, Fibby. For those kindly words I'll stand you a beer. Perhaps two. Shall us to the Station Hotel?"

"I was going there in any case. I want to have a talk with the page-boy. He was in the lounge all morning yesterday. It's just possible he may have heard the murderer inviting her to meet him in the Black Dingle."

They walked down Station Road side by side, Lord Basil towering above the stocky, bowler-hatted super. Passing a furniture shop where rather exotic rugs, carpets and cushions were displayed in the window, Fibkin suddenly stopped and chuckled.

"Good Lord, I do believe they've sold it!"

"Sold what, sweet pippin?"

"That imitation tiger they were showing in the window. It was one of those stuffed velvet arrangements ladies put in their bedrooms when they want to be considered smart. Sort of mascot, you know. Actresses go in for them a lot. It's a modern craze."

"I shouldn't have thought it would have reached North Wales."

"It must have done," Fibkin chuckled. "Someone's bought that stuffed tiger all right. Probably some shop girl who wants to be like a talkie star."

Lord Basil lit a cigarette thoughtfully. Another explanation had occurred to his mind. Had Gravenant with his strange tiger-obsession been the purchaser?

Here was a chance to put that ridiculous suspicion of his to the test. If he could find out who had bought the tiger . . . He started towards the door, but a glimpse of the interior made him turn back. There was a sale on and the counters were six-deep with women. It was not a moment at which to begin harassing the attendants with questions. And in any case he couldn't do much questioning while Fibkin was present.

A few yards down the street they turned in through the revolving door of the Station Hotel and made their way to the lounge. Fibkin looked at the clock.

"Five past the hour and they haven't opened yet. That's unusual. Usually the error's the other way."

It was evident there had been some hitch in the running of the hotel. The manageress was talking to Miss Floss's successor. They were standing before the circular partition of the bar, trying to look through the opaque red glass.

"Where can he have gone?" said the manageress.

"He came in here with the keys," said the barmaid. "I saw him with my own eyes."

Lord Basil and the super seated themselves at one of the little glass-topped tables close to the bar. Fibkin rapped with a coin. The barmaid came up.

"I'm sorry, but we can't get the bar open. The page has disappeared and he's got the keys. But if you'll tell me what you want I'll fetch it from the other bar."

Lord Basil gave the order. Hebe returned bearing two silver tankards crowned with foam. She lingered by the table.

"Eddie'll get the push for this. He's supposed to go into the bar a quarter of an hour before I come on duty to put things straight."

"Perhaps he's inside helping himself," Fibkin said jocosely. "When he does come back I want to have a word with him alone. Funny that just the morning I wanted him he should be missing."

He stopped and his jaw fell open in amazement. For a moment he doubted his own sanity.

It was as if a monstrous black bat had alighted from no-where and perched itself on the top of the partition. Its pointed ears almost touched the ceiling. It was glaring down at them with eyes like blue flames.

Such were Fibkin's first shocking impressions of the Black Killer. Then, before he had fully grasped that the bat was a cowled man wearing a long black robe, the apparition came hurtling through the air straight at his throat.

CHAPTER XV

THE FIGHT WITH THE APE

LORD BASIL AND THE BARMAID both had their backs to the partition. To them the arrival of the Black Killer seemed as sudden and cataclysmic as if a mine had been exploded beneath their feet.

Table, chairs, men and tankards were sent flying. Without pausing for a second the Black Killer bounded across the lounge like a great cat and dived bodily through an open window.

Beneath the window was a narrow alley at the back of the hotel. Drawn up with its engine still running stood a long, low car newly painted red. The cowled man leapt in and slammed the door. To remove cowl and robes was the work of a second. There was a crash of gears, the whine of an accelerating engine and in a moment the red-painted car had shot up the alley and swung into the stream of traffic on the Abergele Road.

Lord Basil rose shakily to his feet. He was sick and giddy from a kick upon the back of his head.

Fibkin was still doubled up beneath the wreckage of the table. Then, groaning with pain and swearing at every movement, he dragged himself up.

"Did you see his face?" he jerked out.

"I saw nothing except his back as he jumped through the window. Much damaged?"

"Collar bone and a couple of ribs by the feel of it. He kicked me in his stride. I'll phone the Station, but I don't suppose it'll be much use. He'd a car just outside there. He's in Llandudno by now I should imagine. See to the girl, will you?"

The barmaid had fainted. Lord Basil lifted her on to a settee, then he turned his attention to the partition behind which the Black Killer had been crouching.

A spring and he had grasped the top. He pulled himself up, looked down, and saw what he had dreaded. The page was lying face-upwards on the floor. He had been strangled by the Black Killer within a few feet of where they were sitting.

People were running in the direction of the lounge. Lord Basil swung his long legs over the partition and dropped lightly to the floor. A bottle of Martell caught his eye. As he helped himself liberally he reflected that strangled pages inside a bar were even more conducive to good business than alive pages outside.

In a minute Fibkin joined him, also via the top of the partition. He alighted beside Lord Basil.

"Have you touched the body?"

"Light of my life, what do you take me for? Touched the body indeed! You ask that of the greatest student of detective fiction in England!"

"Then don't. I've phoned the Station. Wilks and the doctor are coming round. I want them to see the body just as it is."

"They won't be able to gather any more than I've done," Lord Basil declared. "Shall I reconstruct the crime for you, Fibby? At about five to eleven, when he knew Eddie was likely to be done in the bar, the murderer drove his car up the alley at the back and parked it just outside the window. Then he waited his chance to get in through the window and found, as he had expected, the lounge was empty, and Eddie inside the bar polishing glasses. He stalked him. I think we can picture him holding Eddie's throat with one hand while he closed and locked the door in the partition behind with the other. Having thus secured privacy, he—er—got on with the business. But he'd miscalculated his time or Eddie took longer to kill than he'd anticipated. Before he could get dear we came in. That was when he donned the cowl and black robes. He hadn't been wearing them, but he had them in his pocket. Look at this . . ."

"What is it?"

"A shred of very fine black oiled silk. I found it adhering to yonder hook. Watch."

Lord Basil elevated his arm and waved it so that the hook touched his sleeve.

"What are you doing now?" Fibkin growled.

"Giving a practical demonstration, sweet pippin. You see the tear happened when the murderer was slipping his robes over his head. As I've already explained, he had them in his pocket when he came into the lounge. Made of that thin material they would fold up into a very small space. Does your wife wear a nighty, Fibby? If she does, you'll be able to understand just how he ripped his sleeve."

"All that's plain enough," the superintendent growled. "But what was his motive? Have you looked in the till?"

"My dear Fibby! What a horrid suggestion to make!"

"My name's Fibkin!"

"Fibby to those who love you though. You must have been overworking, Fibby. Too much reading of addresses on dog collars and shadowing of tobacconists after nine has dulled your mind. Haven't you really twigged his motive? To silence Eddie, of course. Eddie was to him what the sword was to Damocles. Don't you see that Eddie, who spent the greater part of his day in this lounge, was very probably the recipient of Miss Floss's girlish confidences?"

Fibkin stared.

"You think it was the same chap did the murder in the Black Dingle?"

"Of course. The unknown boy-friend you haven't been able to trace. Eddie knew his name—or he was afraid Eddie knew it, which amounts to the same thing."

The superintendent made a gesture of disgust.

"Clever devil! Of all the audacious crimes I ever heard of! Murdered my principal witness under my nose! But where did he get those black robes from? They looked like a sort of fancy dress to me. Like a monk of the Spanish Inquisition might wear. It's a ghastly, filthy business . . ."

He bent over the page's body. There were evidences Eddie had fought hard for his life. He had been a strong youth of nineteen of athletic build.

Something had caught Lord Basil's eye. Three large dirt-encrusted coins that had evidently fallen from the page's pocket. While Fibkin's back was turned he picked them up. They were heavy and of the same size as the one Miss Floss had shown Stan.

"I think I'll leave you to it now, Fibby. From the fairy footsteps outside I deduce your pals from the Station have arrived, to say nothing of the entire hotel staff and half Minrhyn Bay. So pip pip, Fibby. Don't want a statement from me or anything, what?"

"I'll let you know about that later."

"Is that a promise or a threat? Well, pip pip again. I'll be gettin' along."

Lord Basil unlocked the door in the partition and passed out into the lounge. It was crowded. There was a rush to view the body, checked by two uniformed policemen.

Another and larger crowd had gathered outside the hotel. Lord Basil slipped out by a side-entrance and made his way to the alley where the Black Killer had parked his car. There were marks of tyre treads in the grit which conveyed absolutely nothing to Lord Basil, although he gazed at them solemnly for a long time through his monocle.

Disconsolately he wended his way to the Rectory. He found Mona happy over a belated breakfast. Lord Basil slid his hand under her rounded chin and kissed the top of her head.

"The Black Killer has begun his day well," he told her after salutations. "He's strangled the page in the Station Hotel."

He related what had happened. And though he spoke lightly enough Mona, who knew his moods, could see the cold, unforgiving anger hidden beneath the flippant exterior.

An anger all the more formidable for being so rigidly re-pressed.

"So that's that," he concluded. "It only goes to prove what we knew already—that the rumour of the *Cinco Llagas* gold has attracted to Minrhyn Bay the most callous, ferocious, cunning gang of rogues in Europe. They'd stick at nothing to get that treasure. If I could exterminate the whole brood of venomous wasps by pouring boiling water over them I'd do it with pleasure. Devils!"

It was a strange Lord Basil who had spoken. In place of the good-natured, vacuous-looking youth his friends called P.B.C., Mona saw a grim-faced man whose eyes were steely with hate. Then the mask again fell and he became his famil-iar self.

"Quite melodramatic, what? By the way, what d'you make of these? They'd dropped out of Eddie's pocket in the struggle."

During the walk to the Rectory he had scraped and pol-ished the coins. They shone dully on the white tablecloth.

"More of the *Cinco Llagas* treasure!" Mona cried.

"Yes. Eddie must have got them from the same source as Miss Floss got her coin. Eggington is right. Saratini hasn't got the treasure yet. Someone else got there first. The Count's letter was pure bluff. By the way, I haven't read you that yet. I got it this morning along with a cheque for ten thousand pounds which I took the liberty of burning."

He read the letter aloud. When he had finished he looked at Mona.

"What do you say, old thing? Genuine or a bluff?"

"A bluff," Mona said without hesitation.

"Then the three of us think the same way, and the fact of Eddie's having those coins seems to me to clinch the matter. So that's the position as it stands at present. A third person—none of us know who—has got the treasure. Saratini is de-voting his energies to tracking that person down. And—most mysterious and formidable of all—there's Gravenant who's playing a lone-handed game. He seems to be out for the treasure and also out for revenge on Saratini's gang. The commander has got a theory that Gravenant and Saratini are the same person, which doesn't seem to me to hold water. I got an extraordinary idea this morning, but—"

He hesitated. Mona looked at him inquiringly.

"No, I don't think I'll tell you what I thought. You'd consider my idea very ridiculous and far-fetched, and I don't want to cast suspicion on an innocent person unless I've some proof of what I say. But if what I suspect *is* right we're dealing with a man endowed with superhuman nerve and cunning. A devil compared to whom Saratini himself is as harmless as a guinea-pig . . . *Heavens!*"

He clapped his hands to his head and groaned.

"Whatever is the matter?"

"I've suddenly remembered something that had completely slipped my mind. Really, I am a piffling ass. I never showed you this, and it may turn out to be the most important thing in the whole show. This note. Someone left it here on the night you were kidnapped. I got it from Mrs. Galbraith."

He took the ill-spelt scrawl from his note-case and handed it across the table. Mona read it aloud.

"But who's it from?" she cried.

Lord Basil returned the note to his note-case.

"I shouldn't be at all surprised if the writer wasn't the person who has got the *Cinco Llagas* treasure," he said impressively. "The mysterious being from whom Miss Floss and Eddie got those coins. And, for another guess, I should say that it was he who won Minrhyn Castle its reputation for being haunted."

Lord Basil's next move was to Minrhyn Head. Mona had pleaded to accompany him, but for once Lord Basil had been adamant.

"Too risky," he told her. "It's quite on the cards that Saratini's letter was a trap. I'm going to take the chance, but I can't let you take it too. Stay here like a good kid while I do a bit of scouting round. I don't suppose I'll be more than two or three hours. Don't leave the Rectory in the meantime for anything or anyone. Promise."

Surprised at his earnestness Mona agreed reluctantly enough. She had no inkling of the dark suspicion that lay at the back of his mind when he exacted the promise.

Out of sight of the castle Lord Basil ran his car into a dip at the side of the road. To enter the castle and see if he could solve some of its mysteries was his intention. After concealing the car as much as possible in a thicket of furze bushes he advanced along the road on foot.

At the entrance gate he got a surprise. It had been closed and secured with a padlock and length of chain. Lying among the long grass just inside the gate was a man whom he recognized as one of the gangsters who had assisted to place him in Saratini's lethal chamber.

The fellow rose as he approached. He thrust his rat-like countenance against the bars and spoke out of the corner of his mouth.

"You clear off, you bloody dude. If you come scroungin' round 'ere you'll get somethin' you don't like. D'you know wot this is?"

"It looks like an automatic," drawled Lord Basil. "Do you know how to use it?"

"Don't I just! You try to get in 'ere, Fido, an' I'll show you."

Lord Basil surveyed him through his monocle. His sneer was the last word in superciliousness and contempt.

"What a boastful, unpleasant little specimen of the lower orders you are," he drawled. "Uneducated, undersized and distinctly odoriferous. When did you have a bath last? Pah! I wonder you dare to speak to your betters, you verminous little worm!"

His lordship's manner would have made a dove see red. Snarling with rage the gangster thrust the automatic through the bars of the gate.

"Speak to me, you blank, rabbit-faced dude! I'll give you a bath, you scented—"

Lord Basil moved like a released spring. He had gone too far; the furious gangster meant to shoot. His dodge sideways would have done credit to a mongoose.

The bullet stung his cheek and drilled a hole in the brim of his hat. But he had the wrist holding the automatic. His other hand shot through the bars and closed on the gangster's throat.

For a second he held the fellow impotent with his feet dangling off the ground. But then he heard a shout and glimpsed two figures in the castle doorway. Evidently Saratini's men were holding the castle in some force.

With a heave Lord Basil sent the gangster sprawling a dozen yards in the grass. Holding a silk handkerchief to his cheek he ran with long, swift strides, keeping to the shelter of the wall. And as he ran he cursed aloud.

"Searching for the gold—that's what they're doing. Great minds think alike. Saratini has tumbled to the idea that the ghost has got it tucked away in some other hiding-place . . . What the deuce was that?"

It had been a dull boom coming apparently from inside the castle.

"He's blowing up the place piecemeal. He must be certain the treasure is still there."

There had been no pursuit. Satisfied on that point, Lord Basil eased up. He had reached the point where the wall encircling the castle grounds turned left and ran along the edge of the cliff.

A grassy ledge ten feet down promised both comfort and concealment. Lord Basil jumped down and stretched himself full length on the springy turf. He selected a Turk from his monogrammed case and lit it thoughtfully.

"Snookered! It was a bad mistake letting them see me at the gate. Looks as if I've got to hang about out here while Saratini methodically blows up the interior of the castle. He's a determined devil. If the gold is there he'll get it."

The thought of his enemy inside the castle and actively pursuing the hunt for the treasure was maddening. Another boom came to his ears. He could picture the gangsters heedlessly blowing up walls and floors in their frantic search to find the gold.

Lord Basil chucked away the stub of his cigarette and stood up. At another moment he might have rejoiced in the beauty of what he saw. Sea and sky rivalled each other in blueness, sea-gulls floated like scraps of torn paper around the cliffs and far below a gentle swell creamed over the rocks.

But his lordship had no eye for scenery just then. He had noticed a patch of rock breaking the evenness of a turf-covered slope a few hundred yards to the left of where he was standing. And although he was too close properly to discern the outline he knew that that patch of rock which disfigured the sheet of turf like some grey, scabrous growth, must be what the citizens of Minrhyn Bay proudly pointed out to unbelieving visitors as the Maiden's Head.

The Maiden's Nose had been the meeting-place appointed by the writer of the note. It was too late now to keep the appointment, but since it was impossible to enter the castle an investigation of the spot seemed the next best thing.

Lord Basil proceeded to make his way sideways along the face of the cliff. After one or two slips when only his strong fingers saved him from glissading down the turf to certain death, he reached the most prominent of the rocks.

The rocks that viewed from the Minrhyn Bay promenade formed the Maiden's profile, were surprisingly large seen at close quarters. The largest of all, the one that formed the tip of the Maiden's nose, attracted Lord Basil's attention. One corner was flat and shaped like a frog's mouth. Underneath was a sort of crevice blocked by a pile of loose stones.

Lord Basil levered out a few of the upper stones. There was a dark space beyond. He thrust his right arm and cane in to their fullest extent and could discern no obstacle.

"Jove, it looks as if it was the mouth of a cave! Now I wonder what that leads to?"

To go in was the only way of finding out. He grasped the overhanging lip of rock and wriggled feet first into the aperture. His feet encountered nothing on the other side. He lowered himself until he was hanging at the full extent of his arms with the back of his head pressed painfully against the uppermost of the pile of stones.

Releasing his hold and allowing himself to drop into that unknown darkness was, perhaps, the nastiest moment of Lord Basil's career. He had visions of himself lying at the bottom of some subterranean pit with a broken leg.

Eight feet down his fall terminated painfully on a slab of rock.

Muttering and cursing Lord Basil struck a match. His jaw dropped and he forgot his bruises.

"I'll be dashed if it isn't a tunnel! Leading straight into the bowels of Minrhyn Head by the look of it. Now where—?"

A chain rattled and something uttered a coughing snarl. Before Lord Basil had realized what was happening a hairy, long-limbed shape that smelt vilely sprang upon him out of the darkness. Huge fangs clashed within an inch of his face.

An ape! Thoughts raced through his mind. Saratini knew of the existence of this tunnel. The shaggy, red-eyed fury throttling him in the darkness had been chained at the cliff-end to act as sentry . . . Probably it had been placed there as a trap to catch Gravenant.

By some miracle his hands had locked on the unseen throat. But powerful as were those white slender fingers, he felt they couldn't retain their grasp for long. The ape was only five feet high, but it had the strength of three ordinary men. It had wound its long limbs about his body and was striving to bury its fangs in his throat.

Unless he could draw his automatic he would be torn to shreds like a rag doll. With a stupendous effort he forced back the brute's head. Savagely he crashed it against the side of the tunnel. His right hand snaked to his gun.

He had it. Pressing the barrel against the shaggy chest he pulled the trigger. The intolerable pressure relaxed. He flung the ape back and fired again. It uttered an uncannily human moan and fell dying.

Had the shots been heard? Lord Basil whirled about and stood waiting.

Tense minutes passed. Then the ape's fingers closing in their death-clutch upon his silk-clad ankle made him jump.

No one was coming. He struck a match and surveyed his late antagonist with a repugnance tinged with pity.

He bent over the squat, misshapen body. And then an expression came on his face Mona had never seen. Red, hair-tingling anger. Above all, he was a lover of animals.

Anything in the nature of cruelty to the dumb creatures roused in him a red-eyed devil of rage.

The wretched creature he had been compelled to kill owed its ferocity to shocking ill-treatment. Someone had tormented it. There were marks on its body as if it had been prodded by a sharp instrument.

And then he heard feet stumbling along the uneven floor. Quick as lightning he crouched behind the ape's body. A tall figure holding a torch had halted two feet beyond the radius of the ape's chain.

Mr. Cusper's intellectual voice spoke from the darkness.

"Do a dance, Joe. I want to see you jump about and gnash your teeth. Oh, you'd like to bite me, wouldn't you! . . . Wake up and dance, you silly brute . . . Wake up—"

He prodded at the shaggy form with the pointed stick he had brought for the purpose. . . . It was great sport to infuriate the ape . . . Most amusing to make him jump and scream and chatter in impotent wrath, knowing he was safely restrained by a thick chain.

"Wake up, you sulky brute . . . Dance . . ."

The chain rattled. Something leapt from the darkness, and then it seemed to Mr. Cusper as if earth, sea and sky had merged into one fist-slamming tornado. He was whirled from one side of the tunnel to the other, picked up and smashed to the ground. The pointed stick fell about him like a red-hot flail. Again he was jerked to his feet. A terrific upper-cut lifted him six inches into the air and sent him spinning unconscious into the arms of the dead ape.

CHAPTER XVI

CAPTURED BY THE LIZARD

"AND THAT IS JOLLY WELL THAT," quoth Lord Basil.

He dusted himself with care, replaced the monocle in his eye, picked up Mr. Cusper's torch and proceeded down the tunnel.

When it seemed as if he had walked about a mile into the bowels of Minrhyn Head, he saw a whitish sheet of cement about the size of a door on the left-hand side. Low down was the aperture through which Hocking had wriggled.

"I thought as much," said Lord Basil with satisfaction. "I'm in the tunnel Saratini mentioned in his letter. I got in at the wrong end."

In a moment he was inside the dungeon. He swung the torch round the original hiding-place of the *Cinco Llagas* gold. It was just as Saratini had left it. The three chests still lay coffin-wise at the bottom of the pit. And just as Hocking had done Lord Basil jumped down and opened them. He knew they would be empty, but he had to verify the fact with his own eyes.

Climbing out again, he sat down to consider the problem. Who had spirited the gold out of the chests? Who or what was the mysterious source by which the coins had reached, of all unlikely people in the world, Miss Floss and Eddie?

He remembered the theory he had propounded to Mona— that the writer of the ill-spelt note had got the treasure. But who was he? How had he secured the gold?

He took the note from his pocket and studied it. The handwriting suggested extreme old age and feebleness. The spelling suggested ignorance. But somehow he couldn't pic-

ture a feeble, ignorant old man using high explosives with
the skill the evidences of which lay before his eyes.

"No, it was either Saratini or Gravenant who blasted the
way into the dungeon," he decided. "That means that the
writer of this note had found another way of getting to the
gold. He didn't come through that sealed-up door—it was
intact until the gangsters blasted a hole through the cement—
and the top of the wall was also sealed up and intact. Therefore Mr. Ghost, as I'll call him, got to the chests at the bottom of the well by some other route. In other words, he got
into the well from underneath, not from above."

Again he sprang into the pit. Someone had left a crowbar
lying on the ground. Armed with this Lord Basil began to
test the side and bottom of the well.

The bottom had been covered inches deep by a layer of
cement dust and fragments of stone which had fallen there
when the lid that had closed the top had been blasted open.
Driving the crowbar through this he heard the sound of iron
striking solid rock. He moved the chests and tested the
ground on which they had rested. It, too, rang solid to his
blows.

He turned his attention to the sides of the pit. They were
formed of huge, roughly-cemented stones. One, a great slab
of slate measuring about three feet by four, rang hollow.

"*Eureka!*" breathed Lord Basil. "I believe I've solved the
mystery!"

Again he struck the slate. The upper edge tilted a few
inches outwards. He grasped it with his fingers and pulled. It
swung towards him, the slate pivoting on an invisible bar
driven through the centre.

He could now see what lay behind. A tunnel of roughly
the same dimensions as the slate. It seemed to slope upwards
in what he guessed must be the direction of the castle itself.
Beyond question that was how "Mr. Ghost" had come to the
Cinco Llagas gold, and also beyond question it was along
that diminutive tunnel he had carried it piecemeal from the
chests.

His intoxication was short-lived. The sobering thought that the gangsters were in the castle in force searching for the gold cut short his impromptu hornpipe of joy.

He stood still and listened. There was a sound of voices coming from outside the dungeon. Then he recognized Count Saratini's soft voice.

"I should like to have a final look—"

Quick as lightning Lord Basil pushed the slate back to its original position. There was only one possible hiding-place. He pulled up the lid of the nearest chest, slipped inside, and gently lowered the lid again.

Men were entering the dungeon. Again he heard that sinister, purring voice. It was now charged with amused contempt.

"My dear Hocking, the one essential qualification for a subaltern in the Royal Household Lancers is that he should have a complete vacuum in his head. Please observe that garment hanging yonder. Superlative cut and the latest style, isn't it? And look at the stub of that expensive Turkish cigarette. Still warm, I observe. Now it's your turn, Hocking. What do you notice?"

"A stink," said Hocking coarsely. "Like the pomade a scented, over-dressed dude of a titled puppy might use."

"Exactly, Hocking. I too observe an effluvium of puppy. Whatever can the cause be? Oblige me by putting a few bullets through those chests, will you? As they're quite empty nobody will get hurt."

The right-hand chest opened and Lord Basil appeared after the fashion of a jack-in-the box. And never had his lordship looked so utterly foolish as he did at that moment.

He made no attempt to rise. Sitting cross-legged in the chest he blew a kiss to Saratini.

"Pip pip, old sweetheart! How's things this bright day? Left the dolls at home, what?"

The gangsters stared down at him as they might have stared at an idiot. One fellow spat expertly on to his lordship's head.

"I was dreamin' about you, Lizzie, old duck," chattered Lord Basil. "Thought I saw you goin' round picking up cigarette-ends. Ridiculous dream, what?"

"Very," said Count Saratini. "I hope it will be a long time before I'm reduced to those straits. Haven't you had my letter saying that I've found the treasure?"

"Of course I have, old flick. Allow me to congratulate you. Oh, I was so happy to hear your news! I began to sing *'Green Hands I loved beside the Shalimar'*. Do you know that song, Lizzie?"

A gangster sniggered. Saratini gave him a venomous glance not missed by Lord Basil. Evidently the Count was sensitive about his hands.

"I'd like to see you buying gloves, Lizzie. D'you ask for flesh-coloured ones?"

The Count yawned.

"Your yapping bores me, Fido."

"You don't say? Then I'll just fade away. Auntie's expectin' me back to tea."

He made as if to rise from the chest, but Saratini waved him back.

"Why trouble to leave your coffin? We should only have the trouble of putting you back again."

"Meaning what, sweet pippin?"

"That my men are going to shoot you where you sit."

For a second the two men stared at one another. Then Lord Basil giggled like a coy schoolgirl.

"You are an old tease, Lizzie. Suppose I took you seriously? I should be quite frightened."

Again he made as if to get out of the chest. Saratini gave an order. Three automatics pointed downwards at his head.

Saratini leaned over the pit.

"You've got three minutes to live, Lord Basil. Three minutes in which to repent your incredible folly. It's your own fault. I warned you repeatedly not to interfere with my plans."

"Mother's boy likes his little joke, doesn't he?"

"This is no joke. One minute is up. You have now two minutes to live."

And Lord Basil knew by the expression on his face that he was in cold earnest.

He thought desperately. He was a brave man, but at that moment life seemed very sweet. Should he make a bid for life by telling Saratini of the tunnel he had just discovered?

No—he'd be damned if he would. Far better death than surrender to this sneering devil ... But, God, if only he could have got Saratini first! Had they been on the same level he would have hastened the end by a leap at his enemy's throat.

But to reach Saratini where he sat was impossible. He could only sit still and wait for those crashing bullets ... Sit still in his own coffin ...

Saratini's eyes were on the minute hand of his watch. He cared as little about killing Lord Basil as an ordinary man would of stamping on a black beetle.

There were ten seconds to go. He raised his eyes to see his lordship screwing something into his eye ... But it was not the familiar monocle. It was a coin that shone dull yellow in the light of the torches. Lord Basil was not looking at the automatics. He was juggling two other coins in the air and they also shone golden as they flew from hand to hand.

Saratini leant forward. He had forgotten to watch the seconds.

"What are those?"

"Elephants, sweet pippin. Can't you use your eyes?"

Hocking spoke hoarsely.

"The damned puppy's been fooling us. Those are gold coins. It's he who's had the treasure all the time."

The gold flashing through the air had fascinated the gangsters. Suddenly Saratini spoke.

"I understand, Lord Basil. You've found the *Cinco Llagas* treasure. Displaying those coins is a sign you are willing to exchange it for your life."

"Right for once, Lizzie. May I come up?"

The Count nodded. In a moment Lord Basil was beside him. He extended the three coins that had fallen from Eddie's pocket on the palm of his hand.

"There you are. Indubitable proof I know where the treasure is. But I warn you that if you kill me you'll never, never be able to find it. Not if you blew up the whole of Minrhyn Head and passed the fragments through a mincing-machine. Do you know why?"

Saratini raised his eyes from the coins.

"Why?"

"Because, my lamb," drawled Lord Basil with a swift glance round, "they don't make mincing-machines big enough."

And his fist went to the Count's jaw like a criss-cross of lightning.

For one apparently so languid, Lord Basil could on occasions move with a celerity positively amazing. The blow that sent Saratini headlong into the pit, the kick that sent the torch spinning from Hocking's hand, and the sweep of the left arm that sent the other two gangsters sprawling back were as nearly simultaneous as makes no matter.

Before acting he had noted the exact position of the hole that was the only exit from the dungeon. And now he dived for it. Slim and active as a weasel he left the dungeon like— as he would have said himself—a bat flitting out of hell.

That was where his luck failed him. By ill-chance the big German called Heinman had arrived at the other side of the wall at the precise moment Lord Basil emerged.

Heinman had just time to grasp the situation. For one of his ponderous, slow-witted type he acted with commendable promptitude. He had an iron excavating implement in his hand. Quick as thought he brought it down on the back of Lord Basil's sleek head.

The German bent over him. There was murder in his eyes as he raised the tool for another blow.

"So! The young swine-dog once again! Take this, Herr Fido . . ."

Had the blow fallen whatever brains Lord Basil possessed must have spattered on the floor of the tunnel. But a strong hand seized Heinman's arm. He turned with a growl to see Hocking.

"Let me the young swine-dog kill."

"Not much, Fritz. I don't give a blank for his precious life, but he knows where the treasure is. If you killed him before we get the secret out of him the Chief would skin you alive."

There was a pause during which they stared at the motionless figure. Then Saratini emerged through the hole. He looked white and shaken and his face was livid with rage.

Even Hocking was appalled by the malignity of his expression. The smiling urbane mask had been ripped away; his hands shook with anger. Going up to the unconscious man he kicked him violently.

"Treacherous puppy! But I'll pay you out for this. I'll make you wish you'd been shot like a rat at the bottom of the pit . . ."

Then with a great effort he regained his self-control. They saw him take the little phial of cocaine from his pocket, shake a few grains on to the back of his hand and sniff. When he spoke again his voice was steady although still charged with hate.

"Tell the men there's no need to continue with the blasting. Providence has sent us a much simpler method of reaching the *Cinco Llagas* treasure. Lord Basil Curlew will conduct us to it himself."

A glance of sinister understanding passed between Heinman and himself. The big gangster licked his lips.

"Going to make him squeak, Chief?"

"Yes, and many times," smiled Saratini. "He's going to squeak until he's squeaked his way into a padded cell. But long before he goes mad he will show us the hiding-place of the treasure."

CHAPTER XVII

WHICH DEALS WITH TORTURE
AND A MARCH HARE

BEING A MODERN HOUSE, built by an architect who had not foreseen the possibility that it might one day be utilized as the headquarters of the most fiendish gang of crooks in Europe, Sperm was not provided with a torture-chamber. The bedroom in which Lord Basil was placed was quite ordinary. Had the blind not been drawn the window would have commanded a magnificent view of the mouth of the Conway, the Great Orme and Puffin Island.

Heinman had been appointed as his guardian until such time as he should recover consciousness. The big German sat crouched on a chair beside his bed, his eyes fixed on Lord Basil's face. He thought to himself what a weak, effeminate-looking dandy Lord Basil was, and he chuckled to think of the alteration Saratini's treatment would effect in the young man's appearance.

"How will you look when you are mad, young swine-dog? You for the robots a good match will be. No teeth, no tongue and only half a nose. I don't think the little English girl you any longer will love . . ."

He had spoken aloud. Lord Basil's eyes opened. "Mornin', Rose. Got my tea?"

Heinman chuckled. Secure in the knowledge that Lord Basil's hands were bound, he seized his nose and shook it roughly.

"Wake up, Herr Fido. You in your own kennel are no longer. We have brought you to Sperm."

Lord Basil raised his head and stared at him. His face was blankness personified.

"Do you mind repeating that?"

"You're in Sperm, Herr Fido."

"My name is Curlew, Lord Basil of that ilk. And what may Sperm be? A home for imbeciles? Also, do you mind explaining why my hands are tied, and why I've got this filthy headache?"

"You know as well as I do."

"My good fellah, do you mind being more explicit? I vaguely remember Nero picking at a fence and pitching me on my head in a ploughed field, but that's all. Was I knocked out? Is this a hospital or something?"

"It is a hospital for impudent puppies, Herr Fido. We the good manners to you will shortly teach. Like this, Herr Fido."

He leant over the bed and struck Lord Basil on the mouth. His lordship cursed him with amazing fluency.

"You filthy swine! If you imagine I'm to be treated like this, you're wrong. Are you mad?"

"No, but *you* will be very shortly," Heinman grunted. "I am not deceived. That your memory is lost you to pretend are trying. We shall see."

He rang a bell. After an interval of five minutes, Count Saratini entered the room.

Two pallid-faced, undersized men accompanied him. Saratini's love of the *macabre* had displayed itself in the costumes worn by these minions. They were attired after the grim fashion of medieval torturers, with leather aprons and tightly-fitting black caps. In their hands they carried hideously suggestive implements. Pincers, coils of wire and a long canvas sack.

The Count had no mean knowledge of psychology. He knew that the most terrifying part of an operation is watching the preparations. Slowly and in full view of the helpless man on the bed those grim assistants made their arrangements.

In the commonplace setting of that pleasantly-furnished English bedroom with the afternoon sun filtering through the chinks in the blind, the scene was as fantastic as it was horrible. With much hammering and puffing of bellows the assistants had lighted a little iron stove for burning charcoal. They knelt on each side, heating lengths of wire. The acrid smell of hot steel mingled with the fumes from the charcoal.

A master of the *macabre,* Saratini had spoken no word. Attired in a long dressing-gown, he stood, a strange, sinister figure, at the foot of the bed with his arms folded. His lizard's eyes were watching his victim's face for any sign of fear.

He was not disappointed. The expression of amazement with which his lordship had greeted the appearance of the torturers changed to one of almost ludicrous consternation and terror as he realized the import of what they were doing.

"What the devil are those fellahs up to? What are they heating that wire for?"

Saratini spoke slowly.

"We are going to question you, Lord Basil?"

"Question me? What about?"

"We wish to know the hiding-place of the *Cinco Llagas* gold."

Lord Basil shut his eyes. His head moved wearily from side to side.

"Either I'm completely potty or you are. All I know is I got a spill out huntin' and woke up to find myself on this bed. Is this a lunatic asylum? Heavens, I believe it is. It's a lunatic asylum and you've overpowered the keepers."

"You can't deceive me. Where is the *Cinco Llagas* treasure?"

"In the moon," Lord Basil said cunningly. "Untie my hands and I'll take you to it."

"Don't trouble to keep up that pretence. I can see you're acting. Tell me where the gold is, or we'll—"

Slowly and lingeringly, as if he loved the sickening recital, Saratini described what the torturers would do. Lord Basil's eyes filled with terror. He writhed on the bed and fought vainly with his bonds.

"Mad as hatters, the whole pack. Bally lunatics. Lord, this is awful . . . I tell you it's in the moon . . . No, it's hidden in the garden outside . . . I'll take you there now . . . And I'll give you a million pounds into the bargain. . . . A million pounds for each man here . . ."

"Your last chance. Will you tell us?"

Lord Basil's only reply was a groan. Saratini made a sign to the torturers. Holding glowing lengths of wire, they approached the bed.

"Help——Help—The lunatics—"

Heinman's great hand closed on his mouth, stopping his cries. Saratini made a sign. The two gangsters dressed as torturers, bent down over the bed and began to unlace his shoes . . .

Despite the doctor's protestations, Stan had insisted on leaving the hospital that morning. Feeling sick and shaky and decorated as to the head with a white bandage, he made his way to Rose Bower, only to be told that Lord Basil had gone out and had not returned.

Stan drove thence to the Station Hotel. He was surprised to sec a large crowd of loiterers outside. Two constables were vainly urging the people to move on and not to impede the traffic.

A heavy hand fell on his shoulder. Turning his head he saw the jovial, bearded face of Commander Eggington.

"Well, well, well!" boomed the commander. "Up and about again already! D'you know we gave you up for dead last night? Thought the Black Killer had done you in for sure. Did you see who he was?"

His bright blue eyes were fixed on Stan's. The American shook his head.

"I can remember nothing. When I try it gives me a pain between the eyes. But I certainly do wish I could remember. I've a sort of feeling I got a big surprise . . . It's as if there was something deep down inside me trying to give a warning, but I can't get just what it is . . . The doc says if I don't worry and don't try to think my memory may come back quite suddenly. On the other hand, I may never remember till my dying day what happened at that farmhouse. Concussion's a queer thing."

The commander made no comment. Stan's eyes passed him to the crowd outside the hotel.

"What are all those folk rubber-neckin'? Been a fire?"

"A murder. The Black Killer again. He got Eddie, the page, who used to be in the lounge with Miss Floss."

"You don't say!"

"It's perfectly true. I've been talking to that policeman. Apparently he got into the lounge just before eleven via the window. As it happened, Lord Basil and the superintendent had gone in to have a drink. The Black Killer knocked them both out and got away . . . For sheer nerve and audacity I should say that murder requires some beating."

"I should say so," Stan agreed fervently. "Where is Lord Basil now?"

"Very probably at the Rectory with Miss Vachell. Shall we go and see?"

Without waiting for Stan's consent the commander stepped into the car. The American let in the clutch. He was feeling dull and dazed, very different from his usual alert self.

Another effect he ascribed to his head injury was the sense of impending danger that hung over his mind like a dark cloud. He'd a dim feeling that he was being shadowed, watched. Some unknown peril stalked beside him, but as to what it was he could make no guess.

If only he could remember! His subconscious mind held the key to the mystery. Buried there—all but erased by the effects of the blow—was the knowledge of what had happened at the farmhouse.

But the effort of thinking was almost agony. Dully, almost like a man in a dream, he steered his car in the direction of the Rectory. He was conscious that the commander was watching him closely. His huge right arm was extended along the back of the driving-seat.

"I suggest we visit the castle this afternoon," Eggington said suddenly. "You and I and Miss Vachell. And Lord Basil—if we can get hold of him. By the way, you haven't heard about Saratini's latest move? He sent a letter to Lord Basil this morning—"

They reached the Rectory gate just as his recital was ending. As Stan swung the car to take the turn he felt the commander's hand close painfully on his arm.

"Look! Ahead of us—"

Preceding them up the drive was a weird figure. A small bearded man wearing an indescribably ragged trenchcoat that reached almost to his ankles. He walked very slowly, bent almost double. One hand was clutched to his chest.

Stan caught Eggington's exclamation.

"The March Hare, by thunder! Now we'll hear something."

Mona had been sitting on the porch. She rose and stared at the figure tottering up the steps.

The March Hare raised his apology for a cap. When he spoke his voice was that of an educated man:

"Miss Vachell?"

"Yes, that's my name."

"I've come to tell you something of the utmost importance. I sent you a note, but you never came But you must be quick . . . I—I believe I'm dying . . ."

He was swaying on his feet. Commander Eggington was beside him in an instant. His hand fell roughly on his shoulder.

"You old scoundrel! So you're the fellow pinched that gold? Where have you put it?"

The March Hare's bleared eyes turned to Mona.

"Who is this man? Your friend?"

"Yes, he's my friend. You needn't be afraid of speaking before these two men. But you're terribly ill. Shouldn't a doctor—"

The old beggar laughed.

"I'm passed the aid of doctors, Miss Vachell. Aneurism of the heart—that's what they told me at the hospital. It was when I knew I was dying I decided to tell you about the treasure. I don't want those others to get it. They're devils incarnate. Especially the man they call Gravenant. He's a monstrosity spewed out of hell . . ."

Between them, Mona and Eggington had placed him in a chair. One was on each side, bending over to catch the faltering words. Stan leant against a pillar opposite the group.

His head was throbbing so that he could barely focus his eyes. Alone of the trio he had been unmoved by this latest event. All he felt was an intensification of the sense of impending horror that had haunted him ever since his return to consciousness.

Pressing his hand to his chest as if to imprison something striving to burst out, the March Hare began to speak.

"I must be quick. My name's Atler; I was a schoolmaster in Bristol before I went to the bad. Then I got into trouble. Money, of course. The details don't matter. It's enough to say I first came to Minrhyn Bay ten years ago as a fugitive. The police wanted me on a charge of shoplifting.

"That's why I went to Minrhyn Castle. An ideal hiding-place for a man in my position. I lived up on the Head like a wild beast for over a year. The slate quarries were working then. I begged food from the quarry-men. Then I became bolder and went down to the Bay and begged along the front. I pretended to be an illiterate old tramp a little wrong in the head. It worked well. No one connected me with Atler, the schoolmaster, who was wanted by the police.

"I amused myself by exploring the castle. It's an amazing old place, riddled with secret passages and hidden rooms. Underneath the rock is honeycombed with tunnels and dungeons. I don't suppose that even I have learned all its secrets. But I know most of them. You see, I'd ten years in which to explore the place.

"That was how I found the Spanish gold. Of course, I'd heard of the legend of the *Cinco Llagas,* but I hadn't believed it. Then one day I found a trapdoor in one of the cellars. There was a small tunnel beneath just big enough for a man to crawl along. I followed it until I came against a big flat stone pivoting on an iron bar. I pushed the stone up and found I was at the bottom of what looked like a well or pit. It was covered over, and at the bottom were three big chests lying side by side."

Eggington gave a hoarse exclamation.

"So that's how you got into the pit! Underneath the lid. That's why Saratini found the chests empty when he blew the pit open!"

The March Hare shook his head.

"Saratini didn't come first. It was the big man with the white moustache, the man called Gravenant. He knew the secret of the mantelpiece in the old library. He got down to the tunnel that leads to the Maiden's Nose and he blew a way into the dungeon above the pit with explosives. I knew he must have known the hiding-place, for he went straight to the spot. In one night he got to the chests, but it was only to find them empty. I was there, listening and watching, although he didn't know. How he cursed when he found the gold gone! He behaved more like a mad tiger than a man."

The March Hare laughed harshly and wiped his lips.

"After that things got quite interesting in the castle. Other men came. Saratini and the man like a Jew, called Sylvester. Pretty soon I was able to piece together what was happening. They were after the treasure too. I tried to scare them away by doing my ghost-trick. But these men weren't like the trippers. They were mad for the gold. And I was frightened myself. I knew if they caught me they'd kill me like a rat. But it was fairly simple to keep hidden. You see, I knew the secrets of the castle and they didn't. *Ah!*"

His eyes closed and he fell back. Eggington bent over him. Perspiration was pouring down his face.

"God, I believe he's going . . . Brandy . . . Get brandy, Miss Vachell."

Mona flew. In less than a minute she had returned with a glass. Eggington forced a few drops between the shrivelled lips.

"The treasure," he cried hoarsely. "What have you done with the gold?"

The March Hare opened his eyes and muttered. Twice the commander had to repeat the question before he could get a coherent answer.

"The gold? Oh, yes, I took the gold. Carried it bit by bit along that tunnel and hid it under the floor of the cellar. God knows why. I never tried to sell it; I loved the feel of it too much. I used to gloat over it like a miser. I suppose I was a bit queer in my head. It seemed a great joke to sit begging on the front, knowing all the time I was the possessor of millions of pounds worth of gold. For years I did that—Begging for crusts during the day and wallowing in the gold at night . . . Yes, I wallowed—literally . . . Used to take my clothes off and roll among the coins . . . My gold! . . . My beautiful red gold! . . .

His eyes glittered and he made clawing motions with his hands. Suddenly his voice became shrill and he began to wave his arms.

"God, what a fool I was. To let myself be bewitched by that filthy metal! We're all fools . . . Saratini, Gravenant, you yourselves, all fools. That gold won't make you happy. Look at me . . . It sent me mad. If I hadn't found that treasure I might have been a happy healthy man . . . That filthy gold . . . Not worth one buttercup; not worth one breath of fresh air . . . Yet men waded through blood to get it. They became devils, wild beasts . . . Gold—she's a red witch who turns men and women into beasts . . . Learn the truth from me . . . Fight the red witch . . . Fight her or she'll poison your brain and soul . . .

"Yes, I've learned my lesson. When I became ill and knew I was going to die, my love for the red witch turned to hatred and loathing. I wanted not to live but to stop the pain. That's why I sold those coins, to get money to buy drugs that would ease the agony in my chest. . . . A girl bought a coin . . . Then a young man bought three . . . I felt I was selling them deadly poison . . . But the pain! I—I had to get relief . . . There was a chemist who sold me things . . . He told me I was doomed.

"I felt I couldn't die until I told you the truth, Miss Va-chell. I knew that you were too seeking for the gold. I sent you that note, hoping you would come." He made a harsh sound like a laugh. "I hope you didn't mind the spelling? I wrote it like that on purpose. . . . I didn't want people to know—"

Suddenly his face was contorted by a frightful spasm of pain. He doubled forward, grasping his chest and groaning aloud. Then he raised his eyes to Mona's white face.

"I came here for your sake," he whispered. "I want *you* to have the gold."

CHAPTER XVIII

THE HUMAN TIGER DISCLOSES HIMSELF

STAN BENT OVER ATLER. Opening the ragged shirt, he slipped his hand inside.

"He's not dead, but he's mighty near it. Come on, commander, we'll carry him into the house and phone for an ambulance from the hospital. Will that be all right, Miss Vachell?"

Mona nodded. The tragedy of the March Hare's life as he had unfolded it had affected her so much she could hardly speak.

In twenty minutes the ambulance arrived. The doctor who had accompanied it gave his opinion to Stan.

"He may live another three hours—certainly not more. No, he'll never recover consciousness. Came here begging and collapsed on the porch, you say? It was a walk up the hill killed him. He'd an advanced aneurism of the heart. Has he any friends, do you know?"

"I don't. Er—I'll see to the expenses of the funeral. His name was Atler. Used to be a schoolmaster in Bristol."

After the stretcher had been carried out Stan joined the others. The commander turning a beaming face as he entered.

"Come and congratulate our little heiress. Yes, I consider she's as good as got that gold. It was a wonderful bit of luck the March Hare coming here. If Saratini had got hold of him first we'd have been done."

"That's so," the American nodded. "But if Saratini's crowd are in the castle things are going to be a bit awkward.

We've got to get rid of them before we can handle that treasure."

"I don't know that I do hope to handle it so very much now," Mona said shakily. "That poor man's story has rather put me off the gold. It almost looks as if there were a curse on it."

Stan patted her shoulder with a fatherly hand.

"You'll feel different when you see it, kid. Atler was crazy, anyway. You and Lord Basil are a different proposition. You won't let the treasure affect you the way it did the March Hare."

"I'll try not," Mona smiled. "But in any case, we haven't got it yet. What are our plans? I suggest we wait until Basil comes back."

"Where is his lordship?" Stan asked.

"He told me he was going up to Minrhyn Head to do a bit of scouting 'round. He said he didn't think he'd be more than two or three hours, and he made me promise not to leave here for anyone or anything until he got back."

Stan looked thoughtful.

"Now, just why did he make you promise that, I wonder?"

"I don't know. I think he had some idea at the back of his mind, but he wouldn't tell me what it was. He said something about not wanting to cast suspicion upon an innocent person until he'd some proof. And he also said that I'd consider his idea very ridiculous and far-fetched."

"As it very probably is," Commander Eggington laughed. "If you'll allow me to say so, Miss Vachell, that young man does not impress me as a very profound thinker."

"Which is where you make a mistake, Commander," Stan said. "It amuses Lord Basil to let folk think him soft, but he somehow gets there all right."

Mona shot him a grateful glance. Commander Eggington laughed good-humouredly.

"Well, we won't quarrel about his lordship's capabilities. The immediate question is what are we going to do? I suggest that you and I, Hastings, go at once to Minrhyn Head. Probably we'll find Lord Basil himself. Miss Vachell, will you come with us or not? I think that what we've just heard is sufficient excuse for your breaking that promise."

"No, I think I'll wait here to see if he comes. I'll give him till five this evening. If he hasn't come by then I'll know that something must be wrong and I'll come and tell you. Where will I find you? In the cottage?"

"Yes, in the cottage," Eggington said. "Bring him with you if we miss him and he turns up here. *Au revoir,* till then . . ."

He raised her hand to his bearded lips in mock-gallant salute. She watched the two men pass out to the car. The commander had his hand on the American's shoulder and was talking loudly in his usual jovial fashion.

Stan was feeling more like himself. Apparently the effects of the Black Killer's blow were wearing off, for his head no longer ached and the sense of depression had left him.

As the car swooped upwards from the Bay past the disused slate quarries, he began to share Eggington's optimism. Now that they knew where the treasure was they held a tremendous advantage over both Saratini and Gravenant. At the worst they could wait until the gangsters had gone away in despair and then secure the gold.

They left the car on the road and walked over the heather to the cottage. Commander Eggington flung open the door and stood inside.

"After you, old chap."

Stan preceded him into the tiny kitchen. An addition to the scanty furniture had been made since the night Mona and Lord Basil had sat there. It was a stuffed velvet tiger that had been placed in a prominent position on the table.

Stan stopped dead. It was as if that stuffed tiger had flung a sudden light upon the dark patch in his memory. He knew now whose hand had struck him the frightful blow.

Commander Eggington, *alias* Gravenant. The man they had thought their friend was the Black Killer.

He had stumbled on the truth at the farmhouse. There had been a footprint in the mould under the window through which the Black Killer had shot Crane and Morgan. He had recognized it as Eggington's.

But the commander had been close behind when he had made the discovery. He remembered now snatching at his automatic. But he had been too late. Before he could draw the gun he had felt the shock of the blow.

His thoughts had occupied an infinitesimal space of time. To an onlooker it would have seemed that his first glance at the stuffed tiger and his grab for his gun were simultaneous.

"You're covered!"

Gravenant's snarl made him whirl about. Very slowly his hands rose above his head'

Gravenant was standing with his back to the closed door. He had a heavy army revolver trained on the American. And the blue eyes under the shaggy brows were as merciless as any tiger's.

"Chuck your gun on the floor. No tricks, or by God I'll spatter your brains out."

Stan's automatic clattered on the tiles, Gravenant kicked it across the room. All his movements gave an impression of almost superhuman strength and ferocity.

Suddenly he grasped the blonde beard and removed it with a jerk. His wig followed. He pushed his forefinger inside his mouth and extracted the rubber gums that had altered the shape of his cheeks.

Stan gasped. The transformation had been so complete as to be almost uncanny. In place of the bluff, jovial-looking naval officer he saw a bald-headed, clean-shaven man. There was something feline in the contours of his skull and the set of his pointed ears, which had been completely hidden by the false beard and wig.

The human tiger! The American understood now how he had come by his nickname. There was something revoltingly animal-like in his expression. It was cunning and ferocious. The great white teeth and obtruding jaws hinted at limitless brutality, while the blue eyes, now unnaturally bright with excitement and triumph, spoke of an unbalanced mind.

But Gravenant was not a madman. Despite his strange tiger-obsession, he was as well able to control his actions as Stan himself.

"So it seems I've won the game after all," he said gratingly. "Fooled you nicely, didn't I? I couldn't have done much against Saratini single-handed. It was a bright idea—joining your party. If I hadn't been a friend of Miss Vachell's I'd never have learned what Atler did with the gold."

Stan was again master of himself. His brain was working furiously, plotting how he should outwit this criminal.

Outwit him he must. The thought of Mona falling into his power was too frightful to contemplate. Gravenant looked as brutal and lascivious as a great ape.

"You were certainly smart," the American drawled. "I tumbled to your game last night, but you were too quick with the butt of your revolver. I suppose you thought I was safe to die in the hospital, didn't you? Otherwise you'd have finished me then and there."

"Yes, and Lord Basil too," Gravenant grinned. "But I took a chance on your not recovering because I wanted to play him against Saratini. The young fool! But he was very useful to me. I feel grateful to Lord Basil. Sit down!"

Stan obeyed the menacing wave of the revolver. If he let Gravenant talk perhaps a chance would come.

"I guess you made fools of us all," he said.

"I did," Gravenant grinned. "I wasn't going to be bossed by Saratini. When I broke with the gang, he and Crane sold me to the French police, but I got away from the damned madhouse they'd put me in. I tell you I'd have broken out of hell itself to get back at Saratini. I haven't got him yet, but I will. I tell you as sure as the sun is shining outside I'll get the Lizard and tear him to pieces. I'll teach him to laugh! Damned mountebank with his robots! But he's as clever as the devil. I couldn't have fooled *him* as easily as I did your lot."

Nothing could have exceeded the ferocity with which Gravenant had uttered Saratini's name.

"But he's clever," he said again with a jerk of his head. "If it had been Crane or Morgan or any of the others I'd have gone for them straight away, but not Saratini. I thought it better to send Lord Basil. I hoped Saratini would kill him and get landed in trouble with the police. Poor young boob! He never twigged I was using him as a tool all along."

Stan's eyes flickered. He had remembered the promise Lord Basil had extracted from Mona. Was it possible that a vague suspicion of Commander Eggington had been the reason?

Evidently the thought had not occurred to Gravenant. He was laughing contemptuously.

"Poor addle-pated dupe! With his 'pip pip, old thing,' and his 'sweet pippin' and all the rest of it! Lord, how I used to chuckle to myself! A specimen like that trying to fight Saratini! Dip a clothes-peg in a bottle of scent and you've got Lord Basil Curlew . . .

"Listen, and I'll tell you how I worked it all. I escaped from that madhouse and I got to Minrhyn Bay before Saratini. I was disguised as Commander Eggington. It was a pretty good disguise although I say it myself.

"I lost no time heading for the gold. I got through the fake fireplace in the old library, blew my way into the dungeon and opened the pit, only to find the gold gone. God, how I cursed! I thought then that there'd been some dirty work when the chests were hidden, for the dungeon and the top of the wall had been both intact before I blew them open. Somehow it never occurred to me there could be another way into the pit.

"But if I'd lost the gold I wasn't going to lose my revenge. I mined the fireplace in the old library, hoping to catch Saratini. He'd arrived in Sir Jasper's yacht, but he was taking his time about beginning the search. Then Constandos came. First I knew of that was when I saw him and Lord Basil and Miss Vachell wandering about the castle.

"That was when I got my idea of joining their party to make things more awkward for Saratini. I watched them go down into the cellars, then I shut the door and raved at them—just the way I had raved at the French doctors to make them think me mad. When I opened the door and rescued them it was as Commander Eggington. I'd cut my own wrist to pretend Gravenant had tried to shoot me. They lapped it all up like buttermilk. And I'd a bit of luck that night. They saw Atler moving about the castle with a light and thought he must be Gravenant.

"That night Saratini played his first card. He had Miss Vachell kidnapped to that farmhouse. But I'd been spying round and had learned that some of the gang had moved to the farmhouse. It was too good a chance to lose. I went after them and I got the three, Crane, Morgan and the woman called Jones. Miss Vachell was too quick for me; she saw me on the drive and got away. But I wasn't troubling about her much. It was Saratini's gang I wanted. Especially Crane.

"To puzzle Saratini a bit more and also to keep the police off the track I'd had this made. I can put it on and take it off in a second. Look . . ."

Without lowering the revolver for an instant, Gravenant pulled a bundle of thin black material out of one of the large pockets of his jacket. He shook it out and dangled it before Stan.

"Cowl and robe all in one piece. That's how the person you called the Black Killer came into being. It was useful this morning when I was getting out of the lounge of that hotel. Lord Basil and that fool policeman never got a glimpse of my face.

"Where was I? Oh, yes. After I got Crane and Morgan I went back to my cottage on the Head. What d'you think I found when I got there? Dr. Constandos, lying in my bed as drunk as an owl.

"He'd got tight down at the hydro, and had come back intending to look for the treasure, I suppose. Well, I made short work of him. Know what I did? I carried him into the castle, tied him and put him in one of the chests at the bottom of the pit. A present for Saratini!" He laughed loudly.

"Next morning I met you in the lounge of the Station Hotel. You remember we had drinks with Lord Basil and that girl showed the coin. Hell, you could have knocked me down with a feather when I saw what it was. It was the first inkling I had that the *Cinco Llagas* gold was still somewhere about.

"Well, you know what happened after that. I got the girl to meet me up at the Black Dingle, and when I had her alone I asked her how she got the coin. She wouldn't tell me— damn her. I took her by the throat and choked the truth out of the little fool. She'd bought it from an old beggar called the March Hare. Where he lived or who he was she couldn't tell me . . . I finished her off then . . . Finished her off and hid the body in the wood . . ."

Hardened as he was to all aspects of human depravity, Stan could barely repress a shudder. Gravenant was grinning like a fiend. He looked a veritable human tiger, half-mad with a lust for killing.

"Oh, I was cunning! I fooled you, I fooled the police and I fooled Saratini. That night we went to the farmhouse and you recognized the footprint on the flower-bed. Only that you were wearing that damned slug-proof hat I'd have knocked your brains out. I hit hard enough! I was so dead sure you were dying, I didn't bother to finish you off. But there was another person I knew might be dangerous. Eddie, that page. If the police had got out of him that Miss Floss had been talking to Commander Eggington, they might have questioned me, which would have been awkward. So I took a big risk. Luckily, I knew from something Miss Floss had said that Eddie had to go into the bar before it opened at eleven to get things ready. I drove my car up the alley at the back of the hotel and got into the lounge through the window. You know what happened. I was behind that partition with the body when Lord Basil and the super came in. I transformed myself into the Black Killer, knocked them both silly and got away. I didn't drive far. Know what I did? Garaged the car, strolled back to the hotel and had a chat with the policeman about the murder! Then you came along . . . You damned, trusting blindworm!"

Stan regarded him steadily.

"And what now?"

"Damned if I know. The hand I hold is so full of good things I'm puzzled which card to play first. But one thing's certain. I'm going to wipe out your bunch. Now I know where the treasure is I don't need your assistance any longer. I can deal with Saratini myself. When that kid with the bobbed hair comes up here this evening—"

He passed his tongue over his lips and grinned evilly.

"Nice little bit, isn't she? Know what I'd like? To have you and Lord Basil tied up in here watching while I made love to her."

"You devil!"

The bestial face behind the revolver was wreathed in smiles.

"That's what I'll do. I feel I owe you something, you pack of smugfaced hypocrites. Yes, I'm a devil all right. Before I go back to hell I'm going to have a bit of fun. Do you know what I'll do with her. I'll—"

Stan laughed aloud.

"You won't, Gravenant. Lord Basil is behind you, you're covered."

Gravenant swung round with a snarl. On the instant Stan hurled himself bodily, chair and all, to the floor.

The revolver roared. He heard the bullet sing past his ear. Before Gravenant could fire a second time he had kicked the gun from his hand.

A cloud of white smoke filled the room. Dimly he glimpsed the huge figure bounding at him like a tiger. He crouched and then shot upwards straight into the air. Right, left, right. Three lightning kicks delivered in mid-air. They had landed full on Gravenant's face. He went reeling back against a dresser.

One hand caught at a shelf. Over came the dresser with a cascade of falling china. Again the lighter man leapt in. His swift bone-smashing blows hailed on the feline head.

Out again. Roaring with rage, Gravenant was plunging at him across the room. Once let those hands get their hold and he was done . . . Must knock him out . . . Kick him on the jaw . . .

Stan's bound would have done credit to a ballet-dancer. Up and round came his right foot, lashing at Gravenant's jaw with every ounce of weight and strength he possessed. Something cracked and he heard Gravenant scream like a maddened stallion.

He was still on his feet, staggering with out-flung arms. As Stan touched the ground, he flashed forward and in. His fists played a devil's tattoo on the huge man's face. One terrific kick aimed at Gravenant's face and he was again clear at the further side of the room.

By heck, he was winning this fight! He had the giant staggering and blind. But if they closed. . . . He knew Gravenant had the strength to tear him asunder with his hands . . .

Could he reach the door? He sprang towards it, stumbled and fell headlong. And then like a human avalanche, Gravenant was on him.

Gorilla-like hands compressing his throat and a knee boring into his chest until it seemed his ribs must snap. Through a mist of blood he saw the human tiger's face hovering above his. Bloodstained and frightful, it appeared to float grinning in the air. Blood that was not his own dripped about his cheeks.

"Got you!" Gravenant was mumbling through broken teeth. "Got you, got you, got you . . ."

His grip was tightening. The American felt unconsciousness rise about him like a dark sea. Then his outflung hand touched something hard. Automatically his fingers closed. They recognized the familiar feel of the butt of a revolver.

If he could raise it and fire! Desperately his brain signalled its message along the relaxing muscles. But he was weakening fast. His hands seemed unable to obey his will. He *must*. With one last tremendous effort of the will he raised the gun. His fingers fumbled round the trigger. The pull felt as if it weighed a ton. Curse those army revolvers! If it had been his own gun . . .

Gravenant had seen the revolver. He had lifted one hand from his victim's throat and was snatching for the gun.

Stan sent his last remnant of strength into his finger and heard a click as the striker struck harmlessly against an empty shell.

Five o'clock had come and gone and there had been no sign of Lord Basil. Mona stood by the drawing-room window in an agony of indecision, her anxious eyes watching the gate.

Half-past five and he had not appeared. Suddenly she felt she could bear the strain of waiting no longer. Something must have happened or he would have returned before this. She would go to the cottage on the Head and consult with Stan and the Commander.

Stan heard her car coming along the slate road. Sitting bound and gagged on a chair in a room adjoining the kitchen, he was unable to give her any warning.

Had it been possible he would have shot her dead rather than that she should enter that cottage. He wrestled madly against the rope. In vain. He had been bound and gagged while still unconscious by expert hands.

One faint hope remained. Was Lord Basil with her? Stan prayed that he was. He had a strange confidence in "Poor Blooming Curlew."

He stopped his vain wrestling to listen. She must be near the cottage now, coming over the heather. Suddenly he heard her call.

"Are you there, Commander? Basil hasn't turned up." Stan's heart stood still. He would have given all he possessed or ever hoped to possess to be able to utter a warning cry. It was mental agony such as even Saratini had never devised, to have to sit there impotent while she walked into the human tiger's lair.

Mona rapped at the door. No answer. She walked into the kitchen and stood staring at the damage caused by the fight. A low laugh from behind made her swing round. The human tiger was standing with his back to the door, laughing like a fiend incarnate.

CHAPTER XIX

IN WHICH BLOOD FLOWS AND GOLD GLITTERS

MONA STOOD AS IF TURNED TO STONE. For the first time in her life she knew the meaning of the word "fear". Not even when she had seen the Black Killer for the first time at the farmhouse had she felt as she did now. She was trapped. The huge man with the bald, egg-shaped head blocked the door and there was no window by which she could escape. Her eyes went to the beard and wig lying on a shelf and she knew the truth.

Gravenant took a step forward and spoke in the voice he had used when playing the role of Commander Eggington.

"So here you are, little lady! Welcome to my humble abode. May an old sailor have the privilege—?"

Before she knew what he intended, he seized her shoulders and kissed her on the mouth. When he did that his eyes glowed with desire.

"Pretty little bit, aren't you?" he said thickly. "Too pretty for that clothes-peg with the monocle. Shall I take you with me when I've got the gold? Take you to South America for our honeymoon?" He gave a loathsome chuckle.

It was as if she had been caressed by an animal. Sick with loathing she shrank away across the room. Gravenant followed, his arms outstretched.

"Come here, you little fool. You liked me when I was the commander."

"I didn't. I thought you an old ass. Now I think you're a—a—"

"What, darling?"

"A devil."

Gravenant laughed loudly. He had been drinking heavily during the interim between the fight with Stan and Mona's arrival.

"Devil, am I? Well, I've been too clever for the whole damned pack of you. Talk of running with the hare and hunting with the hounds! Saratini's the only one who's a match for me. But I'll get him, too. I don't care how much blood I have to wade in to get the gold. Five people have died so far. Don't shrink, little lady. I wouldn't harm you. Come here, ducky . . ."

He had seized her again and despite her struggles was pressing his lips to her face. He felt as repugnant to her as some ape with blood-matted paws. Suddenly she went limp.

Gravenant carried her into the room where Stan sat bound. The American watched in impotent rage while he tied her to a chair and gagged her.

Gravenant surveyed his handiwork.

"There you are. It only needs little Lord Basil to complete the picture. I expect he'll be coming before long if Saratini hasn't killed him. When he does come he'll find his old naval pal waiting to receive him. Well, now I'll say *au revoir* for a little, Mr. Hastings. Pleasant thoughts . . ."

From where he sat, Stan could see Mona's face. He watched her eyes open and saw terror dawn in them with returning consciousness. Then they rested on himself and he saw a look of swift relief.

"Glad to have a companion, anyway," the American thought. "It's mighty little I can do for her, though. Gravenant may be a bit crazed, but there's not much he doesn't know about tying people up."

He had tested his own bonds to the limit of his strength and had found them inescapable. They were tight, cruelly tight. Evidently the human tiger had intended to run no risks where he was concerned.

His eyes fell on Mona's wrists which had been secured to the arms of the chair. By the faint movements he could see she too was trying to free herself.

"Plucky kid," he thought. "She hasn't an earthly, though. She'll only hurt herself for nothing."

But the movements persisted. Stan watched fascinated. Her right hand appeared to have a good deal of latitude. It came to him that Gravenant had not considered it necessary to devote nearly as much care to the binding of Mona as he had to the binding of himself.

Backwards and forwards, this way and that, the sunburned little hand was wriggling. Again Stan met Mona's eyes. They were determined, the eyes of a game fighter who sees a chance of victory ahead.

As clearly as if she had spoken the words aloud he caught the message.

"Buck up! We'll do him yet."

Gravenant was standing outside the cottage. Once more he had disguised himself as Commander Eggington.

Saratini had not exaggerated when he had described him as being a marvellous actor. When he donned the beard and wig and the other appliances that so effectually altered his appearance, it was as if his whole personality also underwent a change. No one seeing the big, bluff-looking man in the homespun knickerbocker suit, who had apparently emerged from his cottage for the purpose of enjoying the last rays of the setting sun, would have dreamt he was a ferocious criminal of doubtful sanity.

From where he stood on a slight rise, Gravenant could see the whole plateau of Minrhyn Head. The only living creatures within sight were the sheep and seagulls.

He looked towards the castle. The thought of the gold lying there filled him with fierce impatience. There was no sign of either Lord Basil or any of Saratini's people. His prisoners could not escape. He decided to leave them where they were and go to the treasure.

Having barred the cottage door against intruders he set off at a trot across the heather. Suddenly he dropped like a stone and lay motionless. He had caught sight of the figure of a man standing in the shadow near the castle entrance.

For all his bulk the human tiger could move as silently and swiftly as a snake. He had recognized the stout figure in plus-fours. It was Sir Jasper Goldburg, Saratini's chief accomplice.

Only the rippling of the heather marked the human tiger's passage. Standing where he was, Sir Jasper could see down the straight drive to the expanse of moor beyond. A direct approach was impossible. Gravenant turned right-handed, making a detour that would bring him to the rear of the castle.

It was impatience and greed mingled that had induced Sir Jasper to visit the castle alone that evening. He was vain enough to believe that although Saratini had failed to find the treasure he might succeed. And being one of those people who believe they can only do themselves justice when they are unassisted, he had deliberately omitted to bring any companion.

A foolish decision. One half-hour in those echoing, bat-haunted rooms had effectually quenched his lust for treasure-seeking. He had over-rated his own nerve. Although he had brought a powerful flash-lamp, he had not even dared to venture down to the cellars.

And then horror had seized him. Horror of the darkness and those bright-eyed rats. Sweating like a frightened horse, he had dropped the torch and fled headlong out to where it was still light.

Cursing, he lighted a cigar with hands that shook. He had given his chauffeur instructions not to return till nine. He couldn't wait till then—not for a million pounds he couldn't. Those bats! The way they had brushed his face in the darkness like ghostly hands . . .

Nor did the plateau of Minrhyn Head look very inviting for the lonely walk down to the Bay. The sun was now low and there was a sea-fret hanging above the moor. From the left an ominous cloud was drifting slowly towards the Head. Already its advance guard, white tentacles of fine, stinging moisture, were coiling around the castle.

City-bred man as he was, Sir Jasper knew that before long the whole Head would be enveloped in a blanket of white mist. No pleasant thought either. With yawning cliffs on either side the place would be a veritable death-trap.

The thought spurred him to action. He rose from the step just outside the door where he had been sitting.

Instantly two hands fell on his shoulders. Gravenant had crept noiselessly upon him from behind. To Sir Jasper it felt as if the castle itself had seized him.

He turned with a bleating cry. It rose to a squeal of terror when he saw the cowled apparition towering above him.

Before approaching the human tiger had slipped on the black robe that was his insignia of murder. All Sir Jasper could see was the cowled head, looking with its pointed ears for all the world like the head of a great cat, and those flaming blue eyes glaring at him through the slits.

He thought of his automatic. But no sooner had he drawn it than it was torn from his hand and hurled contemptuously away. He was lifted in gorilla-like arms. More dead than alive, he felt himself being borne through those empty rooms where the owls fluttered and the bats squeaked.

Darkness and a vault-like smell of damp. He knew now whither he was being carried. Down to the dungeon where the *Cinco Llagas* treasure had once been hidden.

They were in the pit. He heard the clang of a great stone rolling over and he heard Gravenant's grunt of satisfaction. Again he was lifted and forced into what seemed to be a narrow tunnel.

For the first time Gravenant spoke. He had been ferociously enjoying his victim's terror.

"Crawl ahead of me, you little rat."

The discovery that his captor was human and not, as he had half-believed, the spectre belonging to the castle, gave Sir Jasper a grain of courage.

"Who are you?" he stuttered. "What does this outrage mean?"

Gravenant laughed harshly.

"Perhaps you've never heard your pal, Saratini, speak of the human tiger? Not a bad name either. I'll prove to some of those fools before I've done that I deserve it."

"You're—you're Gravenant. The man who escaped—?"

"The tiger who escaped," Gravenant snarled. "Yes, I've come back and up-to-date I've won every move in the game. Do you know where I'm taking you now? To the *Cinco Llagas* gold. You'll have the satisfaction of seeing it before you die."

It was a nightmarish crawl for Sir Jasper. Bent double, whimpering in almost imbecilic terror, he fled before the human tiger, like a rat being bolted by a ferret.

Thanks to his smaller build he made the better speed. Suddenly he came to where the tunnel led into what seemed to be a shaft built in the thickness of a wall.

He felt the surface of a door. Then Gravenant pushed him aside.

"This will be where Atler carried it. The hidden room under the cellars."

They were in the room. Gravenant had produced a flash-lamp. Its beam swept round the den where the March Hare had lived all those years like a wild animal.

There were still a few pathetic signs of his tenancy. A pile of rags in a corner, cooking utensils that looked as if they had been salvaged from the beach. A cracked plate on which there were mouldy fragments of food stood on a shelf beside a pile of tattered books.

But it was not at these things Gravenant looked. He had fallen on his knees and was passing the beam over the slabs of cement comprising the floor. One was obviously loose. Sir Jasper saw him prise it up and hurl it aside.

He thrust the torch into the cavity. And then Sir Jasper heard his almost insane yell of triumph.

"It's here! The *Cinco Llagas* gold! Look at it, you little rat . . . Raw red gold. . . . A million pounds' worth of solid gold . . ."

Curiosity overcame Sir Jasper's terror. His eyes bulged as he stared over Gravenant's shoulder into what seemed a veritable Aladdin's cave of riches. Atler must have spent many happy hours burnishing and polishing that gold. It shone red in the light of the torch, saving a few of the coins which were still coated with dirt.

Gravenant seemed bewitched. With hoarse cries of rapture he began to scoop out the gold. Ingots and bars and handfuls of gleaming coins showered on the floor.

The pile grew. He had pulled up his sleeves so that he could enjoy the rich sensuous feel of the metal against his skin. His gold! The gold he had waded through blood to win.

Beneath the cowl his face was like that of some triumphant demon. He was laughing in a frenzy of excitement.

"See that? It's an altar I've made—a golden altar, ready for the sacrifice. And the victims are ready. Two of them—trussed up and waiting in the cottage. I'll bring them here and sacrifice them to the tiger. The gold's on fire and the flames must be quenched with blood . . ."

With a thrill of horror, Sir Jasper realized that he was alone with a lunatic. The sight and feel of the gold had completely overthrown Gravenant's ill-balanced mind.

Once before in the castle he had pretended to be mad, but this was no pretence. It was as if at sight of the gold the devil that had always lurked at the back of his mind had broken down all restraint and taken complete possession of his senses.

The torch had fallen on the floor, but it was still alight. It showed Sir Jasper the monk-like figure kneeling before the altar of gold. His arms were outstretched to embrace it.

Suddenly he turned and Sir Jasper saw his eyes like blue lamps through the slits. With a scream he fled towards the door. But like a cat on a mouse the human tiger was after him. He dragged him, screaming, across the room and forced him backwards over the mound of gold.

From some recess in his clothing Gravenant had produced a knife with a curved blade. He brandished it in the air, then slashed downwards at Sir Jasper's throat. There was a frightful, gurgling scream. A river of smoking blood cascaded down the gold.

As if the fury that obsessed him had been momentarily sa-tiated, Gravenant became calmer. He wiped the knife and returned it to its hiding-place. Picking up the torch, he flashed it upon the mound of gold now crowned with a twitching corpse.

"That's another of them. Hell, how I wish it had been Saratini! Never mind. I've got two others trussed up and ready. Yes, I'll bring them here . . . Safer than the cottage . . . The girl can scream her heart out, but she won't be heard . . ."

To drag his captives along the narrow tunnel from the pit would be difficult. But there must be some other way into this room—the way by which Atler had first come. He glanced round. For the first time he noticed a rough ladder leaning against the wall.

In a second he was up the ladder and pressing at the trap-door above. It opened with a crash. After a long lingering glance at the gold he sprang through into the cellar above.

He knew the way now. Rats scampered away and owls fluttered as the cowled figure passed with swift tigerish strides. He was walking quickly, purposefully, muttering to himself that the tiger was hungry for sacrifice.

As he passed through the main door he stepped into a world of fine white moisture in which it was impossible to see more than a few yards ahead. The cloud Sir Jasper had noticed had closed round Minrhyn Head.

After a few moments Gravenant stopped, uncertain of his direction. Had he passed beyond the gate or not? He stood still, listening to the anxious foghorns hooting through the mist.

More than once Mona had been criticized for devoting too much time and energy to the playing of games, tennis in par-ticular. Serious-minded people had rebuked her for wasting the priceless hours of youth in the pursuit of an elusive ball, when she might have been doing something really useful—exactly what was not specified.

Stan Hastings could have told those serious-minded people a thing or two. Their one hope of salvation lay in her nerve, gameness and physical strength. And the fact that she possessed those three qualities in abundance was due to her devotion to the white queen of outdoor games.

For nearly an hour Stan had sat raising a mental hat in tribute to her pluck. Perhaps his was the worse ordeal. The suspense was nerve-wracking. Every second he expected the door to open and admit Gravenant.

One little brown hand was free. But her ankles and the other wrist were still secured. He watched her fingers plucking at the hard knots.

They defied her strength. Stan shut his eyes. Perspiration poured down his forehead.

Minutes passed, every second of which seemed to the American an eternity. His imagination began to play tricks. Gravenant had stolen into the room. He was standing behind Mona's chair, watching her efforts with a devilish smile.

So vivid was this mental picture that he had to open his eyes to assure himself of its reality. Gravenant was not there, but Mona had freed her other hand. She was bending forward to untie her ankles.

Another minute of frantic suspense and she was free. She had left the gag to the last. Her hands were fumbling with it as she darted into the other room in search of a knife.

She was back. Stan heard the steel sawing through the rope. The painful pressure on the wrists and ankles relaxed. He rose with a feeling of thankfulness too profound for words. His hand shot out and seized Mona's.

"Miss Vachell, if you're ever in need of a friend you can count on me," he said hoarsely. "That was a great piece of work. I was stiff with fear Gravenant would come back."

"So was I," Mona confessed. "I daren't let myself think or I'd have gone frantic."

Stan went into the other room. He picked up his automatic which still lay upon the floor.

"If Gravenant comes now he'll get what he deserves. I'm not taking any more risks with that lunatic. First chance I get

I'll pump lead into him till he rattles. He's as dangerous as a mad dog."

"And as cunning as a fox," Mona supplemented.

"You've said it. By cripes, he had us fooled properly. Those semi-lunatics are always the worst. The way he pulled that old sailor stuff on us! I could kick myself when I think about it."

"We must warn Basil. Wherever can he be?" Stan was silent. He had come to the conclusion that Lord Basil must have fallen into Saratini's hands. Mona glanced at his face.

"You—you don't think anything can have happened to him?"

"No," Stan lied. "I guess Lord Basil can look after himself all right. It's the mist that's delayed him."

He had opened the outer door and was gazing at the dense white fog that now shrouded the moor.

"What about staying where we are, Miss Vachell, until that lifts? You don't need to worry about Gravenant any more. If he turns up now I'll shoot him dead. We'd be safer in here than groping about out there."

"But I'm worried about Basil. And these mists sometimes stay on the Head for days. Oh, do let's try to find our way down. I want to get back to civilization."

Against his better judgment, Stan yielded. Despite her efforts at concealment, he could see she was terrified.

"All right, then. It certainly wouldn't be any picnic sitting here and waiting for Gravenant. We'll make for the road. Give me your hand. Mustn't get separated whatever happens."

Hand in hand they advanced into the whiteness. The mist was denser than Stan had expected. After walking for a minute he looked back and found the cottage had vanished from sight.

They passed on through the knee-deep heather, their clothes saturated with moisture. The mist was still rolling in from the sea, cloud upon cloud. The only sound was the mournful, incessant hooting of the Liverpool steamers.

Stan spoke.

"We should have struck the road before now. I've been counting. We've come pretty well half a mile."

"It's my fault. I was a fool to suggest leaving the cottage."

"If it hadn't been for you we would never have left it again—either of us. Are these mists a feature of this locality?"

"Yes. They're the great danger of the North Wales mountains. They come up so suddenly. Even the shepherds get lost."

Something blundered against her legs and she shrieked.

"A sheep," Stan said. "I don't know how you feel, Miss Vachell, but I'd give a thousand dollars right now to hit that road."

He knew now that they were walking in circles. Suddenly he stopped.

"Better stay where we are until it lifts. I've a notion we're near the cliff."

They stood still. And then from the swirling whiteness ahead came a crazy laugh.

Stan's automatic leapt into his hand. From what direction had the sound come? Owing to the mist it was impossible to see.

Again came that peal of insane laughter. Gravenant must be quite close. It came to Stan that he could see them while he himself was invisible.

The American was circling round, striving to locate the human brute he guessed was stalking them through the mist. His senses of seeing and hearing were deadened as if by layers of cotton wool.

Suddenly there was the muffled report of a service revolver. He yelled a warning to Mona.

"Lie down. For God's sake—"

He couldn't see if she had obeyed. She, too, had been swallowed up in the blinding whiteness.

And then a huge black shape showed itself for a second. *Crack, crack, crack.* Three splitting shots from an automatic instantly answered by the muffled roar of the heavier gun.

But Gravenant was coming on. He was now raving and screaming at the top of his voice, firing as he ran.

Something struck Stan with frightful force on the shoulder. He staggered wildly and then the world seemed to drop from beneath his feet. He clutched at empty air and felt himself dropping like a stone.

Mona found herself alone. Confused and blinded she began to run like a mad thing. The heather caught at her legs, she stumbled over unseen boulders.

If only she could find the cliff. She would have flung herself over without hesitation. It would be a merciful death compared to what she might expect from Gravenant.

He was following her. She could hear him howling and cursing as he stumbled over the uneven ground.

For the moment the human tiger had missed the trail. His voice sounded more distant. A faint hope flickered in her heart. She threw herself down in the heather, panting and terrified, like a hunted deer.

And then—when long minutes had passed and she had begun to imagine herself safe—a huge hand closed on her arm and she heard a bestial chuckle.

"Got you," said Gravenant. "Got you, my little darling."

He nozzled her face in a tigerish caress, making a hoarse, purring sound as he did so.

CHAPTER XX

THE DRUMMING DEATH

"I'LL SHOW YOU WHERE the treasure is," Lord Basil groaned.

The gangsters, attired like medieval torturers by Saratini's whim, paused. They looked towards the Count.

"Well?" Saratini asked. "Where is it?"

"Hidden in the moon. Hire an airship and I'll take you straight there."

Saratini stared at the man lying bound on the bed. Was it conceivable that this effeminate dandy could bluff in the face of torture itself? They had removed his shoes and tickled the soles of his feet with the glowing wires, and he had still persisted in the pretence that he had lost his memory and didn't know what they were talking about.

Hocking's mind was made up.

"He's not acting, Chief. If that cissy-boy could tell us where the gold is he would. The rap Heinman gave him has wiped out his memory. A blow on the head often does. I remember once a harness bull slugged me one in 'Frisco an'—"

"We'll have a medical opinion." Saratini cut short the anecdote. "Send for Dr. Constandos."

Dr. Constandos, looking white, unshaven and terrified, was hustled into the room. When he saw the torturers and the bound figure on the bed he shuddered. Then he recognized Lord Basil, and gave a cry.

"They've got you, too?"

"Another looney?" Lord Basil said wearily. "He looks more like an unemployed organ-grinder than a doctor. What's his pet delusion?"

Saratini turned to Constandos.

"I understand there are certain tests by which a doctor can detect whether a loss of memory case is genuine or not. Our little Lord Fido has had a blow on the back of his head. I want you to apply tests and give your opinion, your *true* opinion. If I suspect that you're trying to bluff me—"

Instead of completing the sentence he made a gesture towards the torturers, which made his meaning abundantly clear.

He beckoned the other gangsters.

"I believe it not etiquette for outsiders to remain in a bedroom during a medical examination. When you're satisfied about the case, be good enough to ring that bell."

They filed out. Constandos and Lord Basil were left alone. The doctor bent eagerly over the man on the bed.

"It ees terrible they 'ave taken you too. Now there ees no 'ope. But you try to trick them—yes? 'Ave no fear. I will 'elp. I will swear you 'ave lost your memory."

"You think you're my friend, do you?"

"Yes, yes. Of course I am your frien'. I am ze brave Constandos."

"Then go and fetch help. Quick, before those other men come back. They're mad as hatters. They seem to think I've hidden some gold or something."

Constandos winked elaborately.

"Vaire clever. But now to pretend there ees no need. We are alone."

"Fetch help, I tell you. Don't stand there winking and whispering."

Constandos felt puzzled. To his trained eyes the bump on the back of Lord Basil's head was far too slight an injury to have produced a complete lapse of memory. He proceeded to examine his patient. He tested his reactions, watched the dilations of his eyes. And the result of his investigations was to make him feel certain his lordship's memory was in as good working order as his own.

"I know you are pretendin'," he said. "Tell me—"

The bound wrists slipped over his head. The wiry wrists pressed with incredible strength against his throat.

Bound as he was, Lord Basil was strangling him. Even at that moment Constandos marvelled at his strength.

The door flew open and the gangsters burst into the room. The foremost got a kick from his lordship's bare heel that almost broke his nose. Then the struggle straightened itself. Constandos found himself facing Saratini, while the other men held Lord Basil on the bed.

"Well?" the Count asked.

"It ees a clear case. There ees some injury to ze brain. Something ees pressin' on ze memory cells. I prescribe rest an' quiet."

He stopped, appalled by Saratini's expression of mocking rage.

"What a fool you are, Constandos! By comparison Lord Fido would make a statesman. He at least had the intelligence to guess that I could overhear every word you said. Yes, I heard you give your true opinion. You said you knew that he was only pretending."

His mottled hands shot out. He had clutched Constandos by the cheeks and was shaking him furiously.

"That you should try to trick me! You wretched little Port Said half-caste! So you thought you were going to lie to me, did you? I'll blow your brains out for that . . . *Now!*"

He whipped a silver-plated automatic from his pocket and pressed the barrel against Constandos's head. His eyes slid round to observe Lord Basil's face.

"I'll spare his life if you say where the gold is."

"Thanks awfully," his lordship drawled. "I'd much rather you shot him though and yourself after."

With a hiss of anger Saratini sent the doctor staggering across the room.

"Take him away. I'll attend to him later. Dr. Constandos, Lord Fido evidently thinks that you're a lunatic. I rather think that before this evening is out he'll have proved a true prophet."

He gave some whispered instructions to Hocking. Constandos was pushed out of the room with the last grim threat ringing in his ears.

With his going Saratini's manner changed. He was smiling as he pulled a chair beside the bed and seated himself.

"I see it's an obstinate puppy I have to deal with," he purred. "A wilful, vicious puppy who must be taught better ways. Well, there are plenty of methods of doing so. For the one that I've decided upon I'm indebted to the late Mr. Jack London. Have you ever read *The Jacket* by that author, Lord Fido?"

Lord Basil made no reply. Saratini went on:

"In *The Jacket* he describes a form of punishment that used to be practised in American prisons. It consists of placing the—er—patient in a canvas bag which laces down the back. A form of strait-waistcoat you understand. When it is laced really tightly the body swells and the pain of the suspended circulation becomes excruciating. No man can endure it. Jack London writes of hardened criminals who laughed at ordinary forms of pain weeping and raving after a few hours in the jacket. They would confess anything in order to get release. It was the most effective form of Third Degree ever invented."

Lord Basil was staring at him in horror.

"I've read the book. It made my flesh creep. But—but you're not going to do that to me?"

"Unless you tell me where the *Cinco Llagas* treasure is, I will."

"But I tell you I don't know," Lord Basil shouted. "I was huntin' and got pitched on my head. I never heard of the *Cinco Llagas* treasure in my life. You're mad."

"An extraordinarily wilful puppy!" Saratini murmured. "Well, we'll see what the jacket will do for you. Lace the puppy up, Heinman."

The sheet of stout canvas was spread flat upon the floor. Despite his struggles Lord Basil was lifted off the bed and placed face downwards in the middle. His hands were unbound so that his arms could lie along his sides. The edges of the canvas were lifted and a length of strong cord threaded through the eyelets bored in the canvas for the purpose.

The lacing commenced. The canvas was too short by three inches for the edges to meet across Lord Basil's back even when stretched to the uttermost. By hauling on the lace until their muscles cracked the gangsters reduced that gap to an inch.

The helpless cocoon was lifted and placed on the bed. Saratini bent over his victim.

"Don't be frightened, Lord Fido. I know you feel as if you were being slowly crushed to death by a steam-roller passing over your body, but I assure you men never die in the jacket. But every minute the pain will get worse. What you feel now is nothing compared to what you will be feeling in an hour's time. When I come back after three hours or so you'll be very, very anxious to tell me all you know about the *Cinco Llagas* treasure. Heinman!"

"Yes, Chief?"

"You will remain here to watch him. The moment he becomes amenable to reason send for me."

"Very good, Chief."

Saratini fixed the German with his sinister eye.

"Remember he's your responsibility. Don't make any mistake. If you do—"

His smile completed the sentence. The big German trembled. He knew something of the Lizard's methods with those who failed to carry out his orders.

But in this case there was no possibility of failure. The prisoner was as helpless as a trussed chicken. All he had to do was to remain in the room until the growing agony of the suspended circulation broke down his will-power.

Anyway, what was there to be feared from that monocled clothes-peg? Heinman heartily despised Lord Basil. He knew he could break that slim, willowy figure between his great hands.

He had one of those brutal natures that delight in the spectacle of pain. When the others had gone he seated himself on the chair beside the bed. He leant forward in gloating anticipation.

He could see a faint movement under the tightly stretched canvas. Lord Basil's hand was moving. Thanks to his slim figure the jacket was not so tight in the region of the waist as it was round the chest and shoulders.

"Well, Herr Fido? How are you feeling now?"

To his amazement Lord Basil was smiling.

"I've won, old horse. Saratini will never learn where the treasure is now. Good-bye, Fritz."

"Good-bye! What is it you mean?" Heinman shouted.

The hands under the canvas were wriggling desperately. The German heard the panting words in which there was a ring of triumph.

"Fooled you! Good old Constandos! You didn't see him slip the syringe into my pocket, did you? Morphia, to escape Saratini . . . I—I . . ." His voice broke into feverish muttering. "Can't reach the damned thing . . . Ah! I've got it now . . . I—"

With a shout Heinman aimed a blow at where his hands were moving under the canvas. He understood what he was doing. He was trying to reach the syringe of morphia Constandos had slipped into his pocket

Perspiration was pouring down the German's face. If he succeeded in injecting the morphia the secret of the *Cinco Llagas* gold would be lost. And Saratini would hold him, Heinman, responsible!

Du Lieber Gott! The English puppy was escaping under his very eyes. His hands were still moving. They were fumbling under the canvas, striving to drive the needle home.

He was finding it difficult. Heinman could tell that by his contorted face. But his eyes were triumphant. It could only be a matter of seconds before he had the instrument of death in the correct position.

Heinman dashed to the door. His shout brought a gangster at the double.

"He's got a syringe of morphia. Quick—help me to unlace him. Must get it away. . . . If he kills himself . . ."

"Too late!" came the shout from the bed. "Good-bye, Fritz—"

The other fellow had grasped the situation. They rolled over the helpless form. A knife sheered through the lace. The canvas was peeled away.

"Where's that syringe? Take—"

The words died in a gasping cry. Slim, manicured hands with fingers like steel wires had closed round his fleshy throat. And only when he felt that fearful grip did Heinman realize the strength of the man he had thought a weakling.

He was lifted like a child and smashed down upon the floor. Quick as a striking snake the Englishman whirled upon the other gangster. His movements were swift as those of a battling leopard.

Nor was there a particle of mercy in his face. Cold-eyed and vicious he sent over a full-shouldered smash to the chin that would have felled a horse. The gangster went down as if he'd been pole-axed. He lay motionless with horribly sagging jaw.

Heinman was struggling to his feet. Again those merciless hands flashed to his throat. He was forced backwards on the bed. The pale, monocled face grinned into his. A drawling, pitiless voice spoke in his ear.

"So this is the end, my friend. A man who tortures others isn't fit to live, Heinman. I'm not killing you for the sake of the treasure. I'm killing you because you're a human ghoul who pollutes the air."

Without perceptible effort those hands whose slimness and whiteness many a woman had envied, tightened their grip until there was the crack of a breaking spine and Heinman ceased to struggle.

The dead German lay upon the bed. The gangster with the smashed jaw had been securely bound and gagged.

Lord Basil tiptoed to the door. He was determined not to leave Sperm until he had settled his account with Saratini for ever.

That devilish Italian was not fit to live. Lord Basil was not vindictive, but he felt that in ridding the world of Saratini he would be doing a service to humanity.

Apparently the sounds of the struggle had not been heard. He turned the handle and stepped out into a dark corridor.

Silence reigned in Sperm. A waiting, sinister silence that reminded him of what had happened the previous afternoon. Those robots! Even now he shuddered at the memory of the child with the severed throat wagging its head and clapping its hands while the strangled man crept down the stairs.

He would have to be wary if he were to catch the Italian. He knew the silent house lurked with dangers like a snake-infested jungle.

Suddenly he stood still. A whimpering terror-laden cry such as a little animal in a trap might have uttered had come to his ears. Seemingly it had come from above.

Saratini was at his fiendish games again! Lord Basil remembered what he had said to Constandos. And he knew from whose lips that cry had come.

Reckless of discovery, he broke into a clench-fisted run. The sound had come from an upper floor. He saw a door marked "Private" and set his shoulder against the woodwork.

The lock gave to his push. He rushed in and saw Saratini himself.

The Count was alone. He was standing motionless in the centre of the room, facing the door. He was smiling, with his head slightly bowed as if he were listening and his arms folded.

The Englishman advanced with his light, cat-like tread. His fists were dangling at his sides ready to strike and death was in his face.

"We meet again, Lizzie! Some puppies have sharp teeth, you know. Put your hands up, you vile swine! You're going—"

He was on the point of aiming a frightful blow at the Count's face when something warned him to stop. Something in Saratini's unnatural immobility.

He stopped and stared. From the back of Saratini's head a thin, all but invisible wire ran up to the ceiling where it connected with an electric cable. What the—? And the truth flashed upon his mind.

It was a marvellous waxwork representation of Saratini he had been threatening. But what was the meaning of the wire running up to the ceiling? Curiosity impelled him to lift a chair and throw it so that it passed above the waxwork's head, snapping the wire in its passage.

There was a crackle, a vivid blue flame and a smell of burning. Lord Basil wiped his forehead.

"Phew! Lucky I noticed the wire before I touched him. I'd been charred to a cinder—electrocuted like a frog on a live rail. So that's how Saratini catches would-be assassins!"

The ingenuity of the device made him laugh. But of whom had Saratini been afraid when he had arranged the death-trap? He could hardly have foreseen that he, Lord Basil, would escape.

No—the explanation was Gravenant. Saratini knew he was prowling in the vicinity bent upon revenge. The trap had been set to catch the human tiger in the event of his breaking into Sperm.

"Bright lads!" thought Lord Basil. "It's difficult to say which of them is the most cunning. But one thing's certain, and that is that they're both human fiends."

Again he went into the corridor and listened. This time he heard sounds at the meaning of which he could not even guess. Heavy feet, slow and methodical as those of a sentry on his beat, were marching on a wooden floor to the accompaniment of the throbbing of a drum.

The pitiful cry he had heard before was repeated. Beyond question the horror, whatever it was, was being staged on the top floor of the house.

The stairway was barred by a grilled gate similar to those used on lifts. It had been chained and padlocked as if Saratini was anxious not to be interrupted while enjoying his devilish amusement.

Lord Basil ran into the room where the waxwork effigy stood smouldering and flung up the window. Three feet below there was a ledge broad enough to walk along.

The ledge brought him to a waterpipe. He shinned up this and swung himself over the parapet on to the roof.

From where he stood the roof sloped steeply upwards for
about ten feet. He clawed up this by means of the leaded
slates and found himself on a level surface where he could
stand upright without risk of being seen from below.

A few yards further on he espied an oval-shaped sheet of
glass level with the roof. The glass was frosted, but not to
such an extent as to prevent a dull red light from the room
below shining through. And he knew without being told that
it was in that room that the unguessable horror was being
staged.

He could hear the marching feet and the rolling drum distinctly now. Mingling with them was another sound that
made his blood run cold. The whimpering, gasping cries of a
man driven almost mad by terror.

To his chagrin he found it impossible to see through the
frosted skylight. Short of smashing the glass all he could do
was stand where he was and listen.

Then he noticed a little window in the centre of the skylight, evidently placed there for ventilation purposes. Lying
flat on his face he drew himself up over the creaking glass
until he could reach the window.

It had not been closed quite flush with the skylight. He got
a purchase with his fingers and pulled. It opened jerkily, a
screw dragging along a ratchet. He could now see clearly
into the room below.

Prepared as he was for something fantastic and bizarre,
what he saw surpassed his grimmest imaginings. The room
below was large and devoid of furniture. It had been flood-
lighted with a deep crimson light that made the walls and
floor appear as if they had been bathed in blood.

And through this uncanny light, marching with relentless
feet to the beat of his drum, walked Death. A skeleton draped
in a black shroud. The Noseless One who follows each man
from the cradle to the grave. He was stalking 'round that
room—the very essence of all terror as portrayed in wax by
Saratini's genius.

Even Lord Basil, who knew the thing to be only a monstrous puppet, felt a thrill of horror. Then he saw Constandos cowering in a corner, looking almost half-crazed with terror, and his feelings changed to fury against Saratini. For the ghastly jest had wellnigh succeeded. The superstitious Greek believed the skeleton to be Death himself and was going mad.

The robot was approaching the corner where he crouched. Evidently Saratini had some means of seeing into the room and controlling its movements. It was reaching out with boney arms to embrace the shrieking wretch.

Suddenly the Greek collapsed on the floor in a faint. Instantly the red light went out and the room was in darkness.

"End of another act," Lord Basil muttered. "How long has that joker been doing that? I suppose when Constandos recovers consciousness he'll start again."

To attempt to call Constandos in his demented state would be useless. He crawled off the skylight and stood up, seeking some means by which he could get down to the room below.

A trap-door showed itself. It was unlocked. He raised it noiselessly and dropped some ten feet on to a landing. Here he paused to make certain of his bearings.

A minute later he was at the door of what he knew must be the room he sought. He drew a bolt and stepped into the darkness.

After a moment's groping he found a switch. The red light came on again, disclosing a spectacle as bizarre as anything a madman's imagination could have conceived. Constandos lay unconscious on the floor. Above him, grinning and frightful with outstretched arms, stood the Death-Robot in a menacing position.

If the Greek recovered consciousness to find himself lying at the feet of Death, his brain would assuredly snap.

Lord Basil carried him out into the passage. Hardly had he got him there when he woke up and began to struggle.

Lord Basil's hand descended on his mouth.

"Be quiet for your life. Saratini is somewhere about. That was only one of his filthy jokes. The thing you saw was a robot worked by electricity."

He had to repeat his whisper again and again before he could make the Greek grasp his meaning. Finally, Constandos became calmer. But he still clung to Lord Basil like a terrified child.

"This 'ouse! For God's sake let us go as quickly as we can. *Bacchos,* I thought that thing was Death himself. They had given me a drug, you understan'. When I woke up in that room with the red light, I thought myself in hell. And you tell me it was only a doll . . ."

"One of Saratini's bright ideas. He hoped to scare you into a lunatic asylum. And I believe he would have done if I hadn't popped along . . ."

He helped the doctor to the roof and left him there. Then he returned in search of Saratini.

This time he went to the left instead of to the right. The door of the room next to that in which the Death-Robot stood was closed. Pausing outside he caught the fragrance of one of the rich cigars he knew Saratini favoured.

Was he alone? Very gently he turned the handle. The room was unlighted. He could just discern the form of Count Saratini sitting in an armchair. With a cigar between his fingers he was gazing out of the window to where the Great Orme stood bathed in moonlight

On a table at his elbow was an instrument not unlike a receiving set. Lord Basil guessed it to be the instrument that sent out the invisible Phontgen rays that controlled the robot. Above it there was a periscope-like tube by which he had been able to watch the effect of his ghoulish joke.

A moonbeam illumined his face for a second. He was smiling like some sleek cat that knows it has a mouse within reach to torture.

An idea came to Lord Basil. Saratini was still in blissful ignorance of his presence. Noiselessly he closed the door.

"I think I'll see how he reacts to his own medicine," he thought. "If he's so fond of jokes he may appreciate this one."

He tip-toed back into the room where the Death-Robot stood. He wrapped himself in the shroud and slung the drum over his shoulder. He pulled up his sleeves so that his slim arms showed white in the darkness.

A moment later he had slipped into the room where Saratini sat. Lost in his sadistic dreams, the Count had not heard his entry.

Lord Basil tapped the drum. He saw Saratini start violently and clutch the arms of his chair. His face had gone the colour of snow. Slowly he turned to behold the hooded form of Death standing at the door.

Like a man smitten by a palsy he rose, shaking, to his feet. His hands went to his open mouth and he uttered a thin, quavering scream such as a very old woman might have uttered in the last extremity of terror.

It was then Lord Basil guessed his secret. This prince of horrors was himself an arrant coward where superstition was concerned. He believed now that Death himself had come to punish him for having usurped his terrors.

Rolling the muffled drum he advanced slowly into the room. Scream upon scream rose from Saratini's lips. He had backed against the wall. His hands were outflung as if they could fend off death.

The horrors he had dabbled in must have sapped his own reason. He was screaming now on one thin continuous note. He was writhing against the wall in an agony of dread far surpassing anything any of his own victims had suffered.

Lord Basil had advanced until he was almost touching the slavering wretch. Slowly he extended his shrouded arm. In a sepulchral voice he enunciated the words, "*I-am-Death.*"

It was a true saying. Before his fingers had touched him Saratini gave one last frightful cry and fell to the ground—literally dead of terror.

CHAPTER XXI

LORD BASIL MEETS A GHOST

HAD LORD BASIL LINGERED in the room where Saratini lay he must have been more than human. He left it hurriedly. His hands were shaking as he rid himself of the drum and shroud.

"Jove, if that wasn't the absolute outside edge! Never dreamt he'd take it like that! Dropped dead of sheer funk! He must have had rotten nerves and a rotten heart."

The success of his impulse to play a prank on Saratini had been almost too complete. It would be a long time before he could forget those screams of horror.

The noise of sledge-hammers striking iron caught his ear. Running to the top of the stairs he saw Hocking and two others of the gang attacking the iron grill. Angry shouts and a fusillade of shots greeted his appearance.

Lord Basil was untouched. He kissed his fingers and sprang back out of the line of fire. As he did so he smelt smoke and heard a dull roar as of fast mounting flames. The men below had also noticed the fire. He heard their shouts of anger change to yells of consternation. He joined Constandos on the roof.

"Sperm is on fire. Hocking and the others will be trapped if they're not devilish nippy. So will we, Standy, unless we get a move on."

They found a fire escape at the other side of the roof. The house was burning with extraordinary rapidity. As they ran down the iron steps flames reached for them from the windows like hungry serpents.

From the Great Orme road Lord Basil looked back at the holocaust.

"The wasp's nest is being destroyed, Standy. I can guess what started that fire. It was a waxwork Saratini had put up hoping to electrocute Gravenant. Something must have fused when I broke the wire. Well, that fire will save Superintendent Fibby's reason. If he'd gone into that house and seen all those dead bodies and robots and things he'd have gone clean off his chump. As it is, the fire will conceal everything."

He smote the doctor between the shoulder-blades.

"Brace up, sweet pippin. Your troubles are a thing of the past. Saratini's gang is bust sky-high. It looks as if we're going to get the *Cinco Llagas* treasure after all. Phew, it's been hot work though! We didn't foresee what a time we were going to have that afternoon you rolled up at the Brig-y-don Hydro."

Constandos contrived a laugh.

"If I 'ad I would nevaire 'ave left Port Said. I 'ave been buried alive an' scared almost out of my senses. They were devil-men who came after that gold. To secure it they would 'ave stopped at nozzing. Even if you 'ave beaten Saratini there ees still Gravenant. I warn you you may find 'im ze worst of all."

Lord Basil nodded gravely.

"I rather agree, old fruit. Gravenant is the unknown danger and therefore the most to be feared. Well, you don't look fit for much more so I'm going to take you back to the hydro. Here's a car. Now if this sweet chappie will oblige us with a lift . . ."

The "sweet chappie" proved obliging. As they drove towards the Bay they passed a stream of vehicles hastening to scene of the fire which could now be seen for miles. They had to drive slowly on account of the sea-fret now rolling inland.

From the hydro Lord Basil telephoned the Rectory. He guessed Mona must be uneasy on his account.

It was Mrs. Galbraith, the Scotch housekeeper, who took the call. Mrs. Galbraith had had a worrying day. There had been too many what she called "goings-on" to please her orderly mind, and she was inclined to put the blame for all the mysterious happenings on Lord Basil Curlew.

The collapse of the March Hare on the porch that afternoon had, so far as Mrs. Galbraith was concerned, put the finishing touch on things. Why she should have considered it Lord Basil's fault that the March Hare had collapsed where he did instead of somewhere else it is difficult to say, but she did. To sum up with a convenient colloquialism, Mrs. Galbraith was "fed up" with Lord Basil.

When therefore she recognized his voice on the phone, she quickly made up her mind what she would say. The truth, that Miss Mona had gone off to that friend of hers at Rhos (that was what Mrs. Galbraith honestly believed to be the cause of the young lady's absence from home) would only have brought him bothering 'round.

Without knowing exactly why, Lord Basil was feeling anxious as he raised the receiver. Of course Mona would have kept her promise and remained in the Rectory, but still—

"Is Miss Vachell there?"

"The puir lassie's asleep in her room this minute," said Mrs. Galbraith dourly. "An' a'hm thinkin' it's a bit of sleep she wants too. Gallivantin' 'roond the toon! Your lordship ought tae be ashamed."

His lordship was grinning with relief. Mona was safe in the Rectory. His vague fears were groundless.

"Thanks awfully, Mrs. Galbraith. Well, I'll trickle round to-morrow morning to give her the news. Sound scheme, what? Pip pip, Mrs. Galbraith . . . Ta most frightfully . . ."

Right joyfully his lordship headed for the bar. If a chappie didn't deserve some liquid refreshment after doing what he'd done that afternoon, he never deserved any at all. Come to think of it he was deuced tired. The soles of his feet were lined with blisters and his chest muscles ached as result of having been compressed by the jacket. Never mind. A tankard of the old and mild would soon put those matters right.

Mona was safe, and that was all he cared.

Tankards, one, two, three were filled and emptied. A plate of sandwiches had been denuded of its contents. Strangers smiled at the slim, monocled young man with the fatuous expression who absorbed beer like a human sponge.

Presently the human sponge felt he'd like a little exercise. Fourth tankard in hand he wandered out of the bar and down a passage. At the end of the passage there was a new bar that had recently been opened. Lord Basil reflected that it mightn't be a bad scheme if a chappie sampled what the beer in this new bar was like.

He pushed open the glass-panelled door. And then the tankard crashed from his hand to the floor. Even more significant, his monocle dropped from his eye.

It was a moment of palpitating horror. Smiling at him across the counter was Miss Floss, the girl who had been murdered in the Black Dingle.

A ghost! This was where a chappie legged it. But before Lord Basil could get through the door the supposed apparition spoke.

"It's all right. I'm not Edna. I'm her sister. We're very alike with the same sort of uniform and all. There's been two or three have thought I was her ghost."

"You're her sister! Jove, what a scare you gave me! Do you mind proving your reality by pouring out a double brandy?"

His lordship had a friendly, sympathetic manner that induced confidences. Before he had been three minutes in the bar the second Miss Floss was telling him her suspicions.

"I believe I know who has done it. What's more, I believe I saw him going off this very afternoon with another chap. Now you read that letter. Edna wrote it the morning it—it happened. No, I haven't shown it to the police yet. I'm going to though. Don't mind the first bit . . . Start there . . ."

Lord Basil began to read the dead girl's letter.

". . . I'll send you the jumper, dear, when it's done. Do you know, I believe I've clicked! It's a scream. He's an old beaver with a yellow beard who says he was in the navy.

Quite the gentleman, too. He's a friend of Lord Basil Curlew, so I suppose he's all right . . ."

An old beaver with a yellow beard who says he was in the
navy! Who could that be but Commander Eggington?

Lord Basil gasped. Here at last was confirmation of the
vague suspicion that had entered his mind that morning. It
had been the commander he had had in mind when he had
warned Mona not to leave the Rectory.

For Gravenant, like Saratini, had under-rated his lordship's intelligence. He had tried to confuse him by advancing
the theory that Saratini was the Black Killer, but his clever-
ness had over-reached itself. Lord Basil had not believed the
theory for a moment. But it had occurred to him to wonder
why Commander Eggington should have been so anxious to
make him attack Saratini?

That had been the pointer that had first directed his suspicions in the right direction.

Miss Floss's sister was speaking again.

"Do you know, I believe I saw a fellow I thought might be
him this afternoon. Not many big men with beards about, are
there? This one looked as if he might be a naval officer. He
was in a car with another chap. The other one had a bandage
round his head."

Lord Basil stared at her.

"Wh—what was the other one like?"

"Clean-shaven, with a brown face. They were driving up
in Brig-y-don direction."

Stan Hastings for a fiver! Lord Basil's fist came down on
the counter with a crash. He was cursing himself for an unut-
terable fool. Stan had been suffering from loss of memory as
a result of the Black Killer's blow. Incidentally, it was what
he had been told about that at the hospital that had suggested
the plan to Lord Basil by which he baffled Saratini.

Why hadn't he warned Stan that he suspected the commander? But he had not imagined the American would leave
the hospital so soon.

"You—you didn't notice which way they went?"

"They were heading up the Penrhyn Road when I saw them."

The Penrhyn Road! That was the road leading to Brig-y-don Rectory. Then had Mona seen them? Or had Gravenant—he was hideously certain Gravenant and Commander Eggington were the same person—driven there with the intention of enticing her into the car?

Thank God he'd made her give that promise. From what Mrs. Galbraith had said he knew she was safely in the Rectory. The human tiger had not caught her . . . But had he caught Stan?

He must speak to Mona at once. No matter if she were asleep—she must be wakened. With a human tiger on the prowl he couldn't stick at trifles.

This time it was Ellen the housemaid who answered the phone.

Lord Basil spoke with an urgent ring in his voice. "That you, Ellen? Oh, I want to speak to Miss Mona at once. I'm sorry if she's asleep, but it can't be helped . . . *What?* . . . Oh, my God!"

He dropped the receiver with something like a groan. Ellen's words had shattered his fond belief that Mona was safe. She had told him the truth—that Mona had left the Rectory shortly after five that evening and had not come back.

"Is anything ze matter?"

He turned to see Constandos. The doctor had found himself unable to sleep and come down in search of company.

"The devil's the matter," Lord Basil snapped. "I've got a shock for you, Standy. We've been fooled all along the line. Commander Eggington was Gravenant in disguise."

Constandos uttered a cry of incredulous amazement.

"Impossible! You must be mistook!"

"I'm not. But there's no time to explain things now. He's got both Mona and Stan. They don't suspect him. For all I know to the contrary, he may have murdered them hours ago. Anyway, they're in ghastly danger . . . Mona in Gravenant's power! . . . I'd a dread of that happening . . ."

"Where do you think 'e 'as taken them?"

"Minrhyn Head for a cert. I'm going there at once."

A man passing along the corridor had caught the last words. He stopped and turned.

"Did I hear you say you were going up Minrhyn Head?"

"What about it?" Lord Basil snapped.

"You won't be able to—that's all. There's a thick mist. You couldn't see your hand in front of your eyes. If you try going up by the road you'll drive over a slate quarry as sure as eggs."

"I see. Thanks."

The stranger walked away. Lord Basil flung up a window. Even at that lower level the mist was now thick enough to render driving a car at more than a crawl impossible. And he knew by experience that up on Minrhyn Head, where the clouds piled round the rock even on clear days, the mist would be a hundredfold more dense.

Constandos made a gesture of despair.

"We can do nozzing. We must wait until ze mist 'as lifted."

"Damn it, man, that may be days. We'll have to borrow a car—I left mine on the Head—and chance the quarries. No—wait a minute. I've a better scheme. We'll take the *Gipsy Queen.*"

"The *Gipsy Queen?*"

"My motor-boat. I'll have a shot at climbing the cliff. It will be quicker than the road."

Constandos gasped. To him the scheme seemed almost tantamount to suicide.

But Lord Basil's mind was made up. The *Gipsy Queen* was beached just below the hydro. By good fortune she was ready for an instant departure moored by the east breakwater.

They were off. Gliding over a mist-shrouded sea with the orange lights of Minrhyn Bay looming on the left. The *Gipsy Queen* was fast. Lord Basil flung the throttle wide and drove her recklessly through an eerie world of white vapour.

Black posts like the legs of gargantuan storks loomed ahead. Rhos Pier—where he and Mona used to fish. Constandos yelled as the *Gipsy Queen* heeled in a right-angled turn with the water bubbling over the gunwale. Another yard and they would have collided with a pier support.

"P.B.C. again," Lord Basil drawled. "I clean forgot the pier. Standy, I ought to be kicked."

Another sickening swerve and they had rounded the pier. He opened the throttle another fraction of an inch. They had left the sheltered water of the bay and were dipping and swinging over fat, oily waves.

Constandos crouched down behind, blinded with spray. He missed the louder roar of the heavier boat bounding towards them. But he felt the *Gipsy Queen* rear like a plunging horse as they caught her swell.

The other boat had passed invisible in the mist. But the sound of her engine was still distinct. She had turned left-handed and was holding a course parallel to their own—heading straight for the unseen mass of Minrhyn Head.

Lord Basil swore in amazement.

"Who the devil can that be? They're racing us to the Head. Surely the police—"

The idea had crossed his mind the police might at last have got on the human tiger's trail. But the mystery craft carried no light. And her engine sounded too powerful to be that of the little launch used by the Minrhyn Bay police upon occasions.

And then he guessed the truth. Saratini's rats were making a last desperate bid for the *Cinco Llagas* gold. Some had escaped the holocaust at Sperm. They had secured the motorboat from Sir Jasper's yacht and were making for the Head with the intention of having a final search.

Here was a new and unexpected complication. He had under-rated the determination of Saratini's gangsters. Or, rather, he had under-rated the power of the lure of that million pounds' worth of solid gold.

There was no time to trouble about the gangsters just then. A dull rumble ahead told where the swell was surging and creaming round the rocks at the foot of Minrhyn cliffs. He shut the throttle and the *Gipsy Queen* glided forward under her own impetus. There was a crash as her nose struck a submerged rock, and then a wall of black, foaming water seemed to leap at them out of the mist.

"Quick, Standy. Jump, man, for your life!"

Constandos jumped blindly, slipped on the glass-like surface of a rock and disappeared in a suffocating smother of foam. An arm like a steel hawser clamped round his waist. He felt himself being dragged over rocks and shingle waist-deep in swirling water.

Out of reach of the waves Lord Basil deposited him on a heap of seaweed.

"Know where you are? If my navigation was correct, we're at the foot of Minrhyn Head, almost directly below the castle. Those were some of Saratini's crowd in the other boat. If they've managed to land they're about fifty yards to the left. Curse this mist! Listen—"

The mist carried the sound of the men's voices to their ears. Lord Basil laughed.

"It's the fellah called Hocking and two others. Determined devils! Question is, did they hear the *Gipsy Queen* and realize who was in her? If so, we may expect them here very shortly."

He drew his automatic and waited tensely. After a minute or so he relaxed.

"I think they're climbing the cliff. Standy, old chappie, I'm sorry, but you'll have to stay here. You couldn't manage the climb possibly. If—er—I don't see you again—well, here's pip pip, and all that."

Constandos grasped the slim hand. For a fraction of a second the clearing mist allowed him to glimpse Lord Basil's face. He was smiling, but his eyes were steely with inflexible determination.

Another second and he had vanished. Constandos sat down to wait. An occasional pebble or fragment of rock falling on the shingle at his side alone apprised him of the man clawing up the rock far above his head.

A scream brought him to his feet. It was repeated—a terror-laden cry echoing through the mist. Seconds later he heard the thud of a body striking against a rock.

Two hundred feet up Lord Basil also had heard the cry. He guessed its meaning. One of the gangsters had missed his footing and fallen headlong from the cliff.

Every sound was uncannily distinct in the mist. As if he were only a few feet away he heard a frightened voice.

"Jim's slipped! Gawd, this ain't no bloomin' picnic. How high is the ruddy cliff, Hocking?"

Hocking's voice answered, coming as far as Lord Basil could judge from some point above the first speaker's head.

"We're past the worst. Bear to the left and you'll strike a gully. So Jim's fallen, has he? Well, I guess there'll be all the more gold for us."

There was a callous laugh and again silence.

Lord Basil had grasped the situation. The gangsters had found the gully he remembered pointing out to Mona the first evening. Inevitably they would be first on top of the cliff.

He was having by far the harder climb. An eight-foot ledge of rock had barred his upward progress. He had to work his way sideways, each step bringing him nearer to the enemy.

A breeze had sprung up. It was blowing the mist back from the cliff-face. A watery moon shone through and he glimpsed a figure crouching on all fours on a ledge.

Hocking! He had reached the top and was waiting for his companion. Lord Basil saw that he himself had still another thirty feet to climb. If Hocking saw him now he would be caught at a hideous disadvantage.

A direct ascent was impossible. He had to keep bearing to the left, each foot bringing him closer to the gangsters. He could see the other man now. Hocking was reaching down to give him a hand.

Something turned under his foot. He hung for an instant by his fingers from a crevice, listening to a boulder crashing its way down the cliff face. Hocking too had heard the sound.

"What the flaming hell? There's someone else on the cliff! To the left and about a dozen yards down."

He ran to the left and threw himself on his face. The beam of a powerful flashlamp swept down the rock like a miniature searchlight. And then Hocking's shout of surprise and anger sounded through the night.

"It's that bloody dude again! Little Lord Fido come to get his gold. You're not coming any higher, Fido. We've had enough of you and your tricks. You kidded Saratini all right, but you're not going to kid us."

He could plainly see his lordship's pale face. Lord Basil was clinging precariously to a slope of rock.

"My dear fellah, do be reasonable," he said plaintively. "It's dashed uncomfortable down here. Can't I come up and—"

"Can that cissy-talk," Hocking snapped. "We know you. I tell you I'm not taking any more risks where you're concerned. If you know any prayers you can say them right now. Don't move. You're covered."

Two automatics pointed directly at the helpless man. Hocking went on, a jeering, triumphant note in his voice.

"Your break's finished, Fido. I guess you'd a mighty long run of luck, but it's petered out at last. I'm going to do what Saratini should have done—shoot you straightway. Yes, I saw the way you mauled Heinman and that other guy. I'll hand it to you, Fido, that you're a dangerous cuss at close quarters. Cripes, you had us all fooled properly with that glass eye and drawling voice of yours. We wrote you down for a regular cissy . . . But we've seen through your bluff now and you're not coming on top this cliff . . ."

He spoke with harsh determination. Looking upwards Lord Basil saw the unwavering muzzles of the automatics, and knew that his fate was sealed.

CHAPTER XXII

IN WHICH "POOR BLOOMING CURLEW" BELIES HIS NAME

HE COULD DO NOTHING save lie there waiting for the blasting agony of the bullets. Those grim men behind the automatics were taking no more chances. They had him at their mercy and they meant to kill.

It was the end. Thoughts rushed through his mind. Bitterest of all was the thought he had failed Mona. Yes, he had let down the girl who trusted him.

But it was too late for regrets. He had made his decision. Rather than wait there to be shot like a starving cat on a ledge he would loose his hold and let himself be smashed on the rocks hundreds of feet below.

Hocking's jeering voice sounded from above. "Said your prayers, Fido? I'm going to count five and then shoot. One . . . two . . . three . . ."

Let go and fall. He willed his fingers to loosen their grip, but the inborn desire for life seemed to hold them clamped. And then he heard Hocking curse. A curling tendril of mist had suddenly blown inwards to the cliff, blotting him from their sight.

Fate had flung him another slim chance of life. He swung himself sideways. Two streaks of red flame pierced the mist. He heard the screaming bullets ricochet from the rock.

By heaven, he'd do those devils yet! Madly he began to claw his way up the cliff. The gangsters were now firing blindly into the mist. Incessant streaks of flame and bullets that zoomed like angry wasps.

If only the mist held . . . One yard, two yards . . . he was nearing the top and making quicker progress as the slope grew more gradual. They had stopped firing, fearful of wasting their ammunition. But he could picture them crouched and waiting, their guns ready and their eyes straining into the mist.

And then another puff of wind spelt the death-knell of his hopes. Again the mist that had divided them lifted. Their figures loomed black through the greyness. He heard Hocking's shout.

"There he is! Don't let him get any higher . . . Shoot—"

As if in obedience to his yell a gun thudded twice from somewhere on the right. He saw Hocking jump and stagger on the edge of the cliff with outflung arms. The other man had fallen forward on his face.

Again the unseen gun spurted flame. There was a rattle of stones and a long-drawn scream of terror. Hocking's body hurtled past, spinning and somersaulting into the darkness of the abyss.

Stan's voice spoke from above. It was drawling, imperturbable as ever.

"You can come up, son. The road's clear."

In a moment Lord Basil was beside him. He made no comment on what had happened. Explanations and thanks must wait till later.

"Mona?"

Stan's left hand closed on his arm.

"Don't take it hard, old man. I guess—well, I guess it's the worst."

"Gravenant?"

The American nodded dumbly. His face was deathly white from loss of blood. His right arm hung useless at his side.

"He was Eggington. The March Hare came to the Rectory and told us where he'd put the gold. Gravenant got us up to the cottage. Myself first, then Miss Vachell. We got away; he trailed us in the mist. There was a gun-fight. I took one in the shoulder . . . I fell over the cliff and lit on a ledge about twenty feet down. I was knocked cold. When I got up there wasn't a sign of either Miss Vachell or Gravenant. But I guess I know where he's taken her. Into the secret room in the castle where Atler put the gold. He's gone clean raving mad . . . Got some crazy idea of making a sacrifice to the tiger . . ."

"You've been there? You tried to follow?"

"I did. I found the entrance to the tunnel along which Atler took the gold. There's a big pivoting stone in the side of the pit where the chests are. The tunnel leading to the secret room under the cellars is behind that. Well, I went there, and—"

"What?"

"I couldn't move the stone," Stan said wearily. "Gravenant has blocked it on the other side. I reckon he did that so that he wouldn't be disturbed while he made the sacrifice. But there must be another entrance to the secret room through the cellars. I was just going to look for that when I heard the firing out here. But—I hate to say it, old son—but I'm afraid we're too late."

It was a few seconds before Lord Basil spoke. When he did there was not a tremor in his voice.

"We must try to find the other entrance. At the least we can get Gravenant. And, Stan . . ."

"What?"

"When we find him he's my meat. Don't forget." They began to stumble through the mist towards the castle.

The cellars were a labyrinth of darkness. The rock beneath the castle had been honeycombed with passages and vault-like tunnels.

Somewhere in the blackness lurked the human tiger they were trailing. Gravenant, the man with the tiger-obsessed brain; the semi-lunatic whose cunning and ferocity had baffled the Continental police for years.

Of all the desperate men drawn to Minrhyn Bay by the lure of the *Cinco Llagas* gold, he was by far the most formidable. Playing a single-handed game he had been the first to reach the treasure and had been mainly instrumental in wiping out Saratini's gang.

But in the moment of triumph his tottering reason had collapsed. He was now all tiger. The cunning that had enabled him to play the part of Commander Eggington had vanished. He had become a ferocious animal mad with a lust for killing.

He had carried Mona to the room where Sir Jasper's body lay upon the mound of gold. Mercifully for herself, she was unconscious. At the frightful moment when he had crept on her in the heather she had fainted.

Leaving her there, Gravenant had gone back to look for Stan. The gold was on fire and must be quenched with blood. One sacrifice would not satisfy the tiger. For a long time he had searched in the mist.

Baffled, he had returned to the castle. One lingering spark of reason had led him to barricade the entrance to the tunnel. Then he had gone to the room where Mona lay.

She was conscious and she had heard him coming. She felt as if she were in a wild beast's lair. But somehow he was less frightful to her now that he was wholly mad than when he had been three-quarters sane. It had been Gravenant the man, not Gravenant the lunatic, who had been so utterly repulsive.

She lay still with her eyes closed. Without a glance in her direction he had gone straight to the mound of gold.

When she opened her eyes she saw the huge, cowled figure kneeling in front of the altar in an attitude of prayer.

She was past terror, almost past caring what happened. As in a dream she listened to his raving voice. He was embracing the altar. She saw him bend his cowled head and press his face against the blood-stained gold.

Suddenly he seemed to remember her. He rose and came towards her with quick, padding steps. A knife gleamed in his hand. His eyes were as if a devil were glaring through blue glass.

"The gold's on fire . . . It must be quenched with blood . . ."

He was lifting her in his arms. And then it seemed she suddenly woke to the full horror of her position. She was young and she craved life. She screamed, pitiful, helpless screams that no one could hear.

And as before it was the name of the man she loved that she cried aloud.

"Basil! . . . Help! For God's sake . . ."

The madman had dragged her to the altar from which he had thrown the other body. He had lifted her on to the mount of the *Cinco Llagas* gold. The knife hovered in the air.

"Help! Basil!"

There was an answering shout and the crash of the trap-door in the ceiling being flung back. With a snarl Gravenant released her. He whirled about to face the man who had interrupted the sacrifice. He saw Lord Basil. Mona's screams had saved her life. They had guided her rescuers to the human tiger's lair in the very nick of time.

For a moment the human tiger stood motionless, glaring. The cowl had been ripped from his face by Mona's struggles. His head was bent forward and from his throat issued rumbling, animal-like growls while saliva dribbled from his distorted mouth.

And then he began to advance. Slowly, mincingly, like some monstrous gorilla shambling out of a forest glade. His hands were extended, his fingers were hooked like a tiger's talons.

Stan's voice sounded from above.

"For God's sake, shoot, man. He could rip you up like a rag doll."

He had his own automatic in his hand, but he was loathe to use it. Fascinated, he watched the spectacle.

Was Lord Basil mad? He had made no attempt to draw his gun. Tall and slender, he was awaiting the human tiger, his body taut as wire, his hands dangling ready at his sides.

He would be torn to pieces! The American spoke with agony in his voice.

"Shoot, you blasted fool! If you don't I will."

He had raised his automatic, but he was too late.

With a blaring sound like the scream of a raged elephant, the human tiger leapt upon the Englishman. The monstrous draped arms wrapped about the lean figure like wings. Like a charging grizzly he bore him before him into the darkness.

They were locked in a dance of death. A terrible, worrying, snarling sound issued from the blackness. Stan leapt to the floor. He was cursing, praying. Which was which in that hellish scurry? He dared not shoot, but he hovered round the struggle with automatic raised.

Suddenly there was an animal-like howl of baffled fury. Stan paused in amazement. It was Gravenant who had howled.

Those lean hands were holding him in a grip even his colossal strength was powerless to break. Suddenly Lord Basil made a lightning movement. Gravenant seemed to shoot head-first along the floor.

With a leopard-like bound Lord Basil was astride the sprawling bulk. His arms snaked round the gargantuan torso. But after a second he relaxed the hold and rose to his feet.

"Dead as mutton. He fell on his own knife and it's pierced his heart. In the circumstances I think it was the best thing could have happened."

"You took a risk not shooting him," Stan commented. "I never knew you were a ju-jitsu expert."

Lord Basil smiled as he screwed his monocle into his eye to survey Gravenant's body.

"Matu himself taught me. Wonderful thing, ju-jitsu— Gives a chappie confidence . . . When a chappie's got plenty of confidence, he doesn't mind playing the goat if it amuses other chappies."

It was a cryptic remark, but the American understood. It's what a man is and not what he seems to other people that really matters.

Lord Basil crossed the room and without a glance at the *Cinco Llagas* gold raised Mona in his arms. And by the look on his face Stan knew that she was the only treasure in the world he cared about.

When Mona came to she found herself lying in a nest of sweet-smelling heather with her lover kneeling at her side. The mist had cleared. It was early morning and the first rays of the sun were shooting across sea and moor while larks carolled joyously overhead.

She smiled up at him. Her terrors had vanished with the mist.

"You look like a rabbit, Basil."

"Thanks awfully. Well, it's game and set and match to our side. The *Cinco Llagas* gold is yours. Stan knows how to get it sold on the Continent without bother. You're an heiress, little Funny Face."

"I'm going to give away most of that gold," whispered Mona. "Hospitals for sick children and things like that. And of course Dr. Constandos and Stan must have a big share each. I don't want a lot of money. I've got you and—"

Suddenly she threw her arms round his neck. In her loving eyes "Poor Blooming Curlew" for all his foibles was a very Perfect Knight.

RAMBLE HOUSE's

HARRY STEPHEN KEELER WEBWORK MYSTERIES

(RH) indicates the title is available ONLY in the RAMBLE HOUSE edition

The Ace of Spades Murder
The Affair of the Bottled Deuce (RH)
The Amazing Web
The Barking Clock
Behind That Mask
The Book with the Orange Leaves
The Bottle with the Green Wax Seal
The Box from Japan
The Case of the Canny Killer
The Case of the Crazy Corpse (RH)
The Case of the Flying Hands (RH)
The Case of the Ivory Arrow
The Case of the Jeweled Ragpicker
The Case of the Lavender Gripsack
The Case of the Mysterious Moll
The Case of the 16 Beans
The Case of the Transparent Nude (RH)
The Case of the Transposed Legs
The Case of the Two-Headed Idiot (RH)
The Case of the Two Strange Ladies
The Circus Stealers (RH)
Cleopatra's Tears
A Copy of Beowulf (RH)
The Crimson Cube (RH)
The Face of the Man From Saturn
Find the Clock
The Five Silver Buddhas
The 4th King
The Gallows Waits, My Lord! (RH)
The Green Jade Hand
Finger! Finger!
Hangman's Nights (RH)
I, Chameleon (RH)
I Killed Lincoln at 10:13! (RH)
The Iron Ring
The Man Who Changed His Skin (RH)
The Man with the Crimson Box
The Man with the Magic Eardrums
The Man with the Wooden Spectacles
The Marceau Case
The Matilda Hunter Murder
The Monocled Monster

The Murder of London Lew
The Murdered Mathematician
The Mysterious Card (RH)
The Mysterious Ivory Ball of Wong Shing Li (RH)
The Mystery of the Fiddling Cracksman
The Peacock Fan
The Photo of Lady X (RH)
The Portrait of Jirjohn Cobb
Report on Vanessa Hewstone (RH)
Riddle of the Travelling Skull
Riddle of the Wooden Parrakeet (RH)
The Scarlet Mummy (RH)
The Search for X-Y-Z
The Sharkskin Book
Sing Sing Nights
The Six From Nowhere (RH)
The Skull of the Waltzing Clown
The Spectacles of Mr. Cagliostro
Stand By—London Calling!
The Steeltown Strangler
The Stolen Gravestone (RH)
Strange Journey (RH)
The Strange Will
The Straw Hat Murders (RH)
The Street of 1000 Eyes (RH)
Thieves' Nights
Three Novellos (RH)
The Tiger Snake
The Trap (RH)
Vagabond Nights (Defrauded Yeggman)
Vagabond Nights 2 (10 Hours)
The Vanishing Gold Truck
The Voice of the Seven Sparrows
The Washington Square Enigma
When Thief Meets Thief
The White Circle (RH)
The Wonderful Scheme of Mr. Christopher Thorne
X. Jones—of Scotland Yard
Y. Cheung, Business Detective

Keeler-Related Works

A To Izzard: A Harry Stephen Keeler Companion by Fender Tucker — Articles and stories about Harry, by Harry, and in his style. Included is a compleat bibliography.

Wild About Harry: Reviews of Keeler Novels — Edited by Richard Polt & Fender Tucker — 22 reviews of works by Harry Stephen Keeler from *Keeler News*. A perfect introduction to the author.

The Keeler Keyhole Collection: Annotated newsletter rants from Harry Stephen Keeler, edited by Francis M. Nevins. Over 400 pages of incredibly personal Keeleriana.

Fakealoo — Pastiches of the style of Harry Stephen Keeler by selected demented members of the HSK Society. Updated every year with the new winner.

Strands of the Web: Short Stories of Harry Stephen Keeler — 29 stories, just about all that Keeler wrote, are edited and introduced by Fred Cleaver.

RAMBLE HOUSE's LOON SANCTUARY

52 Pickup — Two thrillers from 1952 by Aylwin Lee Martin: *The Crimson Frame* and *Fear Comes Calling*

A Clear Path to Cross — Sharon Knowles short mystery stories by Ed Lynskey.

A Jimmy Starr Omnibus — Three 40s novels by Jimmy Starr.

A Roland Daniel Double: The Signal and The Return of Wu Fang — Classic thrillers from the 30s.

A Shot Rang Out — Three decades of reviews and articles by today's Anthony Boucher, Jon Breen. An essential book for any mystery lover's library.

A Smell of Smoke — A 1951 English countryside thriller by Miles Burton.

A Snark Selection — Lewis Carroll's *The Hunting of the Snark* with two Snarkian chapters by Harry Stephen Keeler — Illustrated by Gavin L. O'Keefe.

A Young Man's Heart — A forgotten early classic by Cornell Woolrich.

Alexander Laing Novels — *The Motives of Nicholas Holtz* and *Dr. Scarlett*, stories of medical mayhem and intrigue from the 30s.

An Angel in the Street — Modern hardboiled noir by Peter Genovese.

Automaton — Brilliant treatise on robotics: 1928-style! By H. Stafford Hatfield.

Away from the Here and Now — A collection of SF short stories by Clare Winger Harris.

Beast or Man? — A 1930 novel of racism and horror by Sean M'Guire. Introduced by John Pelan.

Black Hogan Strikes Again — Australia's Peter Renwick pens a tale of the 30s outback.

Black River Falls — Suspense from the master, Ed Gorman.

Blondy's Boy Friend — A snappy 1930 story by Philip Wylie, writing as Leatrice Homesley.

Blood in a Snap — The *Finnegan's Wake* of the 21st century, by Jim Weiler.

Blood Moon — The first of the Robert Payne series by Ed Gorman.

Calling Lou Largo — Two hardboiled classics from William Ard: *All Can Get* (1959) and *Like Ice She Was* (1960)

Chariots of San Fernando and Other Stories — Malcolm Jameson's SF from the pulps are featured in the first book of the John Pelan SF series.

Chelsea Quinn Yarbro Novels featuring Charlie Moon — *Ogilvie, Tallant and Moon, Music When the Sweet Voice Dies, Poisonous Fruit* and *Dead Mice*. An Ojibwa detective in SF.

Cornucopia of Crime — Francis M. Nevins assembled this huge collection of his writings about crime literature and the people who write it. Essential for any serious mystery library.

Crimson Clown Novels — By Johnston McCulley, author of the Zorro novels, *The Crimson Clown* and *The Crimson Clown Again*.

Dago Red — 22 tales of dark suspense by Bill Pronzini.

David Hume Novels — *Corpses Never Argue, Cemetery First Stop, Make Way for the Mourners, Eternity Here I Come*. 1930s British hardboiled fiction with an attitude.

Dead Man Talks Too Much — Hollywood boozer by Weed Dickenson.

Death Leaves No Card — One of the most unusual murdered-in-the-tub mysteries you'll ever read. By Miles Burton.

Death March of the Dancing Dolls and Other Stories — Volume Three in the Day Keene in the Detective Pulps series. Introduced by Bill Crider.

Deep Space and other Stories — A collection of SF gems by Richard A. Lupoff.

Detective Duff Unravels It — Episodic mysteries by Harvey O'Higgins.

Dime Novels: Ramble House's 10-Cent Books — *Knife in the Dark* by Robert Leslie Bellem, *Hot Lead* and *Song of Death* by Ed Earl Repp, *A Hashish House in New York* by H.H. Kane, and five more.

Don Diablo: Book of a Lost Film — Two-volume treatment of a western by Paul Landres, with diagrams. Intro by Francis M. Nevins.

Dope and Swastikas — Two strange novels from 1922 by Edmund Snell

Dope Tales #1 — Two dope-riddled classics; *Dope Runners* by Gerald Grantham and *Death Takes the Joystick* by Phillip Condé.

Dope Tales #2 — Two more narco-classics; *The Invisible Hand* by Rex Dark and *The Smokers of Hashish* by Norman Berrow.

Dope Tales #3 — Two enchanting novels of opium by the master, Sax Rohmer. *Dope* and *The Yellow Claw*.

Double Hot — Two 60s softcore sex novels by Morris Hershman.

Dr. Odin — Douglas Newton's 1933 racial potboiler comes back to life.

Evangelical Cockroach — Subversive fare from Jack Woodford

Evidence in Blue — 1938 mystery by E. Charles Vivian.

Fatal Accident — Murder by automobile, a 1936 mystery by Cecil M. Wills.

Ferris Wheel Hussy — Two from Aylwin Lee Martin: *Death on a Ferris Wheel* (1951) and *Death for a Hussy* (1952)

Finger-prints Never Lie — A 1939 classic detective novel by John G. Brandon.

Freaks and Fantasies — Eerie tales by Tod Robbins, collaborator of Tod Browning on the film FREAKS.

Gadsby — A lipogram (a novel without the letter E). Ernest Vincent Wright's last work, published in 1939 right before his death.

Gelett Burgess Novels — *The Master of Mysteries, The White Cat, Two O'Clock Courage, Ladies in Boxes, Find the Woman, The Heart Line, The Picaroons* and *Lady Mechante*. All are introduced by Richard A. Lupoff who is singlehandedly bringing Burgess back to life.

Geronimo — S. M. Barrett's 1905 autobiography of a noble American.

Hake Talbot Novels — *Rim of the Pit, The Hangman's Handyman*. Classic locked room mysteries, with mapback covers by Gavin O'Keefe.

Hollywood Dreams — A novel of Tinsel Town and the Depression by Richard O'Brien.

Hostesses in Hell and Other Stories — Russell Gray's violent tales from the pulps. #16 in the Dancing Tuatara Press horror series.

I Stole $16,000,000 — A true story by cracksman Herbert E. Wilson.

Inclination to Murder — 1966 thriller by New Zealand's Harriet Hunter.

Invaders from the Dark — Classic werewolf tale from Greye La Spina.

J. Poindexter, Colored — Classic satirical black novel by Irvin S. Cobb.

Jack Mann Novels — Strange murder in the English countryside. *Gees' First Case, Nightmare Farm, Grey Shapes, The Ninth Life, The Glass Too Many, The Kleinert Case* and *Maker of Shadows*.

Jake Hardy — A lusty western tale from Wesley Tallant.

Jim Harmon Double Novels — *Vixen Hollow/Celluloid Scandal, The Man Who Made Maniacs/Silent Siren, Ape Rape/Wanton Witch, Sex Burns Like Fire/Twist Session, Sudden Lust/Passion Strip, Sin Unlimited/Harlot Master, Twilight Girls/Sex Institution*. Written in the early 60s and never reprinted until now.

Joel Townsley Rogers Novels and Short Stories — By the author of *The Red Right Hand: Once In a Red Moon, Lady With the Dice, The Stopped Clock, Never Leave My Bed*. Also two short story collections: *Night of Horror* and *Killing Time*.

Joseph Shallit Novels — *The Case of the Billion Dollar Body, Lady Don't Die on My Doorstep, Kiss the Killer, Yell Bloody Murder, Take Your Last Look*. One of America's best 50's authors and a favorite of author Bill Pronzini.

Keller Memento — 45 short stories of the amazing and weird by Dr. David Keller.

Killer's Caress — Cary Moran's 1936 hardboiled thriller.

Lady of the Yellow Death and Other Stories — Tales from the pulps by Wyatt Blassingame. #14 in the Dancing Tuatara Press series.

League of the Grateful Dead and Other Stories — Volume One in the Day Keene in the Detective Pulps series. In the introduction John Pelan outlines his plans for republishing all of Day Keene's short stories from the pulps.

Man Out of Hell and Other Stories — Volume II of the John H. Knox pulps collection.

Marblehead: A Novel of H.P. Lovecraft — A long-lost masterpiece from Richard A. Lupoff. The "director's cut", the long version that has never been published before.

Master of Souls — Mark Hansom's 1937 shocker, introduced by weirdologist John Pelan.

Max Afford Novels — *Owl of Darkness, Death's Mannikins, Blood on His Hands, The Dead Are Blind, The Sheep and the Wolves, Sinners in Paradise* and *Two Locked Room Mysteries and a Ripping Yarn* by one of Australia's finest mystery novelists.

More Secret Adventures of Sherlock Holmes — Gary Lovisi's second collection of tales about the unknown sides of the great detective.

Muddled Mind: Complete Works of Ed Wood, Jr. — David Hayes and Hayden Davis deconstruct the life and works of the mad, but canny, genius.

Murder among the Nudists — A mystery from 1934 by Peter Hunt, featuring a naked Detective-Inspector going undercover in a nudist colony.

Murder in Black and White — 1931 classic tennis whodunit by Evelyn Elder.

Murder in Shawnee — Two novels of the Alleghenies by John Douglas: *Shawnee Alley Fire* and *Haunts.*

Murder in Silk — A 1937 Yellow Peril novel of the silk trade by Ralph Trevor.

My Deadly Angel — 1955 Cold War drama by John Chelton.

My First Time: The One Experience You Never Forget — Michael Birchwood — 64 true first-person narratives of how they lost it.

Mysterious Martin, the Master of Murder — Two versions of a strange 1912 novel by Tod Robbins about a man who writes books that can kill.

Norman Berrow Novels — *The Bishop's Sword, Ghost House, Don't Go Out After Dark, Claws of the Cougar, The Smokers of Hashish, The Secret Dancer, Don't Jump Mr. Boland!, The Footprints of Satan, Fingers for Ransom, The Three Tiers of Fantasy, The Spaniard's Thumb, The Eleventh Plague, Words Have Wings, One Thrilling Night, The Lady's in Danger, It Howls at Night, The Terror in the Fog, Oil Under the Window, Murder in the Melody, The Singing Room.* The complete Norman Berrow library of classic locked-room mysteries, several of which are masterpieces.

Old Times' Sake — Short stories by James Reasoner from Mike Shayne Magazine.

One Dreadful Night — 1940s suspense and terror from Ronald S. L. Harding

Pair o' Jacks — Two works by Jack Woodford: *Find the Motive* and *The Loud Literary Lamas of New York.*

Perfect .38 — Two early Timothy Dane novels by William Ard. More to come.

Prose Bowl — Futuristic satire of a world where hack writing has replaced football as our national obsession, by Bill Pronzini and Barry N. Malzberg.

Red Light — The history of legal prostitution in Shreveport Louisiana by Eric Brock. Includes wonderful photos of the houses and the ladies.

Researching American-Made Toy Soldiers — A 276-page collection of a lifetime of articles by toy soldier expert Richard O'Brien.

Reunion in Hell — Volume One of the John H. Knox series of weird stories from the pulps. Introduced by horror expert John Pelan.

Ripped from the Headlines! — The Jack the Ripper story as told in the newspaper articles in the *New York* and *London Times.*

Robert Randisi Novels — *No Exit to Brooklyn* and *The Dead of Brooklyn.* The first two Nick Delvecchio novels.

Rough Cut & New, Improved Murder — Ed Gorman's first two novels.

Ruled By Radio — 1925 futuristic novel by Robert L. Hadfield & Frank E. Farncombe.

Rupert Penny Novels — *Policeman's Holiday, Policeman's Evidence, Lucky Policeman, Policeman in Armour, Sealed Room Murder, Sweet Poison, The Talkative Policeman, She had to Have Gas* and *Cut and Run* (by Martin Tanner.) Rupert Penny is the pseudonym of Australian Charles Thornett, a master of the locked room, impossible crime plot.

Sand's Game — Spectacular hard-boiled noir from Ennis Willie, edited by Lynn Myers and Stephen Mertz, with contributions from Max Allan Collins, Bill Crider, Wayne Dundee, Bill Pronzini, Gary Lovisi and James Reasoner.

Sand's War — The second Ennis Willie collection

Satan's Den Exposed — True crime in Truth or Consequences New Mexico — Award-winning journalism by the *Desert Journal.*

Satan's Sin House and Other Stories — Dancing Tuatara Press #15 by Wayne Rogers – Gore and mayhem from the shudder pulps.

Gelett Burgess Novels — *The Master of Mysteries, The White Cat, Two O'Clock Courage, Ladies in Boxes, Find the Woman, The Heart Line, The Picaroons* and *Lady Mechante.* All are edited and introduced by Richard A. Lupoff.

Sam McCain Novels — Ed Gorman's terrific series includes *The Day the Music Died, Wake Up Little Susie* and *Will You Still Love Me Tomorrow?*

Sex Slave — Potboiler of lust in the days of Cleopatra by Dion Leclerq, 1966.

Shadows' Edge — Two early novels by Wade Wright: *Shadows Don't Bleed* and *The Sharp Edge.*

Sideslip — 1968 SF masterpiece by Ted White and Dave Van Arnam.

Slammer Days — Two full-length prison memoirs: *Men into Beasts* (1952) by George Sylvester Viereck and *Home Away From Home* (1962) by Jack Woodford.

Sorcerer's Chessmen — John Pelan introduces this 1939 classic by Mark Hansom.

Star Griffin — Michael Kurland's 1987 masterpiece of SF drollery is back.

Stakeout on Millennium Drive — Award-winning Indianapolis Noir by Ian Woollen.

Star Griffin — 1987 SF classic from Michael Kurland gets the Ramble House treatment.

Strands of the Web: Short Stories of Harry Stephen Keeler — Edited and Introduced by Fred Cleaver.

Suzy — A collection of comic strips by Richard O'Brien and Bob Vojtko from 1970.

Tales of the Macabre and Ordinary — Modern twisted horror by Chris Mikul, author of the *Bizarrism* series.

Tenebrae — Ernest G. Henham's 1898 horror tale brought back.

The Amorous Intrigues & Adventures of Aaron Burr — by Anonymous. Hot historical action about the man who almost became Emperor of Mexico.

The Anthony Boucher Chronicles — edited by Francis M. Nevins. Book reviews by Anthony Boucher written for the *San Francisco Chronicle, 1942 – 1947.* Essential and fascinating reading by the best book reviewer there ever was.

The Best of 10-Story Book — edited by Chris Mikul, over 35 stories from the literary magazine Harry Stephen Keeler edited.

The Black Dark Murders — Vintage 50s college murder yarn by Milt Ozaki, writing as Robert O. Saber.

The Book of Time — Classic novel by H.G. Wells is joined by sequels by Wells himself and three timely stories by Richard Lupoff. Lavishly illustrated by Gavin L. O'Keefe.

The Case of the Little Green Men — Mack Reynolds wrote this love song to sci-fi fans back in 1951 and it's now back in print.

The Case of the Withered Hand — 1936 potboiler by John G. Brandon.

The Charlie Chaplin Murder Mystery — A 2004 tribute by scholar, Wes D. Gehring.

The Chinese Jar Mystery — Murder in the manor by John Stephen Strange, 1934.

The Compleat Calhoon — All of Fender Tucker's works: Includes *Totah Six-Pack, Weed, Women and Song* and *Tales from the Tower,* plus a CD of all of his songs.

The Compleat Ova Hamlet — Parodies of SF authors by Richard A. Lupoff. This is a brand new edition with more stories and more illustrations by Trina Robbins.

The Contested Earth and Other SF Stories — A never-before published space opera and seven short stories by Jim Harmon.

The Crimson Query — A 1929 thriller from Arlton Eadie. Perfect way to get introduced.

The Curse of Cantire — Classic 1939 novel of a family curse by Walter S. Masterman.

The Devil Drives — Odd prison and lost treasure novel from 1932 by Virgil Markham.

The Devil's Mistress — A 1915 Scottish gothic tale by J. W. Brodie-Innes, a member of Aleister Crowley's Golden Dawn.

The Dumpling — Political murder from 1907 by Coulson Kernahan.

The End of It All and Other Stories — Ed Gorman selected his favorite short stories for this huge collection.

The Fangs of Suet Pudding — A 1944 novel of the German invasion by Adams Farr

The Ghost of Gaston Revere — From 1935, a novel of life and beyond by Mark Hansom, introduced by John Pelan.

The Gold Star Line — Seaboard adventure from L.T. Reade and Robert Eustace.

The Golden Dagger — 1951 Scotland Yard yarn by E. R. Punshon.

The Hairbreadth Escapes of Major Mendax — Francis Blake Crofton's 1889 boys' book.

The House of the Vampire — 1907 poetic thriller by George S. Viereck.

The Incredible Adventures of Rowland Hern — Intriguing 1928 impossible crimes by Nicholas Olde.

The Julius Caesar Murder Case — A classic 1935 re-telling of the assassination by Wallace Irwin that's much more fun than the Shakespeare version.

The Koky Comics — A collection of all of the 1978-1981 Sunday and daily comic strips by Richard O'Brien and Mort Gerberg, in two volumes.

The Lady of the Terraces — 1925 missing race adventure by E. Charles Vivian.

The Library of Death — By Ronald S. L. Harding, Dancing Tuatara Press #20.

The Lord of Terror — 1925 mystery with master-criminal, Fantômas.

The N. R. De Mexico Novels — Robert Bragg, the real N.R. de Mexico, presents *Marijuana Girl, Madman on a Drum, Private Chauffeur* in one volume.

The Night Remembers — A 1991 Jack Walsh mystery from Ed Gorman.

The One After Snelling — Kickass modern noir from Richard O'Brien.

The Organ Reader — A huge compilation of just about everything published in the 1971-1972 radical bay-area newspaper, *THE ORGAN.* A coffee table book that points out the shallowness of the coffee table mindset.

The Poker Club — Three in one! Ed Gorman's ground-breaking novel, the short story it was based upon, and the screenplay of the film made from it.

The Private Journal & Diary of John H. Surratt — The memoirs of the man who conspired to assassinate President Lincoln.

The Secret Adventures of Sherlock Holmes — Three Sherlockian pastiches by the Brooklyn author/publisher, Gary Lovisi.

The Shadow on the House — Mark Hansom's 1934 masterpiece of horror is introduced by John Pelan.

The Sign of the Scorpion — A 1935 Edmund Snell tale of oriental evil.

The Singular Problem of the Stygian House-Boat — Two classic tales by John Kendrick Bangs about the denizens of Hades.

The Smiling Corpse — Philip Wylie and Bernard Bergman's odd 1935 novel.

The Stench of Death: An Odoriferous Omnibus by Jack Moskovitz — Two complete novels and two novellas from 60's sleaze author, Jack Moskovitz.

The Story Writer and Other Stories — Richard Wilson, #2 in John Pelan's SF series

The Technique of the Mystery Story — Carolyn Wells' 1913 book on mystery writing.

The Time Armada — Fox B. Holden's 1953 SF gem.

The Tongueless Horror and Other Stories — Volume One of the series of short stories from the weird pulps by Wyatt Blassingame.

The Tracer of Lost Persons — From 1906, an episodic novel that became a hit radio series in the 30s. Introduced by Richard A. Lupoff.

The Trail of the Cloven Hoof — Diabolical horror from 1935 by Arlton Eadie. Introduced by John Pelan.

The Triune Man — Mindscrambling science fiction from Richard A. Lupoff.

The Universal Holmes — Richard A. Lupoff's 2007 collection of five Holmesian pastiches and a recipe for giant rat stew.

The Werewolf vs the Vampire Woman — Hard to believe ultraviolence by either Arthur M. Scarm or Arthur M. Scram.

The Whistling Ancestors — A 1936 classic of weirdness by Richard E. Goddard and introduced by John Pelan.

The White Peril in the Far East — Sidney Lewis Gulick's 1905 indictment of the West and assurance that Japan would never attack the U.S.

The Wizard of Berner's Abbey — A 1935 horror gem written by Mark Hansom and introduced by John Pelan.

Two Kinds of Bad — Two 50s novels from William Ard: *As Bad As I Am* and *When She Was Bad*, featuring Danny Fontaine

Wade Wright Novels — *Echo of Fear, Death At Nostalgia Street, It Leads to Murder* and *Shadows' Edge*, a double book with *Shadows Don't Bleed* and *The Sharp Edge*.

Welsh Rarebit Tales — Charming stories from 1902 by Harle Oren Cummins

Through the Looking Glass — Lewis Carroll wrote it; Gavin L. O'Keefe illustrated it.

Time Line — Ramble House artist Gavin O'Keefe selects his most evocative art inspired by the twisted literature he reads and designs.

Tiresias — Psychotic modern horror novel by Jonathan M. Sweet.

Totah Six-Pack — Fender Tucker's six tales about Farmington NM in one sleek volume.

Trail of the Spirit Warrior — Roger Haley's historical saga of life in the Indian Territories.

Ultra-Boiled — 23 gut-wrenching tales by our Man in Brooklyn, Gary Lovisi.

Up Front From Behind — A 2011 satire of Wall Street by James B. Kobak.

Victims & Villains — Intriguing Sherlockiana from Derham Groves.

Walter S. Masterman Novels — *The Green Toad, The Flying Beast, The Yellow Mistletoe, The Wrong Verdict, The Perjured Alibi, The Border Line* and *The Curse of Cantire*. Masterman wrote horror and mystery, some introduced by John Pelan.

We Are the Dead and Other Stories — Volume Two in the Day Keene in the Detective Pulps series, introduced by Ed Gorman. When done, there may be as many as 11 in the series.

West Texas War and Other Western Stories — by Gary Lovisi.

Whip Dodge: Man Hunter — Wesley Tallant's saga of a bounty hunter of the old West.

You'll Die Laughing — Bruce Elliott's 1945 novel of murder at a practical joker's English countryside manor.

RAMBLE HOUSE

Fender Tucker, Prop. Gavin L. O'Keefe, Graphics
www.ramblehouse.com fender@ramblehouse.com
228-826-1783 10329 Sheephead Drive, Vancleave MS 39565

CPSIA information can be obtained at www.ICGtesting.com
Printed in the USA
LVOW042224021212

309770LV00002B/289/P